TRAIN TO YESTERDAY

TRAIN TO YESTERDAY

NELL DUVALL

FIVE STAR
A part of Gale, Cengage Learning

GALE
CENGAGE Learning™

Detroit • New York • San Francisco • New Haven, Conn • Waterville, Maine • London

GALE
CENGAGE Learning™

Set in 11 pt. Plantin.

Printed on permanent paper.

LIBRARY OF CONGRESS CATALOGING-IN-PUBLICATION DATA

DuVall, Nell.
   Train to yesterday / Nell DuVall. — 1st ed.
     p. cm.
   ISBN-13: 978-1-59414-663-3 (alk. paper)
   ISBN-10: 1-59414-663-2 (alk. paper)
   1. Time travel—Fiction. 2. Railroads—History—Fiction.
   3. Canals—History—Fiction. 4. Ohio—History—Fiction. I. Title.
   PS3604.U83T73 2008
   813'.6—dc22
                                             2007036137

First Edition. First Printing: February 2008.

Published in 2008 in conjunction with Tekno Books.

ACKNOWLEDGEMENTS

Special thanks to John Helfers, Alice Duncan, and the Five Star staff for making this novel into a book. The libraries of the Ohio Historical Society, Coshocton, Columbus, Upper Arlington, and Ohio State University provided access to records and newspapers of the period and assisted in verifying a variety of information.

Finally, thanks to the members of Novels in Progress and especially to Lyn, Becki, Aileen, and Sally for their support and encouragement.

CHAPTER 1

Darkness descended, sudden and complete. Penny Barton shivered. She strained to pierce the black wall around her as fear wrapped its coils tight and squeezed her chest.

Water? No, no water. Her sweaty palms slipped against something smooth and hard. Heart racing, she stretched out a hand and touched wood, not rough rock.

As those impressions registered, someone coughed, and her panic subsided. She pressed against the wooden seat, glad for its firm, reassuring presence. Trotman's Cave loomed only in her past, not the present. She had nothing to fear from it or from Gerald. Here she faced the overwhelming memories, but not the reality of the black, rising waters that had once sought to envelop her.

Gradually, daylight seeped back into the railroad car as the train emerged from the tunnel and into the light. Her breathing slowed, and she unclenched fingers that ached from the sudden release. Indentations showed on her palms where her nails had dug into the flesh. She rubbed her hands together, anxious to hide the evidence of her momentary panic. To her vast relief no one in the crowded railroad car paid her the least attention.

She smoothed the skirt of her silk dress. The sales clerk at the costume shop had assured her the misty blue taffeta represented the prettiest and most stylish of the shop's mid-nineteenth-century stock. The matching feathered hat covered her short auburn hair, obviating the need for a heavy wig. She had refused the confining corset. Blue photographed well, too, the clerk had observed.

Relaxing, Penny surveyed her fellow passengers. Mostly men and middle-aged, they came from various railroad clubs. They had the money to indulge in an expensive hobby, and well-to-do men meant potential investors for HyperTrans. She had planned this trip to use the nostalgia of the old steam engines to promote HyperTrans' new high-speed rail link. This trip should do just that. But, Penny promised herself, she would make sure they used a route without tunnels next time.

Yes, her boss, Jim Whalen, the current CEO, would be very pleased, and he couldn't give the credit to her father for this one. Whalen persisted in his belief that the CEO had only hired her as Vice President of Marketing because of her dad's role as a major investor. He conveniently ignored the HyperTrans anti-nepotism policy. Hard work and creativity had won her a place in a male-dominated business, and she would not let a man like Whalen ruin it. He came from the old school that preferred to see women as assistants or low-level subordinates rather than decision makers.

The success of this trip could provide HyperTrans with a rosy future. If the company didn't recruit more investors, the line would fail and Penny would have to find another job. She wouldn't give Whalen that dubious satisfaction.

"Hey, Penny."

She looked up as stocky, redheaded Ryan O'Connor, president of the Coshocton Railroaders' Club slid onto the oak seat beside her. She pulled her voluminous skirt a little closer to give him room.

He lifted the long tails of his frock coat as he settled back. "Great job. We're having a super time. You know, I could almost believe we're really riding the original Steubenville and Indiana Railroad."

Penny smiled, gratified that someone as knowledgeable as Ryan appreciated all her hard work. "Thanks. Your advice and the equipment from Magna helped make it authentic—almost too authentic." She shifted her weight to get some circulation back in her legs.

"Yeah." Ryan grinned. "The railroads of 1855 didn't waste money on frills for their passengers."

Penny shifted again. The hard oak seats, suspiciously like Puritan church pews, gave little comfort. With every mile traveled, the bench grew harder and more uncomfortable. Why hadn't she thought to bring a pillow? "Magma should at least have provided upholstered seats."

"A little early for that." Ryan laughed. "Anyway, the railroad provided a stove for winter, not that we need it today." He pointed to the squat potbellied fixture at the front of the car. "Besides, most folks only rode between towns, less than an hour for the most part."

"And I had to plan a four-hour trip."

"Hey, it's great. I'm a rail buff, remember? I love these old trains. Nice of Magna to offer us costumes—not that we needed them," Ryan continued. "They should know reenactors already have that stuff. Anyway, I guess they wanted us to look the part for their filming. Still, it isn't every day we get to ride a steam train—or be in a movie." They both laughed.

"How'd you get HyperTrans to fund this trip anyway?" Ryan asked, a quizzical smile on his face.

Penny grimaced as she remembered Whalen's shout when she proposed the project and showed him the likely cost. "Hard work. My boss had a few doubts, but when Magna Productions offered to supply the equipment and then agreed to share the costs, how could he refuse?"

"He couldn't. Anyway, we get the benefits." Ryan undid the buttons of his vest and rubbed his paunch. Pulling out an antique gold pocket watch from his vest pocket, he flipped it open.

"I told him the publicity would help us get investors and influence the State Legislature. I hope you and your club members will support the draft bill to open the state-owned right-of-ways to private investors."

"I'm thinking about it." Ryan grinned. "A couple of our fellows plan to buy stock in HyperTrans."

"Good, be sure to let me know their names."

He nodded and snapped the watch shut. "Still three hours to Gnadenhutten and that high tea of yours. I'm getting kind of thirsty. Maybe when we stop for water, I'll pick up coffee."

"Good, I could use one, too."

Ryan got up and stretched. "Coffee it is. See you later." He strolled toward the back of the crowded car and stopped to chat with club members as he walked.

Gazing out the window, Penny concentrated on the scenery. At least on this steam train, it didn't pass in an indistinct blur. Magna insisted they not overtax the engine, so they traveled at a leisurely twenty miles per hour. The view through the train window offered a real sense of the rural nature of Eastern Ohio, where prosperous farms and dairy cattle dotted the rolling landscape.

The steam engine, picturesque as she remembered it with its bright green paint and its yellow inverted bell of a smokestack, made slow, chugging progress through the hilly countryside. Sounding a repetitive *shoosh-shoosh*, it wended its way west from Steubenville, Ohio, toward Gnadenhutten, past tall stands of oaks and birches and wide fields of grazing cattle. When they passed an Amish buggy, Penny could almost believe they had traveled back to 1855.

To please Magna, a stickler for authentic details, she had even bought a facsimile leather-bound edition of Brontë's *Jane*

Eyre. She picked it up and began to read. The scenery outside the carriage window passed by without further notice as she absorbed first one chapter and part of the next.

Then, the train began to slow. A loud hiss of escaping steam heralded a stop. Peering out the window, she glimpsed the engineer leaning out of his cab. Outside, a small village of barely more than a few white houses and two stores nearer the tracks filled the view. Trees stood like silent sentinels on the hillside behind the buildings. Leaves, long gone, left bare limbs to brave the cold. Why stop here? She saw no station.

Worry niggled Penny as she reached for her briefcase only to remember she had opted for a velvet reticule as befitted a lady traveler of 1855. She pulled out the folded map of the line from the drawstring purse. Only four wood and water stops had been planned before their final destination, and they had refueled no more than half an hour ago. The next stop lay almost two hours ahead.

She leaned forward in her seat for a better view. Hopefully the boiler hadn't sprung a leak, or whatever it was that old engines did. She shook her head. A mechanical problem would ruin the trip. Being stranded in rural Ohio would not make for contented clients nor would Magna Productions get the film footage it needed. No footage, no funding. She could almost hear Whalen's laughter at that.

The wheels sounded a scratchy grinding noise and then jerked to an abrupt halt. The engine belched a hissing jet of steam. The passengers in the crowded car craned forward and leaned out the windows for a better look.

Frowning, Penny watched a tall man dressed in a dark frock coat atop cream-colored trousers step aboard the carriage. He hesitated at the entrance of the packed car, his top hat held in his gloved hands. His eyes widened as he surveyed the many passengers. The period costume suited his lean frame. Not quite

Tom Cruise or Pierce Brosnan she decided; his nose looked a trifle too prominent for either. He had to be an actor hired by Magna.

The stranger worked his way into the car and stopped next to her seat. He gazed down at Penny with a dazzling smile and eyes the color of dark chocolate. Dazed, she gaped back. That intense regard drew her with him to some private place. Her cheeks grew warm. Suddenly conscious her gaze had turned into a stare, she glanced down to hide her embarrassment.

"Excuse me, madam. Is this seat taken?"

She stared up at him, caught by the rich sparkle in his dark eyes, then gave a little shake of her head and forced herself to look away from his face, past generous lips and a strong, smooth chin to her book. Fantasies of that mobile mouth on hers and those arms holding her to his broad chest made her heart race. Shocked, Penny pinched her wrist.

Get a life, girl, she almost muttered. After Gerald, she had sworn off men. All men. Especially tall, handsome ones. With stiff resolve, she focused on his costume. His wool frock coat covered broad shoulders and framed a cream-colored shirt in fine linen with a high, stiff collar. Every detail had been executed to perfection, even to the impeccably positioned black cravat. Her gaze traveled downward to rest on his polished leather boots.

The man shifted his tall hat in his hand, drawing her attention back to his face. He looked at her with eyebrows raised, a quizzical smile on his lips. Flustered by the amused gleam in his eyes and her own wayward thoughts, Penny quickly looked away again.

"Is this seat taken?"

"Uh, no, it's not." She shifted closer to the window. "Please, sit down."

He folded his long frame into the seat and crossed one leg

over the other, then straightened the crease in his trousers. "I apologize for interrupting your solitude." The man grimaced. "But all other seats in this carriage have already been taken. While I welcome the increased revenue, I'm not used to seeing so many travelers. Rail travel is so new, some people still mistrust it." He sighed. "Too often, the drivers are unable to keep to their established schedules and travelers must perforce seek other means to complete their journeys."

Blinking, Penny folded her hands. This man had to be an actor.

Turning slightly to face her, he captured her gaze with those liquid brown eyes. "My name is Fletcher Dawe. I am a dry goods merchant from Coshocton." Pulling a rectangular case from his pocket, he handed a large card to Penny.

She looked at it briefly, glad of the distraction from his too intense scrutiny, and rubbed her finger over the raised script, smooth and bold against a flat white surface. Magna had really taken authenticity to the extreme.

"How do you do, Mr. Dawe? I'm Penelope Barton from Columbus." She tried to match his formality. Playing the part of a prim and proper lady amused her, but she had to fight the temptation to just stare at him. To cover her confused state, she fumbled for a moment in her reticule and pulled out one of her own cream-colored business cards.

As Fletcher Dawe took it, his fingers brushed hers, sending an electric tingle through her hand and up her arm. He stared down at the card.

"Miss Barton." The warmth of his smile lighted his features and gave a shine to his dark eyes. "It is a distinct pleasure to see one of the fair sex use this mode of transport. My aunt remains one of the few ladies in Coshocton brave enough to chance the rigors of rail coach." He slipped her card into his vest pocket.

"My father's a partner in the railroad, so I could hardly do otherwise, He says we should act an example for others. I take the train whenever I can."

He studied Penny, his face filled with avid interest. "Ah, then we have something in common. I invested in this line and am endeavoring to complete the westward link in a timely fashion. Once finished, goods from the east will reach us more promptly, and we can ship our grain and cattle east more cheaply. Travel to Columbus will be faster and more convenient than by road or canal."

"You've invested in HyperTrans?" Penny studied his face again, but could not identify him. She prided herself on knowing the major investors.

"HyperTrans? I cannot say I have heard of that line. No, I mean the Steubenville and Indiana Railroad. This line."

"Yes, of course." Penny pressed her lips together to keep from laughing. Whoever had written his dialogue had worked hard, or he had a talent for improvisation. She paused a moment, unsure what to say, but the silence worried her even more than her uncertainty. "We have excellent rail access in Columbus. That's one of the advantages of living in the state capital."

He nodded. "I envy you that, but my home is in Coshocton and opportunities for business abound. With the railroad finished, we can only expect more."

"Someone once called the railroads the engines of progress."

Smiling at her words, he nodded. "Yes, that is just what we hope. An astute observation, Miss Barton. You like Columbus?"

Again his intense gaze rattled Penny and made her hurry her words. "I wouldn't give up my view of the bend in the Scioto River for anything. To the north I see the Broad Street Bridge." Conscious of his continuing scrutiny, she struggled to make small talk. "Living in the capital provides plenty of entertainment. Have you been to Columbus?"

"I travel there sometimes on business, but I have not traveled there for almost a year. I must remedy that and soon." He raised one eyebrow as he gave Penny a broad smile.

A warm glow suffused her heart and spread outward. Could he mean that? He's an actor, she reminded herself. She wanted to know more about him, but a sudden unaccustomed shyness restrained her.

Fletcher Dawe glanced out the window. Released from his gaze, perplexity assailed her. She had long ago passed the giddy stage, but her instant response to this man disturbed and puzzled her. After Gerald, she had vowed not to be misled again. Determined to get a firmer grip on her emotions, Penny picked up her book.

"Ah!" Fletcher beamed, looking from her book to her face. "You and my aunt must have common interests. She is a devoted reader of the Bells."

"Bells?" Penny blinked at him, then she remembered—the Brontë sisters had originally published under the name Bell, and her book had the name Currer Bell embossed just below the title. "Oh, yes. I particularly like Currer—" she dredged up memories of her college English Lit. classes. "But Ellis is also a favorite."

He nodded. "My aunt agrees, but she prefers Jane's practicality over Cathy's willfulness. I should like you to meet her. My aunt, that is." His eyes looked wistful.

Penny closed her book, wondering just what he meant by that. "Your aunt?" Did he even have an aunt?

"Yes, Mrs. Emily Dawe. She lives with me and makes my life interesting and ordered." He grinned, reminding Penny of a mischievous boy. "May my aunt and I call upon you on our next visit to Columbus?"

Studying his face, Penny wondered if he meant to visit, or whether he merely played a part? His steady gaze surprised and thrilled her. It had been a while since any eligible man had caught her attention. Now, for the first time in ages, Fletcher Dawe triggered a delicious sense of excited confusion that muddled her thoughts, but in such a pleasant way. Best to stay in character and not read more into his flirtatious manner than was there. An actor had no trouble playing many roles.

Penny lowered her lashes in a suitably modest response. "Of course."

"But I must warn you, my aunt has a very . . . independent turn of mind. She is an ardent advocate of property rights for women and counts Amelia Bloomer, Frances Gage, and Harriet Beecher Stowe among her dearest friends."

"Amelia Bloomer?" He really had gone too far. He must be joking. Well, she could joke, too. What had she learned in her Women's History course? "Yes, she devised some garment or other, didn't she?" Let's see him top that.

Fletcher Dawe sighed. "Indeed, Turkish pantaloons, although some call them Bloomers. My aunt, I am sorry to say, favors this mode of apparel."

Suppressing a laugh, Penny gave him a sideways glance. "Now, Mr. Dawe, surely you can appreciate their practical nature."

"Um, well, perhaps, but I cannot say they flatter the female form, not as much as your lovely gown."

Penny glanced down at the blue taffeta, pleased she had chosen it. "The color is so right," the sales clerk had said. Self-conscious, Penny brushed the feathers of her hat with her left hand, knowing it framed and softened her face. It also heightened the blue of her eyes.

Fletcher Dawe continued to study her. She read approval in his direct gaze and, perhaps, something more. She wanted to explore that, but at the same time wondered if she really wanted to know where it could lead. She didn't need any more failed relationships. Besides, an actor could turn the charm on and off and likely had dozens of willing partners tucked away.

Nonetheless, her pulse raced, and the silk of the dress clung to her back. She reached up to finger the small buttons at the neck of the dress. His eyes followed her hands. Suddenly conscious of the direction of his glance, she pulled her hand back. What was the matter with her, anyway? Stick to business. Distract him.

What had he last said? Harriet Beecher Stowe. Something about her. "Have you read Mrs. Stowe's *Uncle Tom's Cabin*?"

He grimaced and nodded. "My aunt insisted. A degree too sentimental for my taste and perhaps overdrawn, but slavery as an institution is difficult to defend." His face grew solemn. "I can only believe that it must fall of its own weight. In my experience, free men are more productive than slaves."

"I'm glad to hear you say that. This country must support its declaration and its constitution, liberty and justice for all, including—" she gave him a sly glance, "women and Afro . . . I mean slaves."

"Bow-ers-ville." In a robust voice the conductor dragged out each syllable as he walked through the coach. "Bowersville, next stop."

"Oh." Fletcher Dawe frowned and then rose quickly. "I must leave the train here."

Surprise and disappointment rattled Penny. She thought everyone had planned to take the entire trip. Why would Magna arrange for this stranger to join them for such a short time? "You're not going on to Gnadenhutten?"

He shook his head, regret in his eyes. "Not this trip. I have business with a merchant here in Bowersville." He gazed down at her with his mesmerizing look. "But may I call upon you in Columbus? With my aunt, of course."

Holding out her hand politely, Penny wanted something more than such a formal leave-taking, but common sense, despite her fantasies, reminded her she hardly knew the man. "I look forward to meeting your aunt." She lowered her lashes. "And to your visit to Columbus, Mr. Dawe. I would enjoy talking with an admirer of the Bells." *And you,* she refrained from adding. She studied his face, rejoicing in the avid interest she saw there. Maybe he would call her.

"Good, you may count on it." He held Penny's hand just a moment longer than necessary, and his warmth, even through her glove, made her tingle. "It has been a particular pleasure to meet you. I look forward to renewing our acquaintance and soon. Good day, Miss Barton."

He tipped his hat and hurried off as the train started its repetitious *chug-chug* and began to move. He leaped from the carriage and ran a few steps alongside to the window where Penny sat. As the train gathered speed, he stood beside the track and waved to her. She waved back. She watched him standing there as the train pulled away, and he dwindled from sight.

Would he call? Had his interest been real or had the entire meeting been an actor's practice session? But Fletcher Dawe had seemed so . . . so sincere. She wanted him to call. If he had been Magna's actor, she could quiz Tony DiCarlo, her assistant, about the man. However, Tony didn't need to know just how much the stranger had impressed her.

Her perspiring palms and churning stomach disproved her outward calm. She only hoped the encounter disturbed him as much as it had her.

Pulling out his card, she studied it. The name, engraved in raised copperplate, suited the elegance of his clothing and his manner. Inspecting the card again, she found no phone number, no fax number, and not even an electronic mail address. Puzzled, Penny looked out the window and down the disappearing line of track. Bowersville had melted into the horizon, taking Fletcher Dawe with it.

She returned her attention to the card in her hand. His address, at the lower left on the card, read: *202 S. Second Street, Coshocton, Ohio, Purveyor of Fine Dry Goods.* No zip code. Staring at the address again, Penny frowned and then slipped the card into her reticule. He said he would see her in Columbus. A delicious warmth crept over her from her toes to her fingers—anticipation.

"Hey, who was that guy?" Tony DiCarlo, the newest member of the HyperTrans Public Relations Department, wore a smug look.

He smoothed his cravat and tugged on the slightly-too-small frock coat as he plopped down beside her. Penny searched his face for a sign of his involvement in the charade. His expression reflected only sincere interest.

"You tell me." She raised a knowing eyebrow at him, trying to suppress a smile as she waited for his explanation.

He paid no notice to her accusatory expression. Tugging at his tight collar, he shrugged. "No clue. Dressed the part, though, didn't he? Probably an actor." His tone and lack of interest in the stranger implied he knew nothing about Fletcher Dawe.

Disappointment pricked at Penny. She wanted more, but if Tony couldn't help, who could? She paused for a moment, pondering options. "Oh, did you get a list from Ryan O'Connor of the Coshocton Railroaders' Club members? We might need it later." She paused a moment. "Did Magna have any passengers?"

"Not so far as I know. They would have arranged that with you. I'll see O'Connor about a list." Tony got up and ambled toward the back of the carriage.

Satisfied Dawe's name would be on the list and she could ask Ryan more about him, Penny again opened her book. Jane would keep her company until they reached Gnadenhutten. She began to read, but soon her attention drifted. She stared at the page, not seeing the meaningless words. Fletcher Dawe's face appeared on every page, and she found herself pulled into those dark chocolate eyes that offered excitement and passion.

She refused to be swept off her feet by good looks, but Fletcher Dawe had more than that. Much more. He exuded a sense of integrity and a confidence in his own abilities. A man who knew himself and had no insecurity about his own identity or his place in society. His promise to visit her in Columbus made her skin tingle with excitement.

She gazed out the window, but saw only Fletcher Dawe. Fletcher Dawe and his compelling brown eyes.

CHAPTER 2

Coshocton, Ohio
March 20, 1855

Fletcher Dawe wrote at the top of a white page of the brown leather-bound journal lying open before him and pondered the entries to be made. He leaned over his desk, dipped his pen into the ink well, and then stopped. He propped his chin in his left palm and stared at the date penned in deep black where it glared alone on a stark white page. The journal's dark brown edges attested to past heavy use, but the empty page accused him of laxity.

He should consider the store inventory and other entries to be made, but instead a pair of bright blue eyes framed by auburn curls occupied his mind. Too often of late, he found himself thinking of Penelope Barton when he should be doing other things—attending to the store or ensuring the workmen on the rail line didn't slack off. Mooning over a young woman would not do. He sighed and then began to write.

The office door burst open and slammed hard against the wall. It rattled the panes in the window beside Fletcher's desk. Jamie Mathews, panting, nearly fell into the room. He leaned against the doorframe, gasping for breath. The boy, no more than twelve and smallish for his age, tossed his shaggy hair from his eyes and swiped at a trail of sweat creeping down his cheek.

"Mr. Dawe, Mr. Dawe. We've got troubles again with them Farups and Fardowns." Brown eyes open wide, Jamie glanced to the window and then back to Fletcher. He gestured toward the rail yard with a jerk of his head.

Snapping his journal shut, Fletcher tossed it aside and pushed away from his desk. Not again. How many times had Jamie come running, frantic, into his office to tell him the Irish workmen had started scrapping among themselves? Too bad someone hadn't told him about the feuds among the Irish coming from the North and the South of that small island before he hired so many of them.

The boy, ragged in hand-me-down pants, too short and patched at the knees, and a jacket with frayed cuffs, stood just inside the door. His chest heaved up, down, up, down, as he fought to breathe.

"What is it this time, Jamie?" Fletcher dragged a chair nearer the boy and pressed him into it. "Here. Sit for a moment. Try to catch your breath." Balancing on his haunches in front of the boy, Fletcher saw worse panic in Jamie's owl-sized eyes than he had ever seen before.

"You gotta come, afore they kill each other, Mr. Dawe." Skinny fingers clutched at Fletcher's vest. "I run . . . all the way . . . here to . . . tell you. They're swinging mallets." His voice climbed a notch, and he almost shouted at Fletcher, "At each other! Someone's gonna git hurt, 'lessen you stop 'em!" He bounded out of the chair and tugged at Fletcher's sleeve. "Come on, Mr. Dawe! We gotta hurry!"

Fletcher snatched his tall hat from the top of the cabinet and followed Jamie out the door, down the steps of the loading dock behind the store, and then through the alley next to the milliner. Jamie set a fast pace, darting among pedestrians and horses. Once he stumbled over wooden crates stacked outside Whitney's Tavern, but he paused only briefly to catch his breath and look over his shoulder for Fletcher.

Jamie raced past the courthouse square to Fifth Street, where the rail crews worked on the tracks. As they neared the scene, loud shouts, angry curses, and the thud of mallets missing their mark as they hit the ground reached Fletcher. A group of irate men shoved each other back and forth. Flying fists *whoosh*ed through the air and often connected with a jaw or stomach. Erin O'Malley, sprawled on the ground, nursed a bloody and possibly broken nose. Sean Finnerty fingered a black and swollen eye.

"Here, here," Fletcher shouted, shoving his way into the brawl and ducking a flying punch. He reached for one of the crew bosses. "Carmody, what's this about?"

Carmody sported a cut across one eye. An angry red patch on his chin would surely be an onerous bruise later. One look at Fletcher's angry face and he backed away from the other men, "They started it. Them Fardowns won't do a decent day's work. They leave all the hard jobs for us."

"Ain't so, Mr. Dawe," Billy O'Brien interjected. " 'Tis the other way 'round. They started it."

Fletcher shook his head. Disgusted, he surveyed the men, fists on his hips. "No matter who started it, it will stop now, and you will get on with your assigned tasks, or I will fire the lot of you." Fletcher glared at them. "And no wages at the end of the week, either."

The men groaned. A few swore under their breath and several hung their heads. Others looked sullen.

"Do you hear me?" Fletcher raised his voice. Anger made his words almost a shout, and he flexed his hands, determined to keep his temper under firm control. One or two eyed him speculatively, but stepped back.

Carmody and O'Brien averted their gazes and gave slow, reluctant nods as they motioned to their crews. The men backed up and bent to grab tools and jackets and caps tossed aside in the foray, picking up one and then dropping it, or handing it to a mate.

"You men are paid for work done, not for feuding with one another. We have a schedule, a very tight schedule, to meet, and I expect you to keep to it. Any more fighting and you're all finished. I can get new crews within a day. Now get back to work."

He stared at them, his jaw clenched. The workmen looked away or at each other. Carmody and O'Brien gave him sullen nods.

Turning his back, Fletcher stalked away. He dragged his fob chain from his pocket. The watch indicated almost one. "Hmmph!" He cursed under his breath. Only dinnertime and they were fighting already. They should fight on their own time, not his. Fight or no, he had other matters with which to deal. He made a mental note to check on the workers after lunch.

"I thought sure you'd hit one of them again," Jamie said.

"No, Jamie. We want no more accidents to anyone."

"Well, it sure made 'em listen to you."

"Anger and violence are never good answers to a problem. I won't repeat it. No one can justify killing a person except in war or to protect others. Now, you best go on home. Your mother will worry."

Straightening his frock coat, Fletcher walked the few blocks north toward home. The white two-story frame house sat at the end of Second Street, and a brisk walk soon carried him there. He bounded up the steps leading to the wooden porch and opened the door to the front hall. Tossing his hat on the hall table, he took a long, deep breath to steady himself. He had recognized the fear in the men's eyes. They remembered all too well what could happen if they angered him.

Resolutely, he pushed the thought away and focused instead on the tantalizing smells from Aunt Emily's kitchen. Today, the smell of fresh-baked peach cobbler filled the air.

"That you, Fletcher?" his aunt called from the kitchen.

"Yes, Aunt Emily, I'm home. Something smells good."

"Of course." She came through the kitchen door carrying a large tureen. Her gray hair, pulled tight away from her temples, rested in a twisted knot on top of her head. A carved wooden pin held it in place. The bright calico apron hid her gray dress, and a smudge of flour graced her right cheek.

"I made chicken and dumplings. Mr. Harkins killed a few today so I decided we could use a change from salt pork and ham." She wrinkled her nose.

Fletcher nodded. He too had grown tired of the all too familiar salted meats. She placed the tureen on the dining-room table.

"Now you hurry and wash up so we can eat." Turning toward the kitchen she looked over her shoulder. "You're late today. No problems, I hope?" Her arched eyebrows echoed her question.

Fletcher shrugged. "Some."

Aunt Emily could always read his worries. She knew the effort it took to run his store, oversee the rail crews, and act as mediator at least once a week for the constantly feuding Irish.

"We can discuss it over dinner. I'll just wash my hands."

Hanging his coat over a hook in the hall, Fletcher then climbed the stairs to his bedroom. He filled the basin with water from the pitcher standing ready and laved his hands. As he sloshed water around the basin, his thoughts returned to the fight at the depot site. He would not allow them to push him to violence. If they forced him, he would hire other workers. A man of his word, he would act, but unfortunately the men had families, and he had no desire to see wives and children suffer or the work on the rail line delayed. Too many delays would exhaust the available funds. Already the investors demanded explanations, and at least two had asked for the return of their money.

He grabbed the towel and dried his hands. No, somehow he would have to ensure the present work crews finished on time. He shook his head. A formidable task, that. When had the Irish ever set aside their feuds and curbed their tempers?

Dropping the towel to the table, Fletcher left the water in the basin. He straightened his cravat and went downstairs to join his aunt in the dining room. At the table he said a brief grace and then took a long drink of water from the glass beside his plate. His eyes wandered past the steaming tureen of chicken as his thoughts turned to scheduling the first run for the new rail line.

First unfolding her napkin, Emily Dawe next passed her plate to Fletcher. "So? How are things with the railroad?"

He grimaced as he ladled chicken and dumplings onto her plate. "Not well. Just before lunch, Jamie Mathews burst in to tell me the crews were fighting again. I threatened to fire the lot. It makes me wonder if we will ever get this line finished. We only have the track from here to Newark to complete, and it is all easy grade—no tunnels and only the one bridge. What they would do if the going were rough, I cannot even imagine." He sighed.

Emily stared at her plate, troubled line creasing her forehead, and then looked up at him. "Fletcher, you know how the Irish are. It's religion, family, or both. You have the Protestant Fardowns and Catholic Farups both working for you, and they hate one another."

Sighing, she shook her head. "Besides all that, every Irishman comes from a different area, and they despise everyone else. According to Brigid O'Brien, their stories celebrate cattle stealing. They have no cattle to steal here. Now they can only fight and maim each other to prove their superiority. I hate to say it,

Fletcher, but better they take their anger and frustrations out on each other than on their wives and children."

"Then they should do it on their own time. The schedule does not allow for such childishness. If Carmody and O'Brien cannot control their men, I must get someone else." He set his fork down and glared at his aunt.

"Now, Fletcher," she patted his arm, "simmer down. Both those men have families, and they need the work. It cannot be easy for them to keep those men from fighting. They try. I am certain of it."

"Um, I suppose."

For a few moments Fletcher returned his attention to his food. He enjoyed his aunt's cooking. While he regretted the death of his favorite uncle, Emily's coming to live with him had proved fortunate in many ways. An intelligent woman, she could talk with him about business matters, and he valued her commonsense approach. She knew most of the people in Coshocton and had saved him from more than one bad decision.

Reaching for the peach cobbler, Fletcher proceeded to fill dessert plates for each of them. "I have been thinking, Aunt Emily. We have not visited Columbus for quite some time. I have business with Harry Sells. We could go to a few bookstores and, perhaps, call on that young lady I met on the train."

"Young lady? Oh, you mean Pen . . . Penelope? What was her name? Oh, yes, Penelope Barton you spoke of last week. I thought you had forgotten her." His aunt had a sparkle in her blue eyes that told Fletcher she meant to tease him a bit.

"Well, it has been a hard winter and, with the work on the railroad, I could not get away, but we are close to finishing, and I could manage a few days."

Emily grinned at him. "Yes. What is it they say? 'In the spring a young man's fancy turns to love'? There's no reason you should not go, but I have my tutoring, and I cannot leave my students that long." She sighed as she laid down her napkin. "They forget enough as it is between lessons. Yet they want to learn, and how else to provide them with any future without the skill to read?"

Blinking, Fletcher then stared at his aunt. "I cannot believe you would forgo the opportunity to visit Columbus!"

"I have no great reason to make the trip just now. Perhaps later in the year when the railroad is operating, I might be tempted to go. You go without me. No sense dragging along an old lady to cramp your style."

"Old lady?" Fletcher laughed. "I hardly think so. Besides, it would be improper for me to call upon a young, unmarried lady without a female companion. In any event, I told Miss Barton we would both visit so the two of you could discuss your interest in the Bells."

"Um, I see." Emily reached for her cobbler. "Well, I will give you a note to deliver to her with an invitation to visit us. Will that do?"

Emily's refusal to accompany him puzzled Fletcher. Normally, nothing would keep her away. "If you really will not come, I guess it must suffice. I must see Sells, despite the feuding Irish." Frowning, Fletcher pushed his empty plate away. A few days away would not hurt, and he had promised to call upon the fascinating Miss Barton.

Finishing her cobbler, Emily began removing the dishes. "While you're there, you could match that lavender silk for me. You know how I despise doing those kinds of things, but I need some ribbon to trim my bonnet. I'll give you a swatch to match against."

Grinning, Fletcher nodded. Unlike other women, Aunt Emily took little pleasure in maintaining a stylish wardrobe. She preferred to argue politics whenever she could engage him, or even cook or tutor, if she could not. He regarded politics as necessary, but to be avoided as much as possible. He admired her interest in the welfare of the Irish workmen's children and assisted her in buying books and materials so that she could tutor them. He would miss her company on the long journey to Columbus and he hated to postpone her assessment of Miss Barton. The young woman's inviting smile and sea-blue eyes had captivated him too deeply for him to adequately assess her character.

Dinner finished, Fletcher took his leave of Aunt Emily and began the short walk to his store. The day had begun sunny and promising, but now looked overcast and ominous as he set out. He strolled, head down, against the wind, and almost without conscious thought, detoured to the Canal Ticket Office. With or without his aunt as companion, he looked forward to the trip, and the thought of seeing Miss Barton again made him smile to himself.

Entering the cramped ticket office, he wrinkled his nose at the musty smell; the place needed a thorough cleaning. Blue smoke from a cheap cigar filled the air. Dan Hudson, the black-headed lockmaster, with his customary cigar hanging from his mouth, sat with his feet propped up on the potbellied stove. His boots had a muddy crust not yet dry. His wooden chair, tilted back on two legs, groaned and squeaked resistance to his weight as he turned toward Fletcher.

He pulled at the bristly mustache framing his sullen mouth and gave Fletcher an insolent look. "Afternoon, Mr. Dawe." Dan did not rise from his chair as he took another puff on the cigar and blew out a cloud of gray smoke.

Fletcher ignored Dan's lack of interest and his rudeness. "Good afternoon, Dan. How is the canal business these days?" He turned and studied the canal packet schedule scrawled on a board hanging from the wall.

"Kind of slow, this being our off season and all, but I've had the boys out working on the tow path, and we started running last week. 'Course we can't get up to Cleveland yet, but we can get you downriver if you've a mind to go that way," he picked at a fingernail, "seeing as how the railroad isn't operating yet." Dan flashed a half smile, but his narrowed eyes and raised eyebrow gave it an impudent twist.

Sighing, Fletcher resolved not to let Dan bait him. He refused to respond to the snide remarks, but the taunts stung, especially with the delays in laying the track. "The railroad will be running soon. Then you won't have to worry about frozen waterways."

The chair hit the floor with a thud as Dan reached for a log to throw into the stove. The iron door creaked as he opened it and tossed in the log. "No, s'pose not. I see how hard your crews work. Like earlier, just today, as I passed the site, but then you know how to make them work." His mouth twisted sideways as he leaned back in his chair.

Dan's hint he had seen the crews feuding made Fletcher flinch, and the veiled reference to that unfortunate accident last month rankled. He gritted his teeth. Never would he discuss such matters with Dan.

At his silence, Dan shrugged. "Get a bad snowstorm, and the railroad don't run, either."

"Perhaps, but the tracks can always be cleared with a shovel or two." Fletcher glanced back at the schedule board. "I want to book passage next week to Columbus."

Dan's face reddened, but he nodded. "We'll keep a berth for you. What day do you plan to leave?"

"Tuesday. I see you have a packet going." Fletcher nodded toward the board and waited as Dan shuffled through a few papers.

"Don't pay no attention to the board up there. Likely as not, I forgot to update it." He continued to shuffle papers, slowing to scan a letter or two. "But you're in luck. The *Mary Sue* will be passing through on her way to Portsmouth, and she's got room. So early in the season, not too many travelers just yet. However, wait much longer . . ." Dan struck a match and relit his cigar. ". . . and you'll have to wait for a reservation." Dan fingered the embroidered strap of his watch.

Raising an eyebrow, Fletcher stepped back to the door. "I shall remember that, and I will see you on Tuesday. Good day, Dan." Fletcher reached for the door handle and turned to leave.

"Good day to you, Mister Dawe." Dan's voice carried a sarcastic note.

Monday, a week after the Sunday train trip, Penny Barton sat at her office desk in Columbus tying up various loose ends from the trip. HyperTrans had given her a large corner office with two window walls. The phone shrilled.

"Hello. Penny?" The familiar gruff voice needed no identification. Only Jim Whalen, the CEO, had her direct number and would fail to identify himself.

"Yes, have you seen the proposed ad compaign?" Stray thoughts about uncompleted tasks raced through her mind.

"Not yet. Magna's on my back about some guy who rode on that steam train trip of yours. Seems they want him for a commercial."

Sighing, she drummed on her desk with the pink eraser-end of a pencil as she balanced the phone between her ear and shoulder. "Which guy? We had more than a hundred people on that trip."

"They got a copy of a video from one of the club members. Nobody seemed to know him according to Magna. They sent me a blowup of one frame. Meg dropped it off at your office."

"What do you want me to do?"

"Find him. That's an order. Magna's making noises about

reducing their contribution, and you know what that means."

"I'll do my best."

"See that you do. The shortfall in Magna support would just about equal your salary."

The phone disconnect underscored Whalen's implied threat. Penny picked up the folder of incoming mail and rifled through it. The large brown envelope came from Whalen's office. She opened it and pulled out the contents.

For a moment she stared down at the grainy photo. Despite the poor quality of the picture, she immediately recognized Fletcher Dawe's profile. Well, for once she and Whalen wanted the same thing. Since Magna didn't know who Dawe was, she needn't check with them.

She dialed information. "Coshocton, Ohio, the number for Fletcher Dawe, please." Penny spelled out both names and waited.

"Checking," a mechanical voice sounded from the other end of the line. She switched the phone to her other ear. "Fletcher? F-l-e-t-c-h-e-r?" The operator pronounced each letter, slowly and distinctly, reminding Penny of Mrs. Forbes, her second grade teacher.

"Yes, that's it. Fletcher Dawe." She rolled her eyes. After all, how many ways could you spell Fletcher?

"No, no listing for a Fletcher Dawe. Only a Francis Dawson. Nothing at all for an F. Dawe. Would you care to try another spelling?" The operator sounded annoyed.

Penny hesitated. "No business listing? The man I'm trying to locate operates a store in Coshocton."

"Ma'am, I've checked twice." Penny heard the operator draw a deep breath. "Either the location is wrong or the name is incorrect."

"All right, thanks for checking." She set the phone in its cradle and straightened the kink in her neck. She bounced the pencil one final time before jamming it in the pencil cup.

This is crazy, she told herself. She had only talked with Fletcher Dawe for a short while, but she couldn't force his image from her mind. Her glance trailed across the mounds of paperwork on her desk. She hadn't touched the public relations plans Tony had asked her to approve. Two stacks of magazine slicks she promised to have back to the advertising department by Friday rested on the edge of the credenza. She had thought of little else except Fletcher Dawe, and now Whalen insisted she find him or risk her job.

"Crazy," she repeated. She leaned back in her chair, twisting and untwisting a lock of her short hair.

Her thoughts drifted to the commemorative railroad trip and the fascinating stranger. Her reaction to him—the sense of expectation and exhilaration he had raised—still buoyed her spirits and made her want to find him. Most women would call him handsome, but something far more than mere good looks had touched her. He knew his history and literature and spoke in words of more than one syllable. He had a mind as well as a body, not that she objected to his tall, lean frame—far from it. It added to his attractiveness.

Penny stretched her arms out before her and then slumped deeper into the chair. But what about Fletcher Dawe made him so different, somehow special? His eyes? His manner? Both really. His eyes had spoken to her, called to her, and awoken sensations she had long suppressed. He made her tingle with excitement and anticipation she struggled to stifle.

Grappling to identify why, she puzzled over his actions and words. She smiled as she recalled his formality. Then she remembered the words of a conference speaker: " 'The most precious gift anyone can give another is to listen, truly listen.' " Fletcher Dawe had done that. He had given her his complete attention. He had absorbed her every word as though he enjoyed their conversation and found her as fascinating as she had found him. Yet he hadn't tried to make a pass at her.

Her friends urged her to relax her standards a little, but after the fiasco with Gerald, she couldn't. Was it too much to expect a man to be good-looking, educated, and interesting? Fletcher Dawe had an indefinable something. He had shown more than a superficial, nice-to-meet-you interest. It had been as though he wanted her, as though he cared about her as a person as well as a female body.

Some men only wanted someone to feed their egos by telling them how good they were or by sleeping with them, sometimes both. Those men never saw her as a person with needs and interests of her own. She could never relax with them.

Penny ran her hand through her hair. "What am I doing? Manufacturing the perfect man from just one brief encounter?"

The more she considered Fletcher Dawe, the more confused she grew, but somehow his image stayed in her mind. He had said he would contact her, but he hadn't. Yet. And now Whalen had as much as said find him or find another job. Damn!

Glancing from one end of Kitty's saloon to the other, Dan Hudson observed the assembled men. On payday most of the dockworkers spent all their money long before they reached home. Today appeared no different. This day, though, he recognized quite a few railroad workers drinking. Dawe's men. Dan sauntered farther into the room. A few of his own crew stood in a corner holding frothy mugs while several sat at tables along the wall near the window, but the railroad men outnumbered them two to one.

Carmody and three of his crew sat around a broad oak table, dealing poker. Across the room O'Brien and his men leaned into the bar tossing down whiskeys. Dan grunted. Likely as not there'd be a fight before the night ended. After a few ales, Carmody and O'Brien themselves would probably be into it. For several long seconds, he studied O'Brien's face. Briefly their eyes met, but O'Brien turned away quickly. Dan chewed at his bottom lip. Hopefully O'Brien would have the sense not to drink too much. If he did, then he might start talking. It wouldn't do O'Brien or Dan much good if Dawe or his toadies discovered their plans.

Dan looked back to the men playing cards. Two he recognized, one he wasn't sure about, and the other he couldn't recall having seen before. His eyes slid to the pile of coins and cards strewn across the table, and he sneered. Even his own workers, well paid as they were, didn't make enough money to waste on poker. Dawe must be paying his men a good sum. No wonder some of the dockworkers grumbled and threatened to quit the locks. The ones who had would be sorry one day. Dawe would not be as fair to them in hard times as Dan had been. Hadn't he come to Jake Baker's aid when his wife and kid got real sick? Even gave him some extra cash out of his own pocket. Dawe was too much of a hardheaded businessman to do that.

Shouldering his way down the length of the bar, Dan made his way through the crowd of men standing elbow to elbow. At the far end where there appeared some space close to the fireplace, he squeezed in between two other patrons. He angled himself toward the warmth of the roaring flames, bent slightly, and then cupped his hands to light the cigar in his mouth. With a loud sucking sound, he drew on the cigar and turned round slowly to warm his face and hands.

Too late in the season for such blustery weather. And if the northern section of river didn't thaw soon, he'd have to let half his men go. Even the six he had just hired last month. As it was, less business had been promised the canals and locks—much less than last year. Everyone knew the railroad had contracted with some influential businessmen back East for freight hauling the canal should have had. Now they had the Steubenville-Indiana line to contend with. Word had it that it might become as profitable and as successful as the Baltimore.

Dan spat into the fire. Maybe Fletcher Dawe wouldn't be so cocky and self-assured if he knew the problems he'd have running the railroad. Even in the east, they had had their share of explosions and derailments. Besides, in a heavy winter storm, the trains couldn't run, either. Maybe the rivers froze, but snow on the tracks offered just as much of an obstacle. Surely it would be the same for Dawe. At best, the railroad would cost him a lot of his personal investment. Then, when everyone had their fill of railroad problems, they'd come back to the locks. A lot safer and not as likely to blow up as them tricky steam engines.

He laughed and sucked again on the cigar. He'd take back only the best workers then. Wouldn't have to put up with any lazy hands. After everyone saw how bad the railroads were, they'd fight each other to work for him on the canal. Once the men found out how demanding and stingy Dawe was, they'd beg for their jobs back. Dan sneered. Let other men work for Dawe. Business would have to get pretty damn bad before he'd work for him.

"Hudson, what'll it be? The usual?" Klaus Steiner stood behind the bar, wiping wet hands on his apron.

The low-pitched voice of the barkeep startled Dan, and he reeled around. "Naw. Not ale today. Give me a whiskey."

With a nod, Klaus ambled away.

"Better choice would 'e been the ale, Sirrah. It's as good as any I remember from me own town of London."

Dan looked curiously at the man who had spoken. His neat side-whiskers looked recently trimmed. Better dressed than most of the local townsfolk, his silk cravat shone in the firelight, and that cambric shirt must have cost a month's wages. He looked a regular dandy. Nobody dressed like that on a regular workday.

Still, fine gentlemen seldom paid much attention to a lockmaster. Once, one had called Dan "boyo" and yelled at him to carry his valise. Usually the fine ones bought their tickets, left him to handle their belongings, and then went on their way without so much as a backward look, a thank you, or even a tip for his trouble.

The man's voice and dress proclaimed him a foreigner. None of the Easterners spoke with quite that drawl. "London, England?" Dan took a step back and eyed the man again.

"Can there be another? Take my advice, my good man, and have a glass o' the ale." The man lifted his mug and tipped it toward Dan.

"In time. I'll be here a while. What brings you to these parts this time of year?" The man looked like he had been at the saloon a while. His words came slow, and his nose showed a redness brought about by too many glasses of ale.

"First, let me introduce meself." The dandy stood and extended a hand. "I am Doctor Edwin Westcott of England. Lancastershire, actually."

Dan grabbed the extended hand, and allowed the doctor to shake his vigorously.

"And you are?" the blurry-eyed doctor peered at Dan, waiting a response.

"Daniel Hudson. I operate . . ." Dan thought for a half second before saying more, "I'm in charge of the men down at the locks. On the canal." He motioned in the direction of the Walhonding.

"Ah, yes. The canal. I shall take it meself there shortly. Working my way to Saint Louis, I am." The doctor drained his mug and signaled for another.

"Saint Louis? Working your way?" Dan frowned, wondering

what would take a foreigner there. He cocked his head in mild interest, but suddenly glimpsed O'Brien carrying a tall tankard of ale and moving from the bar to a table near the window. Dan prayed Billy O'Brien would go easy on his drink tonight. Scratching his chin, he wondered whether he might have to warn O'Brien.

"Yes, sir. Got something very special, I have. Every doctor hereabouts will be wanting it, too!" The doctor smiled broadly, exposing smoke-yellowed teeth.

Dan snorted. "What could be so special to make you travel all the way from London to Saint Louis?" He lifted his glass and tossed his whiskey down. No figuring some folks.

Looking first right then left, the doctor put his finger to his lips. He leaned close to Dan's ear. The stale odor of ale rose as he lowered his voice. "Chloroform. Best thing to come about for years, it is." The doctor nodded, as if with authority.

"Klora—what?" Dan pulled back and stared at the doctor through narrowed eyes.

"Shh." The doctor pulled him closer. "It's my secret medicine. Chloroform. It will make surgery painless. One whiff and the patient loses consciousness."

"It knocks them out? Whaddaya' mean?" Dan waved at Steiner to order an ale.

"My dear boy, what I mean is it will render the patient sense-less, but only for a brief time, mind you. Unless you use too much and then—" His finger made a quick slash across his throat. "Too much and the patient dies."

Sitting straighter in his chair, Dan opened his eyes wide. "Are you saying that simply by drinking this—this, Chloroform, a patient will sleep? Instantly?"

"Instantly, yes, but not by drinking it. I can show you." The doctor looked around nervously, as if afraid of being caught at some trick. At his feet on the floor sat a black leather satchel, a doctor's valise. He rummaged in it and produced a small brown bottle.

"Seeing you are a professional man and interested, I'll show you." Westcott looked over his shoulder as he uncorked the top of the bottle. He pulled a white handkerchief, neatly folded in a square, from the inside pocket of his coat. "Now only a very small whiff, mind you, or you'll be collapsing here on the floor, and then what would we do?" The doctor cackled loudly. "Be forced to bleed you, perhaps."

Bristling, Dan vowed not to let this drunkard practice on him. Chloroform or not, no one would be getting his blood, or anything else. He bent forward gingerly and sniffed at the wet spot on the doctor's handkerchief. Sweet and pungent, the smell made him giddy. Drawing his head back quickly, he rubbed his nose with the back of his hand and then shook his head to rid it of the fumes.

The doctor laughed again. "Imagine what a bit more might do."

Picking up the bottle of colorless liquid, Dan removed the cork and sniffed. "Doesn't smell bad. Sweet, sort of. But—is that all you do? Hold it to someone's nose?"

"Saturate a rag and have the patient take a long, deep breath. That's it. But—" He wagged his finger and looked stern. "—too much and it's over. A good doctor, though, knows just how much to use." He puffed out his chest.

"And then the patient wakes up." Dan snapped his fingers together. "Just like that?"

"Well, I wouldn't say just like that." The doctor snapped back. "When he wakes, the patient is sick. A little lightheaded, if you know what I mean, and the stomach will be a problem for a while. But it's much better than suffering through a bloody surgery."

The doctor nodded knowingly and narrowed his eyes. He

slapped the cork back into the bottle and stuffed it and the handkerchief into the bag on the floor. When he faced Dan again, his nose glowed a fiery red and his eyes appeared to have difficulty focusing.

Dan stared at the valise on the floor and began to ponder exactly what he might do if he had a bottle of this chloroform. Get rid of bothersome folks for just a while. No bruises to show for it, either. Just creep up and—

After ordering another ale, the doctor turned toward the fire. "Yes, my dear man, every doctor around will be wanting one o' me little brown bottles. But not without a price, you know. One can not get something for nothing these days." He slurped his ale.

"How much?" Dan tried to ask offhandedly, as though just out of mild curiosity.

"More than most men have, you can wager on that. But only doctors can buy it, you know. Not enough to go 'round to just anyone."

Dan leaned on the bar in silence. Even if he had the money, the doctor probably wouldn't sell him a bottle. Just as well. He wouldn't want the doctor or anyone else to know he had the new miracle liquid anyway. He glanced again to the valise on the floor. With a drunken fool guarding it, it should not be too hard to liberate a bottle or two.

"You stayin' round here?" Dan asked the question, expecting the doctor would have accommodations at Brown's Hotel across the street.

"Just for a day or two. At the hotel. Decent place, is it?" The slurred words and the drooping eyes now looked even redder than before and hinted the doctor would do well to find his bed quickly or risk collapse.

"Best in town. But if you really want a good room, you need to get there before it starts to fill up." Dan wanted to have the doctor and his bottles safely stowed. No sense letting anyone else gain access to that chloroform.

The doctor seemed to rally. For a moment he looked alert. "Then I suppose I had better make certain of a chamber there."

"I would, if I were you. And I hear the bath water's hot early in the evening. Not necessarily warm or too clean if you wait too long." Dan winked.

The doctor bent to grab his valise off the floor. Reaching out an arm, Dan stopped him. "Let me. It's the least I can do for such an important visitor in town."

Tossing a few coins on the counter, he then followed the doctor out the door. Under his arm, the valise, full of the dark brown bottles, felt heavy. In his drunken state, the doctor would never miss one small bottle. In the gathering dark, Dan's fingers closed around a slim, cold bottle. He withdrew it with care to avoid a telltale clink from the other bottles and slipped it into his pocket.

The doctor ahead of him stumbled, and Dan reached out a hand to steady him. "Careful there, Dr. Wescott." The doctor righted himself and shook off Dan's hand. "I can manage quite well my good fellow." He brushed off his sleeve and then staggered through the door into the hotel.

CHAPTER 3

Penny stood on the small porch of the stone cottage and pulled her coat tighter to protect herself from the biting cold. Why such stubbornness? To have driven to Coshocton to look up Fletcher Dawe constituted sheer madness. Yes, she had the excuse of picking up the list of reenactors from Ryan O'Connor, but she could have asked him to fax it or mail it. She didn't have to take a two-hour drive to get it, but a break from the office would refresh her. Whalen's snide remarks, and the chance to possibly engineer a meeting with Fletcher Dawe, should she find him, had added that extra little incentive.

Whalen had kept the pressure on her. He made sure she knew her lack of success in locating Dawe endangered the payments from Magna, the film company. Anything that cost the company money caught Whalen's attention. It could give him the excuse he wanted to get rid of her, but she wouldn't let that happen. She'd find Dawe.

To her bitter disappointment, Ryan O'Connor, the head of the Coshocton Railroaders' Club, had found no record of a Dawe among the reenactors. Further, he didn't remember the name or recognize Penny's description of the man. Disgusted, she had made several attempts to locate Dawe and his store. Now, here she stood on Second Street ringing a stranger's doorbell.

Looking down at Dawe's card again, she noted once more the absence of a fax number, an E-mail address, or even a telephone number. Every card she received these days had all three and some even had multiple phone numbers and E-mail addresses. Well, if she failed to find Dawe, she could always visit that Amish quilt shop on the way back and look over the quilts.

Impatient and cold, she punched the doorbell a second time. No response came from within the stone house at the end of Second Street. She turned on the tiny porch and surveyed the neighborhood. Looking toward the center of Coshocton, she observed little traffic. Maybe the owners worked. She tapped one booted toe, anxious to resolve the Dawe problem and get on with her life.

Pulling back her coat sleeve, Penny looked at her watch. If nobody answered, she'd have to give up. At least for today. Three people had already said they had never heard of Fletcher Dawe. One man thought he might know of a Thomas, or was it Hamilton Dawe in Frazeysburg, but then he had reconsidered and decided the name might have been McCaw. In a town the size of Coshocton, she found it hard to accept that everyone didn't know everyone else. So much for small-town stereotypes.

The green wooden door opened with a quick jerk. A silvery haired, middle-aged woman stood framed in the doorway, wiping her wet hands down the front of her jeans. "Sorry, I didn't hear the doorbell." She hesitated as she eyed Penny's coat and the business card in her hand. "You from the insurance company?" The woman frowned. "I thought the appointment was tomorrow."

Penny shook her head. "No, I'm not. I'm sorry to bother you, but I'm trying to find . . ." She proffered Fletcher Dawe's business card to the woman. ". . . this man."

"Hmm." The woman pursed her lips and frowned as she studied the thick, engraved card. "Fletcher Dawe. Interesting name, Fletcher, but I don't know anyone by that name, and I've lived here quite a while." The woman stuck out her lower lip and blew a strand of hair off her forehead. "You're not one of them detectives?"

Smiling, Penny shook her head. "No."

"Guess I've watched too many of those TV shows."

"Perhaps a . . ." Penny struggled to remember the name of Fletcher Dawe's aunt. "A Mrs. Emily Dawe?"

"No." The woman bit at the corner of her thumbnail. "No, but there's a Dawson family here in town. Fairly new, so I don't know much about them. That's as close as I can come to knowing any Dawe." She started to close the door.

"But . . ." Penny shifted her shoulder bag from one arm to the other. ". . . could there be another Second Street? Or maybe a Second Avenue?" The woman shook her head. Penny frowned. "I can't even find number two-oh-two!"

"Two-oh-two? No, you won't find that on this street." The woman rubbed her finger along the edge of the business card as she studied it again. "Honey, somebody's pulling your leg. There's no number two-oh-two, and this town hasn't had a 'purveyor of fine dry goods' for a long time." She chuckled and handed the card back to Penny. "Sorry, I can't help."

Penny nodded in resignation. Now the hunger pangs she had suppressed began again. "Well, maybe you could suggest a place for lunch." She made it more a statement than a question.

"Seeing you're from out of town." The woman paused and cocked her head to one side. "Then I'd go over to Roscoe Village. Most out-of-towners like that Historical Village. They have some interesting things to see there. And you can get a real nice lunch at the Old Warehouse Restaurant. Just follow Whitewoman Street and it'll be on your right."

Still fingering the card in her hand, Penny thanked the woman and trudged back to her car. The cold, dry air chilled her fingers, but aggravation warmed her face. She bit her lower lip and jammed her keys into the ignition.

Damn him! Fletcher Dawe, if that was even his real name, had made a fool of her. Coshocton didn't have a 202 S. Second Street, despite what his business card showed. So why the play-acting on the train? Why waste the time? Maybe he had a penchant for practical jokes. Men!

Her face burned as she thought of him telling the story to a few of his buddies over lunch. No doubt they shared a good laugh. She cursed, but as quickly as it had come her irritation waned. A slow smile crossed her face followed by a loud laugh. *Railroad heiress pursues nonexistent purveyor of fine dry goods.* The thought of such an imaginary headline on one of the tabloid newspapers in the supermarket checkout line amused her, but they'd probably link it somehow to aliens. Well, she could still look at the quilts after lunch. She turned north on Whitewoman Street.

Parking the car in front of an ice cream parlor that appeared closed for the season, she walked to the restaurant across the street. Since her divorce from Gerald two years ago, she had not even wanted to date anyone more than once or twice, and now she pursued a man who didn't exist. What did that say about the state of her mind and her nonexistent love life? Still, she couldn't ignore Whalen's orders or Magna, either.

Penny shrugged and opened the restaurant door. Men of character and integrity no longer existed—anywhere.

A large stone fireplace with a cheerful fire burned and crackled at the far end of the dining room. The waitresses wore period costumes dating back to the 1830s. Waiting for the hostess to seat her, Penny glanced at the drawings and paintings lining the walls. Occasionally an early photograph in an old frame with thick, wavy glass showed life in Coshocton or the surrounding area.

Over lunch, the food, better than she expected and served in large dinner-sized portions, ranked second to the atmosphere.

However, she enjoyed the baked chicken and roasted potatoes and sat back, replete.

"You can get up and take a closer look. Lots of folks do." The waitress, a coffeepot in hand, smiled down at Penny.

"Excuse me?" Penny stared up at her

"The drawings and photos. Big attraction here 'cause most of the drawings date from the 1830s. That's when Roscoe became a port on the Ohio and Erie Canal." The waitress set the pot down and walked over to the wall. "Visitors always try to buy copies. See this." She tapped the glass of a photograph, possibly a wedding picture, of a stern-looking man and woman.

Laughing, Penny anticipated the waitress's next comment.

"Did you ever see such a grumpy-looking couple? Sure hope the marriage turned out a little happier. Back then I guess smiling wasn't the fashion. At least when you faced a camera."

"They didn't have digital photography then. You can only hold a smile so long." Penny grimaced. "They faced tougher times then, and life could be short. Maybe people weren't as happy as they are now." Her words sounded silly. So much for small talk.

"Tough maybe, but I believe folks were a lot more content living in a small town like this one. I think I would have enjoyed living then. Too much stress these days." Coffeepot in hand, the waitress hurried off to another table.

Penny sipped the hot coffee and glanced around the room. The waitress had been right about the pictures. The photos captivated everyone's interest and several diners wandered the room for a better look. Taking her coffee with her, Penny worked her way from one corner of the long room to the other.

Photos of farm machinery, long outdated, clustered along one wall. An artist's rendering of Coshocton as it must have looked in 1835 graced the fireplace, and several small tintypes flanked a window at the back of the room. On the wall opposite her table, Penny stopped to examine a photograph more closely. A group of businessmen, some with bushy beards, stood in front of a white clapboard building. The name on the storefront had been obliterated either by age and the deterioration of the picture, or by a bright shaft of sunlight the photographer hadn't expected. The men's faces looked blurred, too. The top had turned an opaque white.

A hardware store or maybe a pharmacy, she guessed. Then her eyes focused on the clothing the men in the picture wore— their Sunday best, no doubt—dark tailored suits with long coats and matching vests, stiff high collars with cravats. She chuckled to herself. Fashionable enough for *Gentlemen's Quarterly*.

Stretching her neck, Penny squinted and tried to focus the images more clearly. Where had she seen boots like those? Her brow furrowed as she struggled to remember. Her eyes wandered to the card of explanation below the picture.

1851, Coshocton, Ohio—James Hay, David Frew, Fletcher Dawe, other unidentified businessmen in front of the store purchased by Dawe.

For Fletcher, Tuesday dawned less sunny than the previous several days, but bright nevertheless. A brisk wind blew from the west, and he pulled his coat tight as he strode toward the canal. He had tucked Aunt Emily's swatch of lavender silk in his wallet next to the letter she had carefully composed for Miss Penelope Barton. He would find Miss Barton, although he could not remember a Main Street in Columbus. The growing state capital added new streets almost daily.

He continued toward the canal, trying to visualize the streets and landmarks of that city. From her description of her river view, Main Street must be near the Scioto River, possibly just north of Harry Sells' place. Fletcher straightened his cravat, still puzzling.

A swarm of boatmen loaded crates and boxes on board the *Mary Sue,* docked not twenty yards from Dan Hudson's office. Fletcher stood alongside the towpath, waiting for the signal to board the packet. He pulled Penelope Barton's card from his pocket and studied it for the second time that morning.

Penelope Barton
The Waterford, Apt. 7A
155 W. Main Street, Columbus, Ohio 43215
PH. 614-469-0261, Fax 614-469-0270
E-mail: pbarton@hypertrans.com.

Fletcher mouthed the letters "PH" and "Fax." Strange letters followed by a series of numbers. What did they mean? E-mail? Some new service from the post office no doubt. He frowned as he traced the numbers on Miss Barton's card with his index finger.

The Waterford must be the name of her home on West Main, but nothing else made any sense. City folks often did things beyond his comprehension and that he could not explain. Besides, it had been some time since he had last visited the state capital. No telling the changes he would find on this visit. The growing city of Columbus, aided by its role as the capital and by its position on the rail line from Cincinnati to Cleveland, also formed the departure point for gold seekers heading west on the National Road.

Lighting a cigar, Fletcher drew on it until gray smoke rose from the end. He continued to focus on deciphering the odd calling card and trying to place Main Street on the map of Columbus as he knew it. He pulled his watch from his pocket. Judging from the barrels and crates still to be loaded, the packet would leave late. He watched the boatmen work feverishly. At least the trains would run on time and would provide better service than the canal packets.

The *Mary Sue,* painted dark green with white trim, stood in sharp contrast to the now gray clouds scudding behind it across the sky. Perhaps it would rain after all. Fletcher had almost finished his cigar when the crews completed loading, and the captain rang the bell to signal boarding.

Stubbing out his cigar, he picked up his bag and moved toward the gangway. When Fletcher stepped aboard, he observed the packet looked the worse for her many trips up and down the Ohio-Erie Canal. Her once bright paint had begun to peel in more than a few places and left several bare boards on her sides. In addition, repeated passages through the unyielding locks had carved deep grooves in her sides. Less than fifteen feet wide and almost ninety feet long, the boat reminded Fletcher of an overstuffed sausage bulging with cabins at either end.

A team of mules, led by a man in mud-caked boots, hung their drowsy heads as they waited on the towpath for the command to pull the heavy boat along the canal. Every now and then one would lift his head and bray in answer to the harsh cry of the relief mules tethered in the bow of the packet. Fletcher grimaced. At least the railroad would not depend on cantankerous animals. The raucous noise of the mules would surely annoy some passengers and frighten others.

A rough cabin for the crew separated the extra mules from the passenger cabins. A cook's shanty occupied the stern. The man leading the mules on the towpath barked a command, and a crewman jumped to untie the boat.

"Good day for a trip, Mr. Dawe." Dan Hudson held his hand to his eyes as if shading them, even though the sun had ducked behind a growing mass of clouds. " 'Cept for the wind and unless we get some rain." He lowered his hand and resumed checking crates and boxes already on board the boat.

"The wind will die down soon enough." Fletcher glanced

skyward a moment. "Those clouds do not appear threatening. It will be a fair enough trip, and I shall be snug in the cabin." He hurried toward the salon, determined to avoid any more sly comments from Hudson.

Warm, slightly fetid air assailed him as he entered the spacious salon. He would have preferred to travel alone, without conversation, all the way to Columbus. But two ladies, one quite handsome and the other fairly ordinary, already occupied the place. The prettier of the two sat on a settee in front of one of the red-curtained windows. She turned her head as Fletcher entered, and he removed his hat and bowed. Both ladies nodded.

He stowed his bag and his overcoat at the far end of the salon and took a seat beneath a window nearby. Pulling out his copy of *The Coshocton Age,* he began to read.

From beyond the paper, scraps of whispered conversation and giggles reached Fletcher. One of the women, the ordinary one, he thought, had managed to catch the attention of the crewman who served as cabin steward and proceeded to order a coffee. Fletcher focused on his newspaper.

"Coffee, sur?" the crewman drawled. Wearing a large white apron and cropped jacket, he appeared more formally attired than the small number of passengers justified. He leaned backward just slightly, balancing a coffee service on a silver tray.

Fletcher nodded and set his newspaper aside. The man poured a steaming cup of coffee and set it on a built-in table to Fletcher's left. Alongside the coffee he set a roll topped with a generous dollop of butter.

The two women hungrily devoured their rolls and sipped their hot coffee with caution. They eyed Fletcher over the rim of their cups. When they caught his glance toward them, both smiled at him. He nodded, but said nothing. They had dressed in the epitome of fashion for central Ohio with feathered bonnets and flounced dresses edged with black braid. They had overlooked no detail of their traveling costumes. The ordinary one, the taller of the two, wore bright yellow cotton, and the pretty one pink muslin.

The women's modish attire, more than the women themselves, piqued his merchant's curiosity. He always looked for those minute changes that could herald a change in fashion and hence the demands on his stock of fabrics and ribbons. He reminded himself to observe the changes in style and fabrics he might find in Columbus. The state capital encouraged ladies of fashion and provided the models the ladies of Coshocton would surely follow.

Again, he discreetly studied the women's costumes over the side of his paper, scanning the tight-fitting sleeves and high necklines. His aunt cared naught for fashion. As he thought of her, he remembered the swatch of material in his wallet. Most women would not trust a man to select accessories for their wardrobes. He grimaced. In truth, Aunt Emily may have set him the task so he would not reconsider the trip to Columbus and miss the opportunity to call upon Miss Barton.

In memory, Penelope Barton's image rose before him. The fashionable blue gown, the auburn hair topped by the feathered bonnet, but most of all those lively, intelligent eyes. She had dressed stylishly enough. Elegant, but in quiet good taste. Much more to his liking than Sarah Jamison's somewhat gaudy attire. Sarah, meek and plain in features and form, spent an inordinate amount of time and effort on the fripperies the ladies preferred. At the thought of her, he sighed. Much too eager to become Mrs. Dawe. Perhaps that made her emphasize her good points and camouflage any suspected weaknesses. She read *Godey's Lady's Book* and spent more time than prudent with Sally Harkness, the milliner.

"Good day, sir. A fine day for a trip." The tall woman in yellow spoke first. The pretty one giggled as her face glowed the red-gold of a fall apple.

"Yes, it is." Fletcher sighed as he set his paper aside. He would have to introduce himself. "I'm Fletcher Dawe, a dry goods merchant, from Coshocton."

"I'm Letitia Miller and this is my sister Lillian. We come from Akron." The woman paused and arranged her napkin alongside her empty coffee cup. "We are on our way to visit our cousins in Cincinnati and will take a riverboat from Portsmouth. We have never traveled so far before, and it will be our first time on the Ohio River." The sister bobbed her head up and down in vigorous agreement.

"Ah, yes. The Queen City and the queen of rivers, the mighty Ohio. You should have a wonderful time." He reached once again for his paper.

"Have you ever been to Cincinnati, Mr. Dawe?" Letitia tilted her head in a coquettish tease. Lillian said nothing, but fluttered her dark eyelashes.

He nodded. "Yes, I visit there several times a year on business."

"Oh, please, you must tell us all about it," Letitia gushed.

Suppressing a groan, Fletcher feared conversing with these two ladies posed a cumbersome task. Momentarily he thought of Penelope Barton on board the train. They had found a number of interesting topics to share, and her lively manner had made it a double pleasure. Perhaps a longer acquaintanceship with the sisters would show them in a more favorable light.

For the next hour or so, Fletcher described Cincinnati and its buildings, theaters, and shops. The sisters absorbed every word and asked him about details of this and that. They kept up a constant chorus of "*oohs*" and "*ahs*." Letitia kept turning to Lillian and saying "imagine that," and "isn't that just too, too wonderful."

Following lunch, Fletcher retired to the brisk wind on the deck, not so much for a cigar as to rest his tired ears and vocal chords. He wondered how he would survive the rest of the trip. Two chattering women proved tiring. No, not tiring. Exhausting.

The next day the wind died down. When he went outside to smoke, the sisters insisted on following him out of the salon and on to the deck. The younger, Miss Lillian Miller, went into raptures about how she adored the manly smell of a cigar. Was not the aroma just titillating and delicious, and did not her own Daddy just love cigars? For a brief reprieve, Fletcher joined the men on the towpath until driven inside by mud and rain.

After two days, he stepped off the canal packet with considerable relief and on to the dock at the holding basin in Columbus. He set down his bag and stretched. While he usually enjoyed the leisurely trip, the confinement and constant chatter of the Misses Miller had become more than too much. Numb ears and a throat raw from speaking added to his discomfort.

At the end of the dock, a large man dressed in rough work clothes coiled a frayed and soiled rope around a post. His work occupied him, and he paid little attention to the passengers leaving the boat. Fletcher picked up his bag and walked toward him.

"Good day, sir." Still stretching stiff muscles, Fletcher greeted the man.

"Gud day, yerself," the man responded. "Nice day. Glad to see a bit of sun. 'Bout time, I'd say." He meticulously coiled the rope, almost to the end now.

"Yes, it is. Can you tell me where I can find Main Street?"

"Main Street?" The man removed his cap and scratched his grizzled head. Fletcher had mistaken him for a younger man, but he looked forty, maybe older. "Main Street?" the man repeated himself, staring toward the center of town as though trying to see Main Street from where he stood. "I don't reckon I ever heard of that. Leastwise not hereabouts. Are you sure it's in Columbus?"

Fletcher pulled out Penelope Barton's card and studied it. "Miss Barton told me she overlooked the bend of the Scioto River and could see the Broad Street Bridge."

"Um," the man stared at Fletcher then turned and gazed in another direction. "Well, that ought to put her right about here, but this is Canal Street and that one . . ." He pointed to the east. ". . . that's Friend Street. Never heard tell of no Main Street and I've been 'round these parts for ten, twelve years."

"Are there any residences nearby?" Fletcher looked about seeing only the remains of excavation and a sign with block letters, "Backus Sand and Gravel." Beyond that stood two brick buildings once used as the old penitentiary. It would be a strange place for a lady to live.

"Not much hereabouts. Most of the gentry live over on Rich and Town Streets, away from the river. You know how the river can be, come spring and all that snow melts. Since the canal came, they moved away from the noise and the likes of us. Too much drinking and gambling they said." He laughed, revealing the stubs of yellowed teeth, and his portly belly bounced up and down. He pulled out a pipe and a flint to light it. Fletcher waited as the man dragged on the pipe and tamped the tobacco with a callused thumb.

The man looked again at Fletcher. "Maybe you should ask the canal caster or the sheriff. Office over there." He pointed with his pipe to the building next to the lock where the Columbus-Ohio feeder joined the Scioto River.

Fletcher tossed him a penny. "For your time, thank you."

He strode toward the canal master's office. The wooden building, no more than a warehouse really, had a small office at one end where the sign *Canal Master, Pay Tolls Here* hung. As

Fletcher opened the door he noted it needed a new coat of paint. Inside, dried mud covered the floor. The cluttered interior smelled of tobacco and wet ropes and a faint hint of damp wool. From behind a tall desk, a bearded man peered over his glasses at Fletcher.

"You be wanting something, sur?" The squirrel-faced man stared at him, furry eyebrows raised.

"Uh, yes. I'm looking for Main Street." Fletcher approached the desk, so broad it hid all but the man's chest and shoulders.

The man frowned and rubbed his chin. "Don't 'member no Main Street 'round here. Sure you don't mean Bexley village or some other town?"

"Noo," Fletcher drew out the word with hesitation. "That is, I am not quite sure. The card says Columbus, and it is near the bend in the Scioto."

"River's got lots of bends." The man capped his bottle of ink and set his writing instrument aside.

"But with a view of the Broad Street Bridge?"

The man rubbed his jowls. "No, you're right about that. Still, I never heard of no Main Street in Columbus, or even in old Franklinton for that matter." The man spoke with a finality that settled the issue.

Fletcher stood for a moment, uncertain what to do next. He still had his business with Harry Sells and those errands for his aunt. He would stop for a hot supper at one of the taverns. Perhaps someone there could tell him more. "Well, thank you, anyway." Fletcher turned and left, closing the door and leaving the redolent odors behind him.

How strange. Why had Miss Barton given him a card with a nonexistent address? She had said her father was a partner in the railroad. Perhaps a trip to the railway station would lead to him. Surely, if Miss Barton's father held a position of any importance, someone at the station would know of him—possibly even know him personally.

Fletcher walked the short distance to High Street and left his bag at the White Horse Tavern. From there he took the omnibus to the station.

He had no more luck at the station than at the canal master's office. The stationmaster claimed never to have heard of any Bartons and said he knew of none associated with the railroad. Of course, people outside Columbus might have the name Barton. Perhaps they lived in Cincinnati or Cleveland. Surely Mr. Dawe had written ahead to inform the Bartons of his visit?

Fletcher squirmed at the implied breach of etiquette. Because he had decided on impulse to come, there had been no time to write ahead. He thanked the man for his trouble and returned to the tavern.

Throughout supper, he spent lost moments staring down at a lackluster plate of boiled beef and potatoes in the deserted common room. He pondered the problem of locating Penelope Barton. By the time dessert arrived, he wondered if he had imagined the entire incident, or whether she did not want him to know where she lived. The card proved he had met her, but it carried false information.

Strange. She could not have known that they would meet that day. His decision, like this one, had been made only that morning after finishing his business, and what gain could she hope for? He could think of none. Perhaps he should just forget Miss Barton. Had she truly wanted to see him again, she would have given him a proper address. She had appeared so open, so pleasant, and so intelligent. He disliked admitting how much he had looked forward to seeing her again.

Crossing his arms over his chest, Fletcher stared out the window. The evening looked cold and gray, and intermittent rain obscured his view of the city.

Miss Barton had reminded him of Aunt Emily. She had appeared forthright like Emily and almost as fearless. Few other women he knew would chance riding the railroad without a companion. She had traveled alone without even a female friend or a guardian. Perhaps her fearlessness came from duplicity and deceit.

Fletcher moved from his seat by the window to the hearth across the room. He crumpled the cream-colored card in one fist and then tossed it in the fire. Greedy flames licked at the corners of the card, curling its edges and turning the brown print to black. That was the end of Miss Penelope Barton. No point in chasing wild geese no matter how attractive they might appear, especially when he had other business on which to concentrate and the construction of the Steubenville and Indiana Railroad to finish. But as he stared at the fire, the blue of the hot flames reminded him yet again of Penelope Barton's eyes. He clenched his fists in anger and frustration at his misjudgment.

Chapter 4

Several days later in the parlor of the Dawe residence, Emily Dawe jabbed her needle into the velvet pincushion on the small table beside her. "Fletcher," she said, the lacemaker's lamp lighting her hands, but leaving her face partially shadowed. "I suggest you talk with Dan Hudson."

At Dan's name, Fletcher looked up from his paper. Emily pushed her mending aside and bit at her lower lip as she leaned forward in her chair. Something had clearly upset his aunt.

This evening, like most, they had adjourned to the parlor after dinner. Emily occupied her usual place in the rocker beside the fireplace and studied Fletcher's face. The mass of wrinkles on her usually serene brow bespoke her concern.

Returning her gaze for a long moment, he then turned to adjust the Rumford lamp next to him to produce more light. "Hudson? Why?"

She remained silent for a moment longer. "This afternoon when I tutored little Kathleen O'Brien, she asked her mother if that nice man would be by this evening. Young Billy, a bit older and wiser for his age, tried to shush her. You know my insatiable curiosity, so I asked him what man. He told me the lockmaster, Dan Hudson, stopped by now and again to share a jug of ale with his da. According to Billy, Dan always brings sweets for the little ones." Emily looked toward the fire crackling beside her. "Something about Dan's visits to the O'Brien's disturbs me."

"So, Dan shares a jug with Billy and gives the children some treats." Fletcher shrugged, but folded his paper and set it aside. "What do you find so sinister in that?"

His aunt frowned. "A jug, no, that's innocent enough, and even the sweets. But as I gathered my things to leave, Brigid whispered to me she thought Dan was plotting something bad. He makes no secret of his opposition to the railroad."

Fletcher bristled. "Yes, but I cannot do much about that. Many of our goods come by canal packet. I have no desire to antagonize Hudson at present. But once the trains begin to run . . ." He picked up his paper again.

"Perhaps, but do you know who has stirred up trouble among the work crews?" Emily spread her hands, palms up and appealed to him for an answer.

"What?" Fletcher stared at her. "Hmm, are you suggesting Hudson caused the trouble?"

Shaking her head, Emily pursed her lips. "I cannot be sure, but I trust Brigid O'Brien, and Dan spends a lot of time with your men. It makes me wonder. If I remember rightly, he always tried to ingratiate himself with the merchants and businessmen. He bosses the boat crews and workmen. So why should he suddenly become friendly with the railroad crews?"

Fletcher shrugged. "Considering his background, his association with the work crews is only natural. He understands them, and he does not have to be on his mettle with them as he would with his betters. But, you have provided another course to follow. I have little fondness for him, but just because he is insolent and impulsive at times doesn't mean he's acted on his malice."

He sat without speaking for several minutes as he considered his aunt's words. A few discreet inquiries into Hudson's influence and possible involvement should resolve the matter. Perhaps Carmody or one of the others could tell him more about Hudson's behavior. Could it have had anything to do with the clashes between the work crews? Still, even without

Hudson's influence, the Irish never needed a reason for a brawl.

At his dry goods store the next day, Fletcher sorted through bolts of fabric and ribbon. He counted spools of thread, checked drawers and shelves, and by late afternoon had compared all his stock with his inventory forms. It had been a good season, and with Easter not far off, business would be even better. Spring outfits needed those essential finishing touches and fixings. The Coshocton ladies would deplete his supply of laces and ribbon in no time. When hurried steps approached, he looked up in surprise from his check of stock against his order forms.

"Oh, Fletcher," gushed Sarah Jamison as she rushed up to him.

He noted with approval her resplendent forest green Pardessus coat and the Spanish braid used for the intricate decoration. The design outlined her bosom and flared below her waist to terminate almost at her knee. The style suited her. He must remember to add more of the Spanish braid to his list.

"I hoped to catch you," Sarah said. "I need some of that Florentine lace to finish edging the bodice of my Easter dress. I thought I had enough, but silly me, I came up short." She looked down at her black boots and scuffed one foot on the floor.

Fletcher could not resist a smile as he surveyed her blushing face. "Good afternoon, Sarah. You seem to be in some haste." Setting down the bolt of fabric he had been examining, he gazed across the shop. "Florentine lace? Um, yes, I remember the one. It's over there." He led the way to the laces and ribbons, ran his hand along the shelf, and pulled out the ornate Florentine lace. "How much do you need?"

Placing a finger alongside her chin, Sarah considered the lace. "A half yard? Yes, I'm sure that will be enough." She gazed up at him, a broad smile revealing her white teeth in sharp contrast to cheeks the color of a robin's breast.

Fletcher raised an eyebrow. "A half yard?" He had not known Sarah to underestimate yardage. A careful buyer, she measured close, but rarely short. "Mr. Meeks will measure it for you, won't you, Clarence?" Fletcher handed the lace to his assistant, the patent-haired Mr. Meeks, who hovered nearby.

Clarence, his face split in a happy smile, grabbed the lace and made his way to the measuring table. His manner with the ladies made them come often, especially the unmarried ones. However, he paid just a bit more attention to Sarah than to most of the other customers he assisted. Amused by Clarence's admiring glances at Sarah, Fletcher flashed her a parting smile and excused himself to return to his inventory.

A few moments later, carrying a string-tied parcel, Sarah rejoined him and hovered close at his side. "Fletcher, I hope you and Mrs. Dawe can join us for dinner on Sunday. Tabitha is making an apple pie and I know how much you like her sweet potatoes. Papa just butchered a lamb, so we'll have fresh meat. Please say you'll come." Her hazel eyes pleaded, and she clutched her parcel so tightly her fingers shone white.

Studying her earnest expression, he wished she lavished more of her attention on Clarence. No stirring of pleasure rose in Fletcher. In fact, Sarah, despite her smart wardrobe and Aunt Emily's kind words about her, attracted him not at all. A pleasant enough young woman, she lacked his aunt's intelligence, fire, and spirit. Her conversation, mundane and repetitious, roused no desire in him to seek her company. Any husband of Sarah's would have to take care of her—protect and shelter her—almost as one would a child. He could not think of a less desirable situation. He wanted a partner capable of helping with his business, or managing a home, not a fragile flower to cosset.

A small town like Coshocton offered few matrimonial prospects. He had grown up with most of the eligible females of the town, and, while he considered several of them close acquaintances, none suited him as a potential wife. He had met only one woman who had piqued his interest, and she, to his infinite regret, had turned out to be an adventuress.

For a moment, Penelope Barton's face filled his mind, and he saw again her sparkling blue eyes with the soft auburn hair framing an oval face. Then Sarah coughed discreetly, and he looked instead into timid hazel eyes. Courtesy demanded he accept her dinner invitation. Touched by her air of fragility, he could no more wound her by an outright refusal than he could kick a starving cat.

"Aunt Emily may have already accepted another engagement. However, I shall convey your invitation to her this evening, and one of us will call upon you tomorrow. In any event, Aunt Emily will be delighted to know you asked us. Would you give my regards to your mother?"

He wanted Sarah to leave, but she showed no signs of doing so. She simply stood at his side saying nothing, shifting from one foot to the other and playing with the package string.

Fletcher glanced at the parcel she clutched. "I see Mr. Meeks has taken care of your purchase. Can we do anything else to assist you?"

Sarah shook her head, but said nothing.

Frowning, Fletcher grew impatient to resume his work. "Thank you for stopping by." He inclined his head to her as a gesture of polite dismissal. "Please convey my compliments to your mother. Aunt Emily will let you know about Sunday dinner."

He hoped, as he turned his attention to his paperwork, Sarah would take the hint and go. He had nothing to say to her and deemed it best not to encourage her further. Sarah remained for a moment before turning and leaving. He sensed her presence close behind him. Finally, he heard the *swish* of her skirts and the sharp *click-click* of her heels as she marched out of the shop.

As he worked, mechanically jotting notes, he thought again of Sarah. He probably should have told her he could not come to dinner. He liked her well enough, but he found her so uninspiring. With a sigh, he made a note to discuss the dinner invitation with Aunt Emily. He devoutly hoped she had already made other plans for both of them. An unassailable reason for refusing Sarah's invitation would give her less hurt.

Before going home for the day, and remembering his aunt's words of last evening, Fletcher strolled over to the railroad construction site. The day had been fair, but still cool. Most of the snow had melted and left behind only brownish patches here and there. The soft marshy ground squished in spots as he walked.

Pulling his greatcoat tighter, he buried his face in his muffler. A few robins graced lawns, and the buds on the trees encouraged thoughts of spring. Aunt Emily's crocuses sported weak blooms, but little else gave reason to believe good weather would come any time soon. He hoped for fair weather and no more rain until they completed the track laying.

The railroad work site and the ribbon of track lay a few blocks from the center of town where it skirted the edge of settlement and, thus, avoided disruption to the business and main residential districts. Yet the line remained close enough to be convenient for travelers and freight and only a short walk from his store.

Originally, Coshocton had been built near the junction of the Walholding and Tuscarawas Rivers where they merged to form the larger Muskingum River. The Muskingum, which threatened to flood most every spring, ran all the way to the Ohio River. The town sat comfortably removed from its banks with businesses centered on Second Street and residential districts stretching both north and south.

Fletcher smiled. His dream grew before his eyes; the railroad would operate soon. Work on laying track appeared to be progressing well in spite of work stoppages caused by the constant feuds, occasional shortage of materials, and the recent inclement weather. If the construction beyond the bridge over the Muskingum went as planned, the trains would soon run west, all the way from Steubenville to Newark. Then the trip from Steubenville, instead of taking thirty hours by canal packet, would take less than a day.

As Fletcher neared the site, he saw Carmody, the burly Irish laborer, bent over a stack of rails. The man looked at one and then another. Then he returned to the first to examine it again.

"Carmody." Fletcher cupped his hands around his mouth as he called.

Carmody looked up from the stack of rails and waved his arm. "Good day to you, Mr. Dawe. And how be you?"

"Well, thank you, very well. How is your family?"

"Fine, fine. The missus has a bun in the oven." Carmody beamed and puffed out his chest. "This'll be our fourth."

"Four? That makes quite a family." Fletcher pictured the chubby, redheaded Carmodys, all apple-cheeked and smiling.

Carmody nodded. "Aye. We've two fine boyos and a girl. One more to even it out, see." He gave Fletcher a playful poke to the ribs. "And yo' should be thinkin' of a family yerself, eh?" He laughed, one eyebrow raised.

Fletcher sighed. He had no intention of discussing his matrimonial prospects, or rather the lack of them, with Carmody. Instead, he wanted to pursue Hudson and his possible nefarious schemes. "You see much of Dan Hudson?"

"Dan?" Carmody surveyed Fletcher, his eyes suddenly filled with calculation. "You mean the lockmaster? We sees a bit of him now and then."

Fletcher frowned. "Here? On site?"

Carmody shook his head. "No, most times at the tavern. He buys a few drinks and tells a good story. Most of it's bluff. Yo' know Dan and how he makes much of naught. But he has a way with him and a voice sweet as a meadow lark."

Fletcher sensed a lack of ease in the gruff Irishman. "All this at the tavern?"

Carmody rubbed his chin and studied Fletcher's face before responding. "Um, he stops by me house now and again. Always brings a jug and a sweet or two for the littlies."

Just like at O'Brien's. First a stop at Carmody's and then O'Brien's. Fletcher wrinkled his nose. "Hudson say much?"

"Mostly we trade stories. Sometimes he asks about work on the line. Told us about a locomotive blowing up back East. Is he right?"

Staring at Carmody, Fletcher saw nothing except honest curiosity. "I've heard it happens, but the cause lies with inferior equipment or careless operators. You don't need to worry about that. We haven't had one accident on the line yet after almost a year of operation on the sections east of here."

Carmody looked to Fletcher, his eyes troubled. "Said people hereabouts oughta take care riding on a railroad."

Sighing, Fletcher sought to undo Hudson's mischief. "The railroad is as safe—safer—than riding on a canal packet."

Coughing, Carmody glanced to his team of men loading rails onto a wagon before turning back to Fletcher. "Mules, like them used on the towpaths, can be ornery, but they don't explode. Dan says you can count on mules, being as they're God's creatures and all, but you can't count on some infernal machine."

"You agree with him?" Fletcher buried his clenched fists in his pockets and fought to suppress his anger. He refused to let

65

his temper cause more trouble.

"Me?" Carmody's eyes widened. "Sure I'm a God-fearing man, much as the next one, but I like me work. You know I like me work, Mr. Dawe." His eyes turned steely, and his face paled to match the blank sky behind him. "What happens to them rich enough to ride a railroad don't worry me."

Fletcher compressed his lips in a narrow line. "This town has a lot to gain from the railroad—cheaper and faster transport for one, as well as operating all year round." He looked around, but the few men about worked too far off to hear. "Keep you and your men away from Hudson. He's trying to cause trouble. Any man I find associating with him and involved in fighting or work stoppage will be let go without severance and no reference. Pass the word." Fletcher stared hard at Carmody.

"Including them Fardowns?" Carmody's eyes glittered.

"I'm giving O'Brien the same warning. I would not be surprised to find Hudson behind the trouble between you two."

Carmody snorted. "He might add to it, but it's them Fardowns. They hate us, always have. They're slackers, too."

Exasperation burst a bubble of anger inside Fletcher. He had been too nice. "Look, so long as you both do your job, I don't care how you feel about one another." He hardened his voice to match the blue steel rails at Carmody's feet. "But I won't tolerate fighting on the job or disruptions to the work schedule."

"I hear you, Mr. Dawe. But you best watch them Fardowns. I'll take care of my men."

"That's all I ask." Fletcher relaxed. "When is the new child due?"

"Mary says Easter or thereabouts."

"That's only a few weeks away, and a wonderful time to bring a child into the world. I'm surprised you said nothing earlier."

"Well . . ." Carmody looked down at his boots. "After she lost the last one . . . We, that is, Mary told me to say naught.

But with it coming close now, I figured no harm done. Aye, but right now it seems too far off." Carmody sighed and wiped his nose on his grimy sleeve. "Too bad women ain't like bitches. They drop their pups in a few months. Anyway, I'm hoping for another boy."

Fletcher chuckled at Carmody's impatience. "I wish you and Mary luck."

He turned and walked away to look for O'Brien and his crew. Glimpsing a group of roughly clad men half a block off, he quickened his pace. A few mutters and a curse or two reached his ears as he approached the group. Billy O'Brien, his head to one side, listened as another man harangued him.

"Billy, I want a word with you," Fletcher called when a few yards from the group.

Leaving the men, Billy strolled over to where Fletcher stood. "Aye, Mr. Dawe, what kin I do fer you?"

Fletcher eyed the knot of men who stood exchanging remarks among themselves and staring at him and Billy. "I have just spoken with Carmody, and from what I heard, Dan Hudson has tried to stir up trouble by telling lies about the railroad, talking about exploding locomotives, and inciting you against each other."

"Um." Billy focused suspicious eyes on Fletcher. "He warned us about them engines."

Frustration gripped Fletcher. "And the Farups? He talked about them?"

"We-ell . . ." Billy rubbed the uneven stubble on his chin. "A bit now and then. He knows they're a tricky lot, that bunch."

Aunt Emily had read the situation aright; Fletcher sighed. Hudson had set one group against the other, but neither realized it. His anger rose a notch, and he fought to maintain his composure with O'Brien.

"Look, Billy, don't trust Hudson. He wants trouble among

the workmen and wants only to disrupt your work. The man is a liar and out to sow as much discord as he can. I told Carmody any man I learn has been talking to Hudson and fighting or otherwise disrupting the work gets the sack. I am a man of my word, so tell your men."

O'Brien wore a sullen look. "I'll tell 'em, but I can't do nothing about what they do off the job."

"Just remember, I pay only those men who work. Those laid up because of fighting are of no use to me. If you cannot keep your men in line, I'll get another crew boss."

Billy stared at him. "I didna say I couldn't." He paused. "But it's not easy. I can only do me best."

"I hope so, Billy, I truly hope so. I have too much invested in this line not to see it finished. Now you know my feelings about Hudson, I expect you and Carmody to take appropriate action to prevent further disruption." Fletcher paused. "Give my regards to your wife."

He turned on his heel and stalked off for home. He didn't like the undertone in Billy's words. Did O'Brien really believe the rubbish Hudson put about? Couldn't O'Brien see Hudson had deliberately tried to stir up trouble between the two crews? He'd better keep an eye on O'Brien and both crews.

"Hello, Penny Barton?" the familiar voice of Ryan O'Connor roared from the phone.

"Yes. What is it, Ryan?" Penny shoved several folders on her desk aside and picked up a pen to make notes.

"I have something you'll want to see. One of our members found some information on the Stubenville-Indiana Railroad. Guess what?"

Penny sighed. She had too much work waiting to play guessing games. "What?"

"A Fletcher Dawe is listed as one of the investors. Seems he managed the building of the line west from Coshocton. You asked about a man named Dawe."

"But one who took the train trip with us. Maybe he was impersonating Dawe."

"Oh, of course," Ryan sounded disappointed. "I thought you'd like copies of these newspaper clippings and letters about this Dawe."

Leaning back in her chair, Penny twisted the phone cord. "That's not a bad idea. Why don't you send them to me? They might provide some link to the Dawe I met."

Whalen hadn't given up demanding she find the man, but at least the E-mails from Magna had ceased. Her search for Dawe had hit a dead end. Too much work and too little time. Revenge only ranked so high among her priorities. Occasionally Dawe's face came to her in a dream, but she didn't want fantasies and ignored his disturbing presence. If they ever met, she'd pay him back big-time. As for Whalen, she hoped the interest shown by the Railroad Club in HyperTrans might give her an out. New investors would please him.

"Yeah," Ryan's voice interrupted her thoughts. "I'll do that. Seems on the opening run, the lockmaster, guy named Dan Hudson, got himself killed, but they hushed it up. Bad publicity for the railroad. Some locals tore up the track, and he tried to stop the train."

"Interesting. I thought the canals and the railroads were rivals. Why would he save the train?"

"I suppose he had some friends riding it. Anyway, I also called to say we need to get some publicity shots. Could you come here Friday in costume and pose? We've got an old rail car here."

Frowning, Penny flipped open her calendar. "I'm pretty busy just now. We've had some investor queries. I'm sure you can get plenty of others for the pictures."

"Yes, but . . ." Ryan paused. "Well, it's like this, we're trying to interest some of the big-city papers and, with you in the photos, it'll be a snap to get them to run the story. And . . . just think of the extra publicity for HyperTrans. That bill is coming up in the legislature soon for a vote."

Ryan had made the train trip a success, and his club members had also written letters to politicians on train legislation. Whalen hadn't eased up in his demands for results, and the publicity wouldn't hurt. Maybe, just maybe, Dawe would show up, too. That would make Whelan happy.

With a sigh, she initialed "photo shoot" in her calendar. "Okay, Ryan. What time?"

"About noon. See you then."

She made a note to stop by the costume shop on the way home and pulled a file of letters toward her. She'd better send an update about Dawe, but that could wait until after she saw Ryan's clippings.

CHAPTER 5

Friday, Penny stopped her car across the street from the Columbus and Ohio River Railroad office in Coshocton's old red brick depot. She had not returned to the town since her last foray to track down Fletcher Dawe. It still puzzled her how someone could appear and disappear without leaving a trace. She had read the letters and clippings Ryan had sent, but learned little more about the Dawe of the Steubenville-Indiana Railroad and nothing that linked to the present. The honk of a nearby car horn startled her from her thoughts.

Camera equipment, special lights on top of tall poles, extra props for use during the shoot, and a tangle of electrical cords lay scattered about the old depot. Using the station-turned-railroad office for a backdrop had been Ryan's idea. It provided a natural focus for the photos. But the red brick station hadn't been built until more than fifty years after the opening of the Steubenville-Indiana Railroad. So much for Ryan's proposed authenticity. Penny sighed as she opened her car door.

A vintage railroad carriage rested on the well-worn tracks. Wide patches of peeling yellow paint hung from its wooden sides and the bottom of the carriage bowed downward from years of use. Not in the best of condition, but no one could argue about its authenticity. It had been towed to Coshocton and set on the tracks especially for the event. It looked strangely at home.

"Penny! Penny Barton!" Carroty-haired Ryan O'Connor

jogged across the street, flailing both arms. "Can you believe this? I expected maybe ten or fifteen people to show up for this photo session. We must have twenty or thirty. They even dressed the kids in costumes. Isn't this great?" He surveyed the scene with his hands on his hips. His brown eyes sparked with excitement.

She smiled back, enjoying his enthusiasm and good spirits. "You know how I feel about railroads. The more people we interest, the better."

Shaking out the full skirts of her rose silk dress, Penny then adjusted the sash at her waist. "I couldn't get the same outfit I wore for the reenactment. Hope this one will do."

Ryan grinned and looked from her saucy hat to her black boots. "Your costume is perfect. It'll look great in the group shoot, and for the singles it's—" He kissed his fingers.

His response made her smile. Penny reached into her car for her purse and shawl, but then thought better of it. The purse didn't fit the period and the shawl would be too warm, but if she had to wait for a while she might get a chance to read a chapter or two of her book. She snatched up her copy of *Jane Eyre,* untouched since the train trip, and scooped up her skirts. Together she and Ryan crossed the street.

Closer to the old rail car, Penny frowned. She peered inside to rows of wooden bench-like seats and smiled at a blackened potbellied stove bolted to the floor in the front of the car. It looked much like the cars used for the reenactment, but older and in poorer condition. At least Magna keep their old trains in tip-top condition. Despite its need for a good coat of paint, the car provided a perfect setting. Its wooden steps, smooth and worn from years of use, would provide places for people to stand.

"Penny!" O'Connor waved from the raised cement passenger platform. "Grab those people behind you and get ready for the group picture. We need four more men and three women. Choose those with the most authentic costumes."

Gathering several men and women, Penny herded them toward the old car.

"Over here, everybody. Here." O'Connor, like a border collie with a flock of sheep, pointed and directed. "No, just a little left. Better back up. Back, back, back. There. That looks good." He arranged them until all the men and women, and a variety of children, stood posed by the car.

The photographer from behind his camera directed one woman to lift her chin, a man to remove his glasses, and a second woman to push her bonnet back from her face. Satisfied at last, he held up his hand. "Hold it folks, and remember, don't smile."

The images of all those grim people in the pictures at the Warehouse Restaurant surfaced in Penny's memory, but just as quickly she turned forward and smoothed the amused grin from her face. The heat of the sun beat down on her head and shoulders. The unseasonable warmth felt more like a late-June day than April. Holding herself rigid on the first step of the carriage, she sensed beads of perspiration trickling down the sides of her neck. Maybe the global warming crew really had it right.

As she waited, she wondered how things had actually looked in the 1850s, not that it mattered. No one would argue with the authenticity of the pictures. Besides, they would not be presented as surviving photographs from the 1850s, but as publicity photos. They could create interesting art from digital photos.

With a slight shrug, Penny focused on maintaining her pose. Her hands sweated and her stomach growled, a reminder she hadn't eaten breakfast. In front of her, the crowd swirled and reeled into one liquid swarm of color. The conversation from the onlookers fused into a high-pitched hum, and her throat tightened with thirst.

Take the picture, she pleaded in silence to the photographer who had come round in front of his camera to adjust the bow on a child's bonnet. *Just take the picture.* She gripped a handrail beside the carriage steps. Her sweaty palm slipped against the iron railing.

For only a moment the brilliant sun dipped behind a cloud, offering a brief respite from the unseasonable warmth. Just as quickly, it flashed bright again and a blinding beam bounced squarely off Penny's face. The heat, sun, and excited clamor combined to make her view of the passenger platform swim and swirl around her. She could no longer sense her legs as attached to her. Unable to support her body, her legs suddenly gave way. Her shoulders slumped. She could do nothing to stop her forward fall.

She fell a great distance into a bottomless pool of inky water. Drifting past the crowd of chattering men and women and whining children, she fell through the heat of the sun into a cool unfamiliar darkness where a quiet calm settled over her weakened body. From somewhere far away, Ryan shouted.

Not now. Penny ignored him. *Too tired to take more pictures. Too tired.*

She floated in a place where timelessness dangled over her body. Abruptly, a chilly, fresh breeze caressed her face. Her palms had stopped sweating. Energy filled her, and the dreadful heat had fled. She shook her head to clear the thick, dazed sensation and waited for the click of the camera.

The camera in front of her looked different, larger. In fact, the crowd of people in front of her could hardly be considered a crowd at all. Only two or three women and a handful of men stood alongside a single set of railroad tracks awaiting orders from the photographer. All of them looked older and somehow less bright and colorful than the group she had seen earlier that morning. Their clothes appeared faded while the women's severe hairstyles gave their faces a drawn and tired look. But the hats, and especially the shoes, reminded her of the fashion illustrations she'd seen of the 1850s and made her wonder where the reenactors had found them.

In spite of the brilliant sun, a chill brushed her arms. From her step on the carriage she peered into the faces of the people close to her. Where was O'Connor? And what was the photographer doing to the strange box with the black cloth in front of him?

"Miss! Miss!" The photographer walked toward Penny and stood in front of her, frowning. "You must cooperate and stand perfectly still if you expect me to produce a daguerreotype of any quality whatsoever!" His voice sounded gruff and his speech formal. The waxed ends of his mustache twitched as he spoke. "And whatever you are holding there please set it down until after the pose." Penny stared down at the leather-bound book in her hands. Before she could reply to the man, he turned and walked back to his camera.

Camera? Penny's eyes traveled to the huge brown, box-like mechanism positioned on a spindly tripod in front of the impertinent little man. What had he said? A daguerreotype? What was Ryan doing? The man wasn't taking a photo at all! A tintype, an image on metal. But why? She had seen tintypes on the wall of the Warehouse Restaurant in Roscoe. Why would O'Connor choose a tintype instead of a digital photo, which produced a clearer, more versatile image?

Standing perfectly still, Penny stared ahead until the man, mustache still twitching, called for a second group of people to take their places for another pose. She picked up her book and stepped from the carriage. As she walked toward a group of people who earlier had been crowded behind the camera, no face looked familiar; no voice sounded like any she ever remembered hearing. No one approached her to talk, or discuss the origins of their costumes, or the activities planned for Coshocton Rail Days. In fact, no one paid any attention to her at all. Busy with their own conversations or hurrying off in twos and threes, no one stopped to speak with her.

Twirling slowly around, Penny gasped. Nothing looked familiar. The red brick rail station had vanished. She blinked and then blinked again. The station had disappeared. Panic grasped her as she stared about the site.

The carriage, still positioned on the tracks, looked newer and sturdier than she remembered. No passenger station. No elevated platform, either. And the locomotive now on the track had not been part of O'Connor's backdrop for the shoot. Had they moved the carriage when she blacked out? No, she had only had a momentary dizzy spell.

Her heart raced. Her breath came in spurts. She touched her forehead with the back of her hand. No temperature. Surely she would have noticed something as large as a hulking, black locomotive? And the solid reality of a brick rail depot. Had she only imagined the scene in front of O'Connor's office?

Penny sped past a man in thick side-whiskers wearing a dark frock coat. He frowned as she bumped his arm. Her car. She had to find her car and go home. Her mind, in a cruel game, played tricks on her. She would not be a fool. The day had simply been too hot and the sun too bright.

Maybe she needed a rest. She had been working too late, too many long hours. She needed quiet. Time to herself. She turned in a complete circle trying to get her bearings. But where had her car gone? O'Connor couldn't have moved it, could he? It hadn't been parked illegally.

Like the slow opening of a tulip to the early sun, Penny realized that not only was her own car gone, but all the other cars had been moved, too. Where? She looked in every direction as far as she could see. No cars. No buses. No traffic lights. Nothing.

Fear hit her, and her stomach lurched. She couldn't be dreaming. She heard voices, saw color, and smelled the sweet, loamy scent of wet earth. Where was this place? She saw no building, intersection, or vehicle, which looked remotely like any she had seen earlier in the day when she had first driven into Coshocton. Only a few horses and an occasional carriage clop-clopped down the narrow, dirt roadway. All the distant buildings looked like small boxes neatly lined against the horizon.

Suddenly the locomotive belched a thick cloud of black smoke. It wailed a long, slow shriek. Penny jumped. What was this strange place? Where was she? She pivoted slowly, looking first in one direction, then another. Why did this place feel so familiar, yet foreign? Could this still be Coshocton? And if it wasn't, then where? And how did she get to this place?

Hurrying to the bright yellow railroad car, she grabbed the iron railing and climbed inside. She walked the length of the car and back. Her heels echoed against the shiny wooden floor as she passed rows of wooden seats to the potbellied stove and back to where she had entered the car. She pivoted slowly, but nothing changed.

Penny walked out through the door and descended the steps. The scene looked the same as when she had entered the car. The town, small and shrunken, with no telephone poles or streetlights, provided no clues. She turned back to the car again and then jumped down. A few coarsely dressed men in dark, grubby jackets and pants stared at her.

Straightening her shoulders, Penny hurried off. She rubbed her arms. Despite the long sleeves of her dress, the day felt much cooler than she remembered it being earlier. The sun still shone brightly, but a brisk breeze *swish*ed through the trees. The air, damp and chilly, reminded her of the shawl she had left in her car. Her car. Gone, along with everything else she knew.

Keep walking, she told herself. She might stumble into someone or something familiar and walking would warm her. She trailed behind a couple as they headed toward a carriage tethered down the street. She couldn't just follow people around. Penny looked for a sign. Nothing. No stop signs, no billboards, no flyers tacked to telephone poles.

For close to an hour she wandered up one street and down the next. Up Hickory Street, across Main, north on Third Street, back across Chestnut to the east, then down Fourth. At Chestnut and Main stood a small wooden building with an iron bell out front. Above and across the door she read, *Union School, Coshocton, Ohio.* Union School? Penny couldn't remember hearing of any school by that name. But the sign said Coshocton.

A grim realization gripped her. Coshocton, but not the Coshocton she knew. Coshocton as it might have looked—when? Like those old tintypes in the Old Warehouse Restaurant. Had she traveled back in time? She immediately rejected the idea. No. No one could travel back in time. Or forward, for that matter. Impossible. That physicist Stephen Hawking had proved it impossible.

Penny studied the school. She had been to Coshocton often enough to know that a school like this did not sit in the middle of town. She remembered a courthouse at Main and Chestnut, a stone courthouse with broad steps and stores across the street. Penny whirled around. Nothing. No courthouse, no stores.

Overwork and stress had taken their toll and pushed her over the edge. The real Coshocton must exist all around her, but she could not see or touch it. Had she become so obsessed with seeking Fletcher Dawe that she had created this imaginary world? And what did one do in an imaginary world? If she accepted it, wouldn't that just make it worse? She had always been so rational, so attuned to the world she lived in. She did not feel crazy. Did insane people ever doubt their own sanity?

Either she had gone crazy, lost in some mental maze of her own creation, or she had traveled back in time. But to what time? Whose time? Nagging thoughts pulled at the corners of her mind. This surely couldn't be her own time. Of that Penny felt certain. She looked over her shoulder and bit her lower lip. Yet nothing suggested this place could be anything so simple as a restored village or a period reenactment. Everyone and everything she had seen looked almost too solid and real for comfort.

Somehow, she had to find out to where and when she had come. She looked back toward the school. Surely someone would be there. If it wasn't Saturday—or Sunday. Her skirts *swish*ed behind her and wispy tendrils of her short hair strayed into her eyes as she raced across the yard to the front door of the school. Panting, she stood at the door and knocked. No answer. Behind her the bright midday sun slipped westward, leaving a gray, cool afternoon in its wake. She pounded on the door. No sound from within.

She felt like a person in the *Twilight Zone* or a misplaced Stephen King heroine. Everything looked so ordinary and yet so totally different. Was what she saw real or had her mind just made it seem so? Did unseen cars and people swirl around her that she just couldn't see or sense? Practical and rational, Penny rejected the thought that she could be lost in some daydream. She worked hard, but she wasn't stressed out. No, this had to be real and she had no choice but to accept it as such.

Clenching her fists, Penny leaned against the wooden school door. Hot, salty tears rolled down her cheeks. She slapped at them with the back of her hand. Now is not the time to cry, she scolded herself. Any time but now. She refused to give in to hysterics or self-pity.

A square of paper, nailed off to the side of the door, fluttered in a slight breeze. She straightened and moved closer. A handbill. With one hand, Penny smoothed the curling edges of the putty-colored paper and scanned the bold, black print. Her lips moved as she read the handbill out loud. Her eyes widened as she assimilated the words.

Restore Government to Pure American Principles.
American Party challenges Free Democrats to debate.
Sponsor: Denton Jackson, Member, Board of Public Works.
Union School. Half after five, Monday, April 2.

Smaller print at the bottom of the handbill listed topics to be discussed, but her eyes shifted from the date to "American Party" to "Denton Jackson." She stared, her mouth open. Denton Jackson? Hadn't she seen that name in one of the letters Ryan had sent? Penny rubbed her forehead, doubting what she read, but the bold, black print proclaimed its message.

She read the handbill again. Someone had scrawled in the margin: *Shanghai Know Nothings.* Know-Nothings? The Know-Nothings organized some political party in the 1850s. 1852 or '54? Or was it 1856? Penny stood back, her hands on her hips. And what had they been about, anyway? She searched her memory trying to dredge up long-forgotten history lessons.

Miss Ingram, her high school history teacher and a devout liberal, loved the Civil War and had forced her students to learn about the various groups contending for power while trying to influence national policy. Penny could almost hear Miss Ingram's strident voice as she lectured at length on the Know-Nothings. They had been antislavery. And Penny vaguely remembered something about mixing religion with politics, but the specific facts eluded her.

She bent to examine the handbill more closely. It certainly looked new. She reached out and touched the crisp paper. The handbill had not even been rained on or discolored from age. She looked back to the date. April 2. No year.

A thick, cottony lump formed in Penny's throat as the reality implied by the handbill began to penetrate her mental confusion. She had traveled back in time. Stephen Hawking had it wrong. While she couldn't be exactly sure of the year, she knew that somehow she had traveled to the 1850s. And traveling back had something to do with the railroad reenactment, or at least the photo shoot Ryan O'Connor had arranged.

Her stomach lurched. Moisture threaded her palms. Her collar pinched her throat, and the fabric of her dress clung to the skin across her back. Penny swallowed hard. She did not want to be here. She couldn't stay here. Surely, no one would believe she had come from some other time. If this town differed from the Coshocton she knew and the time was not her own, how could she get back?

Back? Make that forward. Penny laughed a high-pitched, hysterical laugh. She glanced nervously up the street. Worse yet, what if she could not go forward? What in the world could she do if she could not find the way to return to her own time? If forced to stay, how could she explain her presence?

For a moment Penny slumped, then slowly straightened her shoulders. Time for that later. She had to find some anchor. She could not stand here forever. She had to do something—anything.

Penny walked around the square and across it. She returned to the handbill twice to reread the date. The list of topics for debate, in small print at the bottom of the sign, glared: *Corruption, Antislavery, Nativism.* Below the topics, in still smaller print, she read *Ladies Invited.*

" 'Ladies invited'?" Penny shook her head and closed her eyes. Somehow she had to get back to her own time.

She crossed the square once again and headed down Second

Street. Few people strolled along the streets and only twice did anyone pass in a carriage. She had no destination. She struggled to match the streets of Coshocton as she knew them to this small, dusty village. She was in Coshocton, the school name testified to that, but as to the exact year she could not be sure.

In the business district, she peered into store windows and studied the display of merchandise. She had only seen dresses like those in the window in pictures or costume shops. Shoes, shiny new, but old-fashioned, at least to her, filled the windows. Advertisements for therapeutic oils and liniments lined the window of the apothecary.

Turning, Penny stared across the street. Most of the small shops and stores had already closed for the day and offered no solution to her immediate problems. Where could she go? She had no money. She could not buy anything to eat or pay for a place to stay. She had only the clothes in which she stood.

Suddenly a sign caught her eye. For several seconds she stood transfixed as the words pelted her mind like hailstones flung from a whirling tornado. Written in elaborate script at the bottom of the sign she read: *Fletcher M. Dawe, Proprietor.* Above that large, dark letters spelled *Dry Goods.* Penny gasped and her palms began to sweat again. The picture in the restaurant had been right; the dry goods store really existed. Not in her own time, but now, whenever now was, here in Coshocton.

Ideas and fragments of information swirled in her mind. Confusion still gripped her, but bits and pieces of what she had seen and read began to make sense. Fletcher Dawe's business card had been correct; the location of 202 South Second Street had existed, after all. Could the man who gave her the card be the real Fletcher Dawe? If she had traveled in time, he must have, too.

She dismissed the thought as too fantastic, then considered the possibility once again. Fletcher Dawe had been so in character; so much so, she had concluded he had played a joke on her aboard the train. No. It just couldn't be, but for a few brief seconds, Penny prayed that it was. She needed some hope, a friendly face. Someone to tell her she had not gone mad and lost all touch with reality.

Her excitement made her shiver. Encouraged and excited, yet skeptical, she stared at the sign. More likely this was a relative of the same name, an ancestor the man she met had impersonated. She shrugged. And if not? She stepped into the street and walked fast, heading toward the store. She had to find out. If he turned out to be the same Fletcher Dawe, whoever he was, then he must know the secret to traveling in time. How else would she have met him? And he could tell her the way to get home.

CHAPTER 6

Penny, still clutching her book, shifted from one foot to the other in front of Dawe's Dry Goods Emporium and tried to summon the courage to enter. Fear chained her feet; she couldn't raise her hand to open the door.

She glanced up the street in one direction and then down the other. Everything looked out of place—strange props on some grandiose stage in a production where she had no part to play. Touching physical objects did nothing to dispel her sense of dislocation. She both wanted, yet feared, to know if she had really met the Fletcher Dawe of this time, because she couldn't begin to guess what that would mean. However, if a descendant had played her for a fool, she would lose all hope of returning to her own time.

Taking a step toward the door of the dry goods store, Penny hesitated again. The building resembled the blurred photograph she had seen at the Warehouse Restaurant, but with a solid reality and spruce appearance. It looked new instead of old and faded. It couldn't possibly be the same building. Penny rubbed her forehead where a headache had just started. The pain only added to her confusion.

Overhead, gray smudges darkened the late-afternoon sky. A sudden wind blew her skirts against her legs, a chilly reminder she would have to seek shelter or find her way home soon. She had no choice but to enter and face Fletcher Dawe.

Struggling to find some direction amid her swirled jumble of thoughts, Penny lacked the will to move. Reality or a dream? She much preferred the latter.

"You look troubled," a woman's voice intruded. "Perhaps I can help."

"What?" Penny reeled, startled to hear anyone address her.

An older woman looked at her with kind blue-green eyes. Her short, full-skirted dress over shiny pink pantaloons made Penny blink in surprise. No one else she had seen wore anything similar. For a moment, the strange fashion illustrations from the nineteenth century rose in memory. In them, the women and men all had large shoulders and diminutive, wasp-like waists. She recalled one not unlike the costume of this strange woman, but even though she had a small waist, she looked real. Not at all like the caricatures Penny remembered in the illustrations. This woman couldn't be more than five feet tall and her short skirt added width where she least needed it, making her look almost as wide as she was high. Unlike the other women Penny had passed today, this lady wore her long locks of silver hair loose under a straw bonnet.

She smiled at Penny, wreathing her mouth with happy laugh lines. "I said, may I be of help?"

Penny struggled for something to say. What? The woman standing in front of her looked so solid, so real as she waited patiently for a reply. Penny couldn't think of any rational explanation for her presence. She had no money, no luggage, no relations, nothing. Indecision held her prisoner as she struggled for an acceptable explanation.

"Uh, I'm . . . I'm a stranger in town . . . and someone stole my luggage, uh—my valise." Penny pulled a handkerchief from her pocket and wiped the corner of her eye, unsure of what to say next. "And my money. I'm—"

The woman's sympathetic eyes reflected concern and worry. "Perhaps we should introduce ourselves. I'm Emily Dawe." She held out her gloved hand.

Eyes wide, Penny stared at the outstretched hand. Dawe? Could this be Fletcher Dawe's aunt? Suddenly aware of the woman waiting for her to speak, she extended her own hand. "Penelope Barton, from Columbus."

"Barton?" Irregular folds creased Emily Dawe's brow, and she gazed at Penny as she recognized the name. "Well, Miss Barton, perhaps we should talk with Sheriff Seton. He prides himself on keeping Coshocton free of unsavory characters."

The woman's words and the underlying implication hit hard. Penny froze. She couldn't very well tell her story to the sheriff. "Uh, I suppose—but what can I tell him?" She fumbled furiously, sorting through a variety of plausible explanations. "When I left the rail car my suitcase wasn't there. I had . . . had packed my money there you see. To keep it safe."

"Rail car?" Emily Dawe stared harder at Penny, her doubt obvious.

"Uh, over a couple of streets." She pointed in the direction from which she had come. "I had just gotten off. A man was taking—" Pictures? Photographs? What had he said? "Uh, daguerreotypes?"

Emily Dawe clapped her hands with a loud smack that made Penny jump. "Oh, how wonderful. Do you think he is still there?" She looked ready to rush off at once. "Let's go and see."

"He rode off in a big wagon . . . and took his . . ." Camera? No. Penny struggled for the right word. "Apparatus. He took his apparatus with him."

Emily grimaced. "What a shame. I would so like to have one taken of my new 'Bloomers.' " She looked down at her pink pantaloons.

"N-N-ew?" Penny stammered and then regained her composure. Old-fashioned sounded more like it, but she reminded herself to watch what she said. "They're . . . lovely."

"Do you like them?" Emily Dawe's eyes sparkled, and she twirled to give Penny a better look. "I'm afraid some of the ladies regard them as too, too outré. I, for one, think Amelia Bloomer has done us a tremendous service. Everyone ought to wear them."

Sighing, Penny nodded. "Some day most women will." When she realized the implication of her offhand remark, she tried to correct herself. "At least I'm sure they will." Images of the women in slacks and in jogging suits, the modern day equivalent of bloomers, but not nearly so flattering to most, paraded in memory.

"You really think so?" Emily smiled and fingered the pink satin. "I find them more practical than sweeping skirts, and more modest, too. But enough of my garments. We must solve your problem. I had not realized the rail service had yet commenced. Fletcher, my nephew, is struggling to complete the line from here to Columbus."

Fletcher? Penny swallowed hard, aware of her faux pas. "No, no of course not, but I came from uh—" She grasped for the name of a town. Where had Fletcher Dawe left the train? Bowerston? Bowerstown? No, it had been "—Bowersville."

Emily nodded. "And you planned to take the canal packet on to Columbus? Yes, I can see that would be reasonable. In that case, perhaps your valise has been taken to the canal office. We should check there."

"Oh, yes, of course. Why didn't I think of that? Where is it?" Penny flushed, aware that every word, every lie, led to a deeper quagmire, but the truth would be even worse.

"Come, I'll take you there."

"Oh, I wouldn't want to impose. I'm sure you had some important errand—"

Emily Dawe laughed, setting her silvery curls to swinging. "Important errand? Nonsense. I only intended to speak with

Fletcher. He is my nephew, you see, but that can wait. Come." Emily took Penny's arm and linked it through her own. "The canal office sits only a short walk from here."

Pulled along by Emily, Penny tried to formulate the details of her story. Surely the investigation of the fabricated loss would provoke questions. Had anyone, besides the photographer, seen her leave the carriage? Several men, with either fist-sized chaws of tobacco or pipes and dressed in soiled work clothes, had stood there. They had ignored her.

Still linked to Emily Dawe, Penny squared her shoulders and continued to walk, glancing this way and that for a familiar cross street or building. Between Emily's multitude of questions and comments, Penny searched her memory for bits and pieces of information about Coshocton's history. When she had planned the commemorative train trip, Ryan's clippings and letters had given plenty of facts and details, but now, walking beside her new friend, she could hardly remember anything at all about Coshocton, the railroad, or the canal.

Emily continued to chatter, apparently unconcerned by Penny's lack of response. She pointed out various buildings in the manner of a well-versed tour guide, including the courthouse and a new hotel. She nodded to several women as they passed, but made no offer to stop or introduce her companion. Penny inhaled a deep breath. Introductions would only be awkward, especially since she couldn't easily or quickly explain her presence in Coshocton.

The squawking of two squabbling crows on the riverbank caught Penny's attention. Emily had guided her to the edge of the Muskingham River, a broader and clearer one than Penny remembered. In her own time, the opaque Muskingham looked dull, not at all like the blue liquid crystal that flowed so swiftly past her now.

"This way." Emily drew Penny toward a square, box-like

building standing to one side of the towpath along the east bank of the river. She doubled her fist and banged the door with impatient raps louder than necessary.

"Dan? Dan Hudson? Open the door." Emily leaned her ear to it, while maintaining her hold on Penny's arm.

A dull thud sounded, and the door opened a crack. Two dark eyes peered out. The crack in the door widened and revealed a stocky man with a shock of disheveled black hair.

"What's all the fuss about? Oh, it's you Miz Dawe. What do you want?"

He eyed Penny with interest, his glance sweeping down from her hat, hesitating on her hips, and then moving to her toes and back up. Before speaking, the intimidating dark eyes lingered for an uncomfortable moment on her breasts.

"This young woman, Miss Penelope Barton, has just arrived by rail and planned to go on to Columbus on the packet. Has her valise arrived?"

"Barton?" Hudson moved his eyes lazily over Penny once again. "The packet?" He hesitated and looked toward the paper-covered table. "Don't have a booking for any Barton."

"I hadn't made it yet," Penny snapped, annoyed at his overt, unwanted appraisal.

Raising an eyebrow, he lounged, arms crossed, against the doorframe. "Then why should your—" He surveyed her again. "—valise be here?"

Determined to put him in his place, Penny used the steely tone that had often set louts like Hudson straight. "Because I told the man on the train I planned to take the packet." She enunciated each word; implying Hudson lacked the capacity to understand.

"Nothing has shown up here. Besides, I don't remember any train due in today." Dan stared at Penny, his black agate eyes accusing and challenging.

"It was a special. Someone had arranged for a pho . . . daguerreologist to make . . . pictures." Blood rushed from her neck to her cheeks. She hugged her book with both arms.

"Daguerreologist?" Blinking, he stared from her to Emily.

Emily nodded vigorously. "You know, Dan. A man who makes daguerreotypes, sort of like portraits, but not painted." Her words hinted at impatience and irritation.

"Oh, oh, them. We don't have no such a person hereabouts."

Emily sighed. "Much the pity that, but apparently the railroad directors decided they wanted some likenesses made. No doubt they sent the man here."

"Yes, yes," Penny burst forth. "That's exactly what he said. He mentioned something about doing a special job for the railroad."

As she tore her gaze away from Dan Hudson's doubting stare, she shifted her position, and her glance ended at the large blackboard on the wall. Penny smothered a gasp as she read the notation scrawled at the top: *Sailings April 1855.*

For a moment her vision failed, and dizziness assailed her. 1855? 1855. Somehow seeing the bold scrawl, white chalk against the blackboard, shook her more than anything else she had seen. The implications of those four digits bore into her consciousness. Reality overcame denial.

It couldn't be. Yet she accepted it. It fit all the various things she had seen—the smallness of the town, the absence of cars, the debate notice, the school, Fletcher Dawe's shop—all fell into place like the slamming of a prison door. Then, with acceptance, came the awful knowledge that in less than two weeks, the man before her would die. His lazy arrogance would not save him. No one could avert the coming tragedy. For him, it lay in the near future. For her, it had already happened and formed part of the colorful past.

An icy shiver crept over her, leaving her cold and numb. Too much had happened. She rubbed her arms, trying to regain warmth and sensation. Emily Dawe gave Penny a sideways glance, a look of concern and sympathy in her eyes.

"Well, Dan," Emily took Penny's arm again, "I suggest you make it a point to watch for Miss Barton's valise. For now, I'll take her home with me." She patted Penny's arm. "She is tired from traveling and could use a nice cup of hot tea."

Penny smiled gratefully. What would she have done if Emily Dawe had not presented herself? Her stomach had been growling for some time and the weather had turned too cool to be comfortable in such a thin dress. "That sounds like heaven."

"Send a boy over when that valise turns up." Emily swept off with Penny in tow, leaving Dan, mouth open, staring after them.

"Have no fear. Dan may be impolite at times, but he knows his business. He will find your valise." Emily paused. "But if not, Sheriff Seton might."

Penny shivered; no way could she allow the sheriff to get involved. "Uh, I hate to trouble anyone. It's just that . . . well, it's all I have and without it . . . I don't know what to do."

"Didn't you sew any money in your petticoat hem?"

"No, I never thought of it." Emily's words make Penny want to smile. So in 1855 petticoats served as a traveler's wallet; what a great way to fool a train robber.

Emily wagged a finger at Penny. "It's a safe way to carry money and keeps your hems in place. Anyway," she patted Penny's arm, "don't fret. We'll work something out."

Penny hoped so. Her mouth suddenly grew dry. Her efforts to reenter the railroad carriage and return to her own time had failed. That left her with only the option of talking to Fletcher Dawe. Fear and desperation made her want to wake from this eerie, inexplicable dream. She must go home.

Walking with firm strides, Emily hurried Penny along. They had gone east from the canal office and now turned north. On either side of the cobbled street stood neat frame houses, all painted white and trimmed in dark green or black and surrounded by deep beds of daffodils and tulips. Occasionally stone or brick houses interrupted the regimented line of clapboard homes, signifying the affluence of a businessman, lawyer, or doctor. In almost every yard, old trees with weighty limbs drooped over roofs and yards.

The town looked more pleasant and prosperous than when Penny had first seen it in her search for Fletcher Dawe. She recognized only one of the homes. The stone cottage near the end of the street where she had stopped to ask about him looked almost new as it nestled among a small stand of young trees.

As they rounded a corner, Penny gazed over her shoulder. Odd she recognized the house at all. In her own time, homes such as these would either be torn down or renovated beyond recognition.

Penny followed Emily to the door of a two-story frame house with white pillars framing the wide front door. Emily led her up a set of limestone steps to the door. Opening it, she stood aside and motioned for Penny to enter.

"Come in and sit in the parlor." She pointed to a room at her right. "I'll put the kettle on and be back straight away." Her bloomers swished as she hurried toward the kitchen.

Entering the parlor, Penny pondered what to do next. Sooner or later Fletcher Dawe would arrive. She had to see him, but right now she would settle for later. The large, rectangular room, with thick wood moldings, tall, slender windows with wavy, pitted glass, and the oak plank floor offered her no clues on what to say to him. A circular rug, obviously handmade, lay beneath a massive library table that appeared covered with piles of books and papers. Penny smiled, thinking of her office credenza with neatly labeled files organized by her capable assistant. Fletcher could use one of those.

Trying to marshal her thoughts, she paced toward a green-striped sofa standing under the front window at one end of the room. Pivoting, she faced a rocking chair and a blue wing-backed chair at the other end, opposite each other and at right angles to the stone fireplace. The cozy setting only added to her sense of dislocation, but it also comforted her. Surely, Fletcher Dawe held the key to returning to her own time.

Above the fireplace, stretching almost to the ceiling, hung a portrait of a stern man with a strong jaw and captivating eyes. The eyes reminded her of Dawe, although the man in the portrait appeared older and stouter. Quick footsteps drew her attention toward the doorway.

Emily Dawe entered and walked to the sofa. She sat and patted the seat next to her. "Now come here and sit down. And take off your bonnet."

Penny perched on the edge of the sofa, set her book beside her, and untied the ribbons of her feathered bonnet. She set the bonnet on top of the book and turned to face Emily.

"Oh my, have you been ill?" Emily stared at Penny's short hair.

For several seconds Penny considered the question, wondering what had led Emily to ask. "Ill?" Then she laughed as she reached a hand to fluff her hair into place. "No, I prefer it this way. It's much easier to care for."

"I'm sure you're right. Washing and brushing long hair takes hours, but most women would never dare cut their hair." The look on Emily's face softened as she continued to stare at Penny's hair. "Although," she said, a finger alongside her cheek, "I believe I like it. Yes, I'm quite convinced I do."

Surveying the room, Penny sought something to say. She had forgotten about the hairstyles of the day. Hers obviously did not conform to the current fashion. Railroads she could discuss, but fashions and local events? Panic again assailed her.

Emily took up the slack. "I noticed you studying the portrait of my brother-in-law, Thaddeus Dawe. Sour old goat. Charismatic portrait, though, I dare say. Still, he knew his comfort and did well by Winifred when he built her this house. The last cholera epidemic took Thaddeus and Winifred, so his son, my nephew Fletcher, asked me to live with him. Do you like English tea?"

"English tea?" Penny stared at her, relieved, but struggling to find solid footing amid the shoals of uncertainty. "Yes, I like most kinds of tea."

Hours had passed since she'd taken any meal, but thirst raged more than hunger. A hot cup of steaming tea, of any kind, sounded wonderful.

"Good, it is one of my favorites. Fletcher bought me some last time he went to Columbus. I'll return in a moment."

Rising, Emily then strode from the room, leaving Penny once again to contemplate the portrait above the fireplace, the room's furnishings, and her doubtful future. Fletcher Dawe had mentioned an aunt named Emily, but the man on the train might be, probably was, impersonating the original Fletcher Dawe. If not . . . She hoped she had met the real Dawe, or she had no hope of returning home.

Penny stared up at the ceiling and expelled a long sigh. Her circular thinking annoyed her; it smacked of insanity. Where had she left logic and cause and effect? She hadn't consciously done anything to transport herself here. Or had she? Had she thought a bit too much about Dawe? But why create such a crazy, detailed nightmare?

A squeal of wheels in need of a good oiling came from the hall. Emily returned pushing a dark wooden teacart on wheels. A lovely china tea service and teapot covered with the calico cozy graced the top along with a tiered plate, carefully set, displaying raisin scones, pudding-filled tarts, and small pink cakes. Penny assumed the cakes to be either strawberry or raspberry.

After pouring the tea, Emily added a generous splash of milk. She handed the delicate cup to Penny. "I always drink my tea English-style, strong with plenty of milk and sugar." She heaped two spoonfuls of sugar into the already brimming cup. "Most Americans drink their tea much too weak in my opinion. But then again, I have an opinion on most things. Please, please help yourself to some sweets."

She stared briefly out the window and then turned back to Penny. "I almost forgot the time altogether. I'm sure you're in need of sustenance after your worry about your lost valise, to say nothing of the exercise from all that walking from the rail depot to town and then back out to the canal and home." She patted Penny's knee with a motherly touch.

The hot, strong tea laced with milk and sugar revived Penny. Her last meal had long since faded to a distant memory. Suddenly ravenous, she filled her plate with a scone, a small cake, and one of the tarts.

"Oh, what's this you're reading?" Emily set her cup on a side table and picked up Penny's leather-bound book. She turned it to the light as she brushed her hand across the cover and opened it. "Currer Bell, how delightful. I have read every book by the Bells that has reached Coshocton. Do you like *Jane Eyre*?"

Her mouth full, Penny nodded. "Um, it's always been one of my favorite novels. Jane fends for herself like a woman should."

"I admire that quality, too. And indeed Jane does." Emily thumbed through the book, riffling the pages. She stared at the endpage, with whatever notation it carried. Penny wondered why her eyes widened as she studied the words. She looked up at her and then down again quickly.

Staring down at the book, Emily remained silent for a moment "You must be tired." She closed the book and returned it to the sofa beside Penny. "Perhaps you would like a rest. We have a spare room, and you may nap there. Although I am not certain about the packet schedules, I cannot allow you or indeed anyone to wait in that dirty office of Dan Hudson's. You rest, and we will talk over dinner."

Hesitation foremost, Penny could think of nowhere else to go. "But I'm causing so much trouble for you."

Much as she welcomed Emily's acceptance and hospitality, she still had no solution to her predicament. If by some chance she took the packet for Columbus soon, what would she find? How could she explain her predicament to Emily? Or to anyone, for that matter?

"Nonsense, it's no inconvenience at all. I love company." Emily rose. "If you have finished your tea, I'll take you upstairs."

Faced with no rational alternative, Penny accepted Emily's offer. If this were an inexplicable dream, maybe a nap would let her wake up in her own time. If not, at least she could use some time alone to work out a credible story.

Placing her cup on the cart, Penny then followed Emily out of the room and up the stairs. The wide staircase rose sharply. At the top Emily turned right, passed one door, and then stopped at the last. She opened the door to reveal a large room painted white. Flowered curtains of rose and white hung at the lone tall window. A small rocking chair, hickory, Penny guessed, stood next to the window. A bed, chest, and dresser, quite ornate and of a dark, rich wood with an oval mirror attached, comprised the other furnishings.

"Here." Emily pulled back the bedspread to reveal cream-colored sheets. "Why not take a nap?" She fluffed the pillows. "If you need anything, I'll be in the kitchen. Sleep well and don't fret. Everything will work out." She smiled at Penny as she turned and then closed the door softly behind her.

The sounds of Emily's descent on the creaking stairs carried through the door. Penny sank onto the soft bed with its soapy-clean smell. Exhaustion washed over her. Emily had been right about the exercise.

Yawning, Penny stretched. Coupled with her confusion and worry, her body and mind demanded rest. She rubbed her gritty eyes and then bent to unlace and remove her shoes. She set them carefully on the rug.

The pillow, soft and thick, reminded her of those her grandmother had used. But that was years ago. Years ago. Her eyes closed automatically.

A soft knock on the door woke Penny. With a start, she sat up and rubbed her eyes. The room looked unfamiliar. Where was she? Then she remembered. The dream still held her; she had not left the past. The same rose and white curtains fluttered at the window. Emily must have opened them while Penny slept. The mirror reflected her image in the bed.

"Miss Barton? Emily Dawe. Are you awake?"

"What?" Penny looked toward the door as it opened slowly, and Emily entered.

"Yes, I'm awake. But it feels as though I've slept so long, too long. What time is it?" Outside, the light had faded. Wide bands of golden sunlight balanced precariously on the edge of the western horizon.

"It's almost six. We'll be dining shortly and I thought you might like to freshen up. There's fresh water in the pitcher." Emily pointed to the dresser. "And the privy is out back."

"Privy?" A note of involuntary surprise crept into her voice; she hoped Emily had somehow missed it. "Of course. And thank you, I'll be right down."

She leaned over and pulled on her shoes as Emily withdrew. Her thoughts wandered past the pitcher and washbasin to the privy outdoors. She grimaced. Maybe she had taken for granted all the modern conveniences back home. The washbasin? No problem. But the privy? The only time she had encountered one was on a camping trip. She rolled her eyes and laughed at herself. No doubt, this age held a number of surprises.

She washed her face and combed her hair, smoothed out the wrinkles in her dress, and then examined her face more closely in the mirror. She looked well rested, but a hint of anxiety haunted her eyes. No one else would notice. Especially since no one could possibly guess her dilemma and the circumstance of her unexpected visit to this younger Coshocton.

Descending the stairs slowly, Penny listened for the sound of voices from the parlor or kitchen. Drawn by the smell of herbs and the unmistakable aroma of onion, she followed the smells toward the kitchen.

Emily stood at the sink emptying a steaming pot of potatoes into a serving dish. "Ah, you look more rested. And now for a good supper." She slapped a creamy mound of butter on the center of the potatoes and turned to stir a pan on the stove. "Just finishing the gravy. Won't take a minute."

Penny nodded, and then turned to the sink to wash her hands. Drying them, she studied the large kitchen. Little resembled the modern kitchen in her apartment. A stove and sink, yes, but how different these looked in cast iron and wood. Against one wall, next to a stone fireplace piled high with logs, stood the shiny-black cast iron range on which rested a mammoth kettle. For boiling water to wash dishes, Penny presumed. On the adjacent wall a wooden counter and sink with a hand pump shared space with a pie safe. The counter, smooth and worn, looked discolored from years of use. The sink, its corners rounded with age, confirmed the number of dishes and pots scrubbed in its deep basin. A wooden table with two ladder-backed chairs sat in the center of the room. A brass oil lamp on the table provided light. No refrigerator, no microwave, no automatic coffeepot.

Emily glanced at Penny from across the room. "If you wouldn't mind carrying the bread we can join Fletcher."

Fletcher Dawe? Suddenly, Penny's dry mouth and stomach twinge cautioned her to proceed with care. She picked up the plate of sliced bread, took a deep breath, and followed Emily. At last, she would meet Fletcher Dawe. The real Fletcher Dawe, whoever he might be.

Emily led the way from the kitchen, across the entry hall, and into the large dining room. At first Penny searched the room looking for Fletcher, but relaxed when she realized he wasn't there. She looked about her with renewed interest.

Unlike the kitchen, this room had an air of formality. Wallpaper, in a muted green and beige with a pattern of trees and houses, covered the walls. A large table occupied the entire center of the room with six mahogany chairs set around it. The needlepoint seats of the chairs matched the wallpaper.

A white linen cloth covered the table. Penny set the bread at one end of the table near the other serving dishes. Dinnerware, a fine grade of china, graced three places. Emily had set out crystal stemware. The candelabrum and place settings looked like solid silver. None of this resembled Penny's all-too-often microwaved meals in plastic trays eaten at her desk.

Emily added the gravy boat, filled to its top with dark, smooth gravy and went to the doorway. "Fletcher, come and meet our guest."

Heart racing, Penny looked toward the entrance. At last she would know.

When Fletcher Dawe came, Penny stared, wide-eyed. She struggled to compose herself, but fear and hope warred. Hope won. This Fletcher Dawe looked exactly like the man she had met on the train. The same build, dark wavy hair, and same intense eyes. Yes, the identical man.

Those eyes widened as he saw Penny. He quickly frowned.

"Miss Barton?" His voice echoed a myriad of unasked questions.

He turned and stared at his aunt. "You didn't tell me our guest was Miss Barton."

Penny sensed, more than heard, a strong undercurrent of accusation in his words.

"Now, Fletcher, I intended to surprise you, and I thought you would be pleased." Emily's voice sounded less sure.

"You have certainly done that." He turned back to Penny, his eyes narrowed. "I must say, Miss Barton, I am surprised to see you. Especially as you gave me a nonexistent address in Columbus."

Penny's mouth dropped open. "Doesn't exist? What do you mean? Of course it does." Then she stopped, sucking in a quick breath.

The address existed in her own time, all right, but in Fletcher Dawe's time? She had no idea. She had not studied the Columbus map of the 1850s, so she had no way of knowing whether the street she now lived on had existed then. "It's south of Broad and west of High."

"So I gathered from your earlier comments about the Broad Street Bridge, but I assure you there is no Main Street at that location."

Emily pulled at his sleeve. "Fletcher, let that rest. You never have shown particular acuity where directions are concerned."

He scowled and fixed a dark look on Penny.

"Dinner is ready and will be cold if we don't eat. Please, do not badger Miss Barton now. We can talk after dinner."

Fletcher held his aunt's chair to the right of the table and then Penny's on the left before taking his place at the head of the table. His eyes, as he passed Penny her plate, had not softened. In fact, his glance accused her of deceit. His anger surprised her. He had said Main Street did not exist. That meant he must have tried to find her, and in his own time, of course, the Waterford didn't exist. It hadn't even been built. She couldn't even remember when the older building next to it, the Cultural Arts Center, a former armory, had been built. Some time around the Civil War, another five years in the future. She had no idea what, if any, buildings might have occupied the site in Fletcher Dawe's time. What a mess!

At once the reason for his mood grew clear. She had given him a card with a nonexistent address. When he tried to find her and couldn't, he must have been confused and then angry with her. He would have thought her a con artist. Now, on top of everything else, she had somehow managed to meet his aunt and sat at his own dinner table. Penny blushed. The delicious mouthful of food suddenly swelled to twice its size and almost choked her.

She couldn't explain her presence now, nor could she explain their earlier meeting. If she told him the truth as she understood it, he would call her insane. Penny tried to force another forkful of food down, but her thoughts remained fixed on her predicament. The entire situation had grown worse.

But she had done nothing wrong! *Why me,* she wanted to yell. *And why now?* She had found her dream man, all right, but he considered her a liar and a cheat, or demented at the very least. None of those characteristics would appeal to a man like Fletcher Dawe.

Emily chatted breathlessly, mostly about some Irish families, students she taught, the weather, anything. She exhibited a steely determination to keep the conversation moving and filled every pause. Penny, occupied with her own concerns, contributed little. Fletcher offered only an occasional noncommittal response.

Penny silently thanked Emily for saying nothing more about contacting the sheriff. He would find no valise. She had no money and no clothes. Surely the sheriff would discover her deception, but then what? Utterly lost, she floundered in a sea of lies. The suspicion in Fletcher's dark eyes when he glanced her way made her situation even worse and more desperate.

After dinner, Penny, eager to avoid Fletcher's searching looks, hurried to help Emily clear away the food. She mechanically dried the dishes as Emily washed. They exchanged few comments. When they finished, they rejoined Fletcher in the parlor, where he stood staring out the tall front window.

"Fletcher," Emily began, "I have asked Miss Barton to stay the night. I have some things of Mary's that should fit her. She is about the same size."

He said nothing and continued to stare through the window.

Emily turned to Penny. "My daughter Mary died a few years ago—in the same epidemic that took Fletcher's parents."

"I'm sorry." Penny cocked her head and tears of sympathy threatened. To add to all her other sins, her visit now forced Emily to relive painful memories. What had she done? Her arrival in Coshocton held an uncomfortable twist for all of them.

"Thank you. It was a sad loss, but it is past." Emily cut Penny short, apparently unwilling to discuss the death of her daughter in any detail. "Come, let us find you something for tonight."

For a moment, Penny hesitated. She wanted to confront Dawe, but his present mood and the little he had said implied he had no awareness of having met her in any but his own time. Emotionally and physically drained, she glanced at the waiting Emily. Too much had happened to her. Fletcher would have to wait until she could think events through. Penny followed Emily.

Taking one of the lamps, Emily again led the way upstairs to the same room Penny had rested in earlier in the afternoon. She tugged open the top drawer of the chest and pulled out a flowered cotton nightdress. She held it up to Penny. "Yes, I think this will do. Tomorrow we can look at the rest of Mary's things and find you some suitable things to wear. You cannot continue to wear the same dress."

"But these belonged to your daughter." Penny flushed. Touching Mary's belongings triggered awkward feelings.

"Mary would not mind." Emily fingered the fine lace at the neck of the nightdress. "I never had the heart to give them away. I have been at fault for letting them waste. I considered cutting them all down and letting out the seams to fit me, but then decided I would not. Mary had a slender figure and more height than I have. I could not bear to ruin such pretty garments."

Emily placed a finger alongside her cheek and stood back, surveying Penny from head to foot. "You have a similar figure to Mary's. These should fit with almost no alteration."

Penny hesitated. "Well . . . just until they find my . . . valise." The lie almost choked her. She took the proffered gown and savored the fine cotton soft against her fingers. "It's lovely."

"Mary liked nice things." Emily smiled. "Until they find your valise then. If they don't find the valise—well, I would rather see the clothes used than molder away."

Turning to leave, Emily paused. "I'll leave the lamp. Just turn the wick down and blow it out when you go to bed."

"Thank you." Penny hugged the gown to her chest as she bit her lower lip. She had an uneasy feeling Emily knew she had never had a valise.

"Good night, Penny. Sleep well." Emily pulled the door closed behind her and left Penny sitting on the bed, the gown still clutched to her chest.

At least she had a place for tonight. Tomorrow loomed before her, a tomorrow she dreaded. Anything she said to Fletcher would increase his doubts about her. It began to seem highly unlikely that he knew anything about time travel. But how had he taken the commemorative train? Had he been whisked into the future yet remained in his own time? How could they have met? Everything she learned only confused her more.

She could think of no acceptable reason to explain her presence. Nothing she could say would bring back Fletcher's lively interest in her. But did she want to stay and change his view?

Damn! The one reasonably attractive man she had met considered her a liar and worse. She had lost all touch with reality and must truly have gone bonkers. Penny punched the pillow. Only in Trotman's Cave had she ever felt so helpless and alone before.

CHAPTER 7

Emily informed Penny when she ate breakfast the next morning that Fletcher had already left for his store. Afterwards, she led Penny upstairs to look through Mary's wardrobe. In Mary's old room, Emily opened the cedar wardrobe. Selecting a pale green dress, she laid it on the bed.

"Now, let's see how this fits."

She frowned as Penny slipped out of her rose silk day dress and into the green one. This young woman wore no corset. Instead she had on some sort of scanty garment that barely covered her breasts. Emily had never seen its like. She wondered at its flimsy construction.

"Would you like to try one of Mary's corsets? The whalebone ribs provide plenty of support." Emily held up one of the lace-trimmed undergarments.

Staring at it, Penny shuddered. "No, thank you. I hate being imprisoned."

"Imprisoned?" Surprise made Emily open her eyes wide. While she had given up the heavily boned versions in favor of a lighter, less tight chemise, young women always sought to enhance their appearances and hide any flaws. Only loose women or the very poor avoided corsets. She added this to the other contradictions she had noticed about Penny Barton. She had never encountered anyone like her.

Circling Penny, Emily eyed the dress and nodded as she moved. "Yes. Yes, this one will do nicely. With just a few minor changes, I believe." She knelt to the floor and adjusted the hem at the bottom of the gown. "One inch shorter. No more, I shouldn't think."

Penny moved toward the tall mirror standing next to the armoire. "You can't imagine how thankful I am. For everything. You've been so wonderful to me, but these clothes—what would I do without them?"

"Charity alone would demand I assist you. However, much as I loved my daughter, I wished she had not spent so much time on her clothing and keeping up with the—" She paused and sighed. "—latest fashions. Improving her mind or helping those less fortunate than she would have pleased me more. The books she could have bought." Emily sighed. "However, now she has left us, I've no doubt she would prefer these garments find a new owner rather than molder away. This was a favorite of hers." Emily moved toward the bed and picked up a bonnet covered in yellow satin.

Fingering the smooth fabric, she then gently replaced it among petticoats and dresses and several pairs of boots. For an instant her eyes misted, and the muscles of her neck tightened as she swallowed hard. "Mary dressed well, the epitome of fashion. You have the coloring and carriage to do her clothes justice."

"You really don't mind then . . . that I wear your daughter's clothes?" Penny removed the pale green dress as she spoke.

"Not at all!" Emily refused to allow herself any but the briefest moments of melancholy, and certainly she had no intention of making this strange young woman more uncomfortable than she already appeared. "We must do something with that hair." She examined Penny's short locks with a critical eye. "Why ever did you have it cut so short?"

"Short?" Penny raked through her hair with her fingers. "Convenience, really. It's trendy. A fun style. Besides, everybody's wearing it—" She stopped abruptly and her face reddened.

Emily leaned forward to listen more closely. Trendy? She silently practiced the word. "Everybody's wearing it," the young woman had said. Not anyone in Coshocton Emily knew wore their hair so short, unless they had suffered severe illness or sold their hair when desperate for money. Yes, a very different young woman, this Penny Barton, but likeable nonetheless.

The young woman quickly turned away and busied herself folding the clothes on the bed. "Emily, I've wanted to ask you something. If my valise, the one I lost—" She pivoted and faced Emily. "—isn't found—and my money, too, of course—I can't rely on your charity. I'll have to earn my keep. I can't expect you and Fletcher—"

"Nonsense." Emily dismissed her protest with a wave of her hand. "If you have no desire to continue on to Columbus, you may stay here until we find your things."

"It's not like I have many options without money." Penny gave her a wry smile. "I have no resources and no friends. All I own was packed in my valise." The distress and indecision on Penny's face touched Emily.

"Maybe I could teach, if anyone would hire me. But I haven't any references." For several seconds she stared ahead and looked deep in thought. "I could work in a bookstore or a woman's clothing store."

Emily snorted. "Sally Harkness can barely eke out a living from her millinery store. She can't afford help. It took most of her inheritance to get her shop started. As I hear now, she may have to close it."

Moving closer, she took the girl's face in both her hands. "Now don't fret about this." For a moment the temptation to hug her grew. Except for the short hair, she looked so much like Mary.

Penny paced to the window. "I could take in laundry. Or maybe open some sort of boardinghouse."

Emily rolled her eyes. "The bookstore sounds more reasonable, even though I cannot say how much business you would have. Let me ask some of the ladies about teaching. I could provide a reference for you." She lifted her chin as if to say "so there."

Penny laughed. "Fine, but meanwhile, I can help you here with cleaning and dishes. Surely there's something I could do."

Again Emily waved in dismissal. "I have an Irish girl who comes in to help with the laundry and heavy cleaning." Frowning, she then paused a moment. "She needs the work and does a good job, but what I lack is someone to talk with about books, current affairs, the Women's Guild. I mean someone who can bring something to a conversation other than local gossip. The ladies hereabouts spend too much time discussing their neighbors, husbands, or children. I have no interest in that sort of thing. From your choice of reading I believe you have the type of intelligence that considers the broader world. Suppose we give each other a three months' trial?"

"A trial?" Penny looked perplexed.

"As my companion and perhaps a co-tutor for the Irish children. Meanwhile, you'll have time to look about and consider other opportunities. Fletcher says with the railroad coming, business will boom."

"But it's an imposition."

"Nonsense, extra help with my teaching and an occasional spirited conversation is just what I need. When I am forced to skip a lesson, the children suffer. Too, while you would have a room and plenty to eat, I'll have to discuss a stipend with Fletcher." Emily sighed and pushed a stray lock of hair from her face.

"But, for me, best of all would be having someone intelligent with whom to talk. Sometimes I am so starved for lively conversation I think I shall go mad. Now that is settled." Emily clapped her hands together as if to seal the pact.

Laughing, Penny Barton plopped down on the bed. "Emily, if it's lively conversation you want, then let's go to the debate."

"Debate?" Emily cocked her head, uncertain what debate Penny meant.

"Just before we met—at Fle—Mr. Dawe's store, I saw a sign about a debate on the school door. The Know-Nothings—I mean the American Party and Free Democrats. Now there's a debate that's sure to be lively. And then some." She bounced on the bed. "What do you think?"

"Well . . ." Emily hesitated and pursed her mouth. "You are correct in one thing. It certainly will be lively. Maybe too lively. Ladies do not generally go to that sort of—"

"The sign," Penny said, interrupting, "read 'Ladies Invited.' Can you imagine? There are so many questions I'd love to ask!"

Emily chuckled at Penny's enthusiasm. "Invited is one thing, but I hardly think we would be offered the chance to ask questions." She studied her houseguest with sharp curiosity. Most of the Coshocton ladies had no interest in political rallies.

"Emily, come on. What can it hurt? Besides, we won't have too many opportunities to hear the Know-Nothings defend their platform."

"What do you mean?" Emily remembered the newspaper articles about the antislavery Know-Nothings. Surely they would have plenty of opportunity to defend their political viewpoints.

"Ah . . ." Penny stammered. "Well, maybe we won't be able to make the next debate. Or maybe they won't invite the ladies, or . . ." She did not finish.

Or maybe Miss Barton knew more than she was willing to say, Emily decided. Her eyes narrowed as she considered the young woman in front of her.

Penny moved from the bed toward the door. "About my staying for three months, shouldn't we ask Mr. Dawe?"

"Later. Fletcher won't return for hours. Besides, let me manage things with my nephew. In the meantime, though, we must first settle something else."

"Settle?" Penny's voice sounded small and childlike. Her eyes reminded Emily of a newborn foal.

"If you are to remain my guest, then we had best determine a credible reason for your visit."

Emily strode to the rocker in front of the window and seated herself comfortably, feet propped on the windowsill, before she spoke. "Penny, surely Fletcher's associates and my friends will ask about you. They will seek details you may or may not want to provide." She watched Penny's cheeks color.

Inhaling sharply, Penny frowned. "I'm simply a friend who has come for an extended visit." The pinkish cast on her cheeks turned cherry red.

Suppressing a smile, Emily raised an eyebrow. "And from whence did you come?"

"Columbus. No, I'm going to Columbus. I came from—" Again Penny paused as if uncertain. "Bowersville. You know that. And if my luggage—my valise—hadn't been misdirected or lost, I probably wouldn't be here at all."

Was Penny speaking faster than usual or had she simply imagined it? And *luggage* did she call it? "Well, you see, Penny, Columbus is not too terribly far, nor is Bowersville. Perhaps, if you had really wanted to, you could have returned by now. Or perhaps you might have sent ahead for some other personal items, since making the decision to stay." Emily turned and looked out the window. "But since you have decided to stay, and, mind you, I could not be more pleased . . ." Anxious to reassure Penny, she smiled a warm, comforting smile. ". . . we must offer some reason for your being here. So unless you have another explanation to offer, here is what I propose."

She dropped her feet to the floor and perched on the edge of the chair. "You are the niece of my dear friend, Clotilde von Wahl. Clotilde lives in the East and has four daughters. She is unlikely ever to visit, so for now we shall say you are Penelope Barton, her niece. From Philadelphia. You have come to Coshocton for a stay of several months. If you decide to make your home here, then I will assume responsibility as your chaperone. How does that sound?"

In a sidelong glance, Emily watched for Penny's reaction. Unless her young charge had a more reasonable story to offer, this would have to do. Emily, having considered all the oddities about Penny and coupled them with Fletcher's initial enthusiasm, decided keeping the young woman close suited her. She doubted Penny could provide a better explanation for her appearance in Coshocton. Regardless of the reason for her secrecy, she intrigued Emily. Her manners and attitude struck an answering affinity, and Emily hoped she might take Mary's place. A place that her nephew Fletcher would question and challenge, and that she must be prepared to defend.

Satisfied with her proposal, Emily smiled at Penny. If she could handle anyone at all, she could certainly handle Fletcher. Besides, getting the better of him now and then did them both good. If this young woman proved to be as stalwart as she seemed, she might make a good candidate as a wife for Fletcher.

That evening after dinner, Emily left to tutor one of the Irish families. Penny and Fletcher adjourned to the parlor.

"Well, Miss Barton, we should discuss your arrival and plans." Fletcher sat in his usual wing-backed chair by the fireplace. Penny, her book clasped in her hands, sat in Emily's usual chair, facing him.

"Yes," she sighed, glad she would at last know for certain

how they had met. Yet at the same time, she dreaded the coming interview. "I agree, but you may find my explanation a bit strange."

"Why not begin by telling me why you are here, and from whence you really come."

Taking a deep breath, Penny then exhaled slowly. The lamplight cast interesting shadows on his face. If only he looked more receptive instead of like a hanging judge. "Frankly, I don't know why I'm here. When I left the railroad car I found myself in this place. I didn't intend to come, although I had been looking for you."

Fletcher's eyes widened. "Surely, if one were in a railroad carriage, one must be going somewhere. At the very least, the train had a destination. You were looking for me? Why?"

"Well . . ." Smiling, Penny looked down at her book. "I enjoyed our conversation and I . . . I wanted to see you again." She looked first sideways at him, and then, chin in the air, she confronted him. Her steady gaze made him blink.

"I said I would call upon you in Columbus. I tried, but . . ." His voice took on a harder tone. "The address on your card does not exist. No one had heard of you or anyone of your name involved with the railroad."

Penny squirmed, wanting to be honest with him, but all too certain of his likely response. "I know." She studied her hands and debated how to tell him what had happened to her when she didn't know herself. He'd consider her a nut. Yet she suspected Emily somehow guessed. Otherwise, why would she have concocted that cover story for her? She took a deep breath and steeled herself to tell him.

He studied her with narrowed eyes filled with accusation and a hint of righteous anger. "You lied to me."

"No, I didn't. I told you the facts. It's just that . . ." She trailed off unable to say "I'm from the future."

"Just what?" He stared at her, his eyes boring into her and demanding the truth.

"You'll think I'm crazy." Reluctant to continue, she fingered the cover of her book. She looked up at him seeking some reassurance or sympathy, but saw none. "I almost think I am crazy, or that somehow this is all a weird dream. This is 1855?"

"What? Of course this is 1855. Why do you ask such a strange question?"

"Because . . . because I was born in 1980, the year President Reagan got elected."

Fletcher's eyes almost bulged, and then he laughed. "Very funny, Miss Barton. Are you sure you don't mean 1830?"

"No, I don't," Penny snapped. "I told you, you wouldn't believe me. Main Street exists. It just won't be called that for a while, and the Waterford was built in the 1980s. I live there. That is, I used to live there. I don't understand this at all." Angry at his disbelief and her own situation, Penny clenched her fists. The utter rejection on his face did it. She burst into tears.

"Miss Barton, please, control yourself." Fletcher pulled out a large white linen handkerchief and handed it to her. His eyes looked less distant now and more concerned. "That still does not explain how we met."

Nodding, Penny lifted her nose from the handkerchief. "I know. I don't understand that, either. You see, I arranged that train trip as a publicity stunt, a reenactment of the opening of the Steubenville-Indiana Railroad. I got a film company to lend us the locomotive and the carriages, and all the railroad buffs agreed to dress in period clothes. We went through that tunnel. I sort of lost it there." Penny shuddered. "I hate dark, closed places ever since—" She stopped, unwilling to tell him about Trotman's Cave.

"Anyway, I started reading my book, and then you got on,

but you didn't stay. I couldn't understand it. And your boots—"

"My boots?" Leaning against the mantel, Fletcher wore a bewildered look. He glanced down at his feet and then back at Penny. "What have they to do with any of this—this fantasy of yours?"

"I only wish it were a fantasy. Well, they matched the period. Didn't you notice? Nobody else had boots like that. Oh, sure, the clothes looked all right. The film company made sure of that. But people wore their ordinary shoes, although nobody wore Reeboks, thank heaven."

"Reeboks?" Fletcher rolled the word in his mouth, as if he didn't like its taste. "What are they?"

"They're running shoes. You know, athletic shoes used for sports—baseball, football, tennis."

He stared at her with a confused, puzzled look on his face.

"They're . . . um, made of nylon cloth and rubber. They're lighter, more flexible, and tougher than dress shoes."

Fletcher walked toward the window and then returned to Penny. He stopped before her, his face furrowed. "I still do not understand about these . . . Reeboks or baseball."

Penny waved that away. "They're not important. Nobody wore them anyway. It's just that the shoes everybody else wore came from the twentieth century, not the nineteenth. You looked and talked so much the part, I couldn't believe it. It was as if you were from 1855."

"Well, I am. How could it be otherwise?" He looked mystified.

Penny shook her head. "But I'm not, and neither were the others. Think, did you see anyone else you knew on that train?"

Again Fletcher paced toward the window and back before replying. "No, I cannot say that I did. The conductor was not the usual man, either." He frowned as he stroked his chin. When he looked back at Penny, his eyes appeared troubled.

"You'd never seen any of us before—because none of us lived in 1855."

He snorted. "That makes no sense. The train stopped, so I boarded and left it as I planned at Bowersville. I live now. I have never lived in any other time. What you suggest is not possible."

"Yes, it is. I'm the proof of it. Bowersville isn't Bowersville. Now it's Bowerston. I even came to Coshocton to look for you, but I couldn't find your store. It doesn't exist in my time."

He stopped pacing and stared at her in surprise. "You came to Coshocton to look for me?"

Penny's cheeks grew hot, and she rubbed her hands. "Magna, the film company, wanted you for a commercial and—well, I wanted to see you again."

He blinked at this bold statement and then scratched his chin. "Um, you say my store no longer exists?"

She nodded. "I asked around town, but no one had heard of you. Then later, at lunch I saw an old, blurry picture—" At his look of confusion, Penny struggled for the right word. Did photographs exist yet? "Um, a reproduction of a daguerreotype, that is, and it mentioned your name in the caption."

"A daguerreotype?"

"Of your store and several other businessmen. Railroad investors, I guess."

"Oh?" He paused a moment. "Yes, we did have one taken last fall. But you said my store doesn't exist?"

"Well, in my time, all the businesses have moved from Second Street. They're on Walnut Street between Third and Eighth."

"There's nothing there."

"Not yet, but with the railroad there will be. You'll see."

"Humph, so far you have only told me things that no one can verify. None of these wild statements prove anything. Just that you have an overactive imagination."

Penny sniffed. "I don't know much about what happens in

Coshocton in the 1850s. I can tell you there will be a war over slavery in about five years. Oh, and someone will try to derail the train on its inaugural run from Coshocton to Newark."

"What?" Fletcher stood stock still, his face suddenly pale, as he faced her. "Who? When?"

"April eleventh. I don't know who tries to wreck it."

Leaning forward, Fletcher skewered Penny with his stony stare. "Look, Miss Barton, someone must have told you this. Where did you hear it? I must know."

"I didn't hear it, I read about it, and I talked to Ryan O'Connor about Dan Hudson." At Dan's name Fletcher blanched even more. "But in the future."

"Dan Hudson?" He said the name with distaste. "You mean the lockmaster?"

"Yes." Penny stared down at her hands. "His family . . ."

"Hudson isn't married." Fletcher sank into his chair and straightened the crease in his pant leg.

"Well, I can't speak for that." She suddenly recalled something about a hidden wife and son, but obviously Fletcher couldn't know that. "But Ryan had the clippings."

"Um, I cannot say much for your choice of friends. Hudson is a troublemaker."

He leaned back in his chair, a frown wrinkling his forehead. He said nothing for a moment and then studied Penny with apparent growing distrust. "I see now where all this is coming from. You are involved in some nefarious plot to sabotage the railroad."

Jumping to her feet, Penny clenched her fists. "No. You've got it all wrong. I'm what I say I am. I'm not involved in any plot."

Fletcher arched an eyebrow in disbelief. "Then prove it."

She stared down at her feet. "I—I can't."

"Of course you cannot, because none of it is true. Well, Miss Barton, I shall have to speak with my aunt about you. I do not know what game you are playing, but it smacks of intrigue and ill will. While you are in this house, I insist you refrain from such schemes."

"Ohh, you are so stubborn! If I can't convince you, that's your problem."

Storming from the room, Penny then took the stairs two at a time. She slammed the door to her room and flounced into the rocking chair by the window. The tears flowed unchecked. So much for the truth. Fletcher Dawe had not trusted her before, and now he discounted everything she said. She had no way to prove the truth of what she had told him until Dan Hudson got killed trying to prevent the derailment. Then Fletcher would just say she had known about it because she was part of the scheme. On top of that, he had provided no clues to either his appearance on the train or any insights into her own transfer.

She would have to find her own way back. But what if one didn't exist? If she remained stuck here, she would have to make the best of it. Trains. She had made them her vocation and avocation. Somehow, she suspected a woman's participation in the railroad business would not be encouraged in 1855. Business belonged to men. Like hell!

There had to be a way to show Fletcher and others that a woman could make contributions. She'd find a way to stop the train derailment. Such an event would not only hurt Fletcher's financial interest, it would kill people. Thoughts of Dan's likely death and the danger to the train passengers struck suddenly. Clearly, Fletcher detested Dan and could not see him doing anything to save the train, but since Dan had done so, perhaps he knew something about the people planning the wreck.

Of course, why hadn't she thought of him before? She'd have to talk with him. Then, Penny remembered how he had looked at her. How his gaze had lingered on her breasts. Well, she knew how to handle amorous wolves. Dan Hudson would not give her any trouble. She would show Fletcher Dawe.

Fletcher stared at the fire watching the flames turn from red to blue and thought about the blue fire in Penny Barton's eyes. He wished he did not find her so damned attractive. With her trim figure and lovely oval face, she made him want to grab her and kiss that soft, silky mouth. He had never felt about another woman like this. Why now? Why this irritating adventuress who probably came only to disrupt the opening of the railroad? But, why tell him? To gain his trust?

His ambivalence toward her disturbed him. He wanted to believe her with all his heart. He feared to believe her, sensing she would break that heart. Why did things have to be so difficult?

As for her story about being from the future, he considered it too preposterous. No one could possibly accept it. She wanted him to believe they had met out of time and that she had traveled back in time. Ridiculous! Such things did not happen.

Too many wanted to see the rail line fail, including Dan Hudson and that snake Denton Jackson, who headed the Board of Public Works. Perhaps one or the other had hired Miss Barton in the apparent belief he would find her attractive and share vital information with her. No one would destroy his railroad, especially not Dan Hudson or Penny Barton.

He tried to remember what she had said. Something about a war over slavery. That brought to mind the words of the Reverend Mr. Henry M. Denison that he had read in an article in the *Coshocton Progressive*. A report on an escaped slave woman, Rosetta Armsted. Denison had said something about the Republic divided and its borders devastated by perpetual war. The man had been upset because the mulatto slave, Amsted, whom he had brought to Columbus had been taken from him and declared a free woman. Surely, the country would not come to war. The South must eventually recognize the folly of slavery and follow the North in abolishing it, although even here some supported slavery. No, neither Miss Barton, nor the Reverend Denison could possibly be right about a war.

And the opening of the railroad? April eleventh? The inaugural run would be before then. No, for reasons known only to herself and her confederates, Miss Barton had made up a series of fantastic lies. Well, he would remain on his guard. He would keep her under a close watch.

Fletcher picked up Penny's book. It had fallen to the floor when she stormed from the room. As he picked it up, the cover fell back, revealing the endpage. He started to close it when the printing on the bottom of the page caught his eye. *Abelard Publishing, Facsimile edition of 1847 printing of* Jane Eyre *by Charlotte Brontë writing as Currer Bell, 2004, all rights reserved.*

Fletcher stared at the printing, wondering if he had gone mad or whether Miss Barton was an even more accomplished liar than he had believed. First her calling cards and now this book. He snapped it shut and set it on the table. Too clever by far. He would catch Miss Penelope Barton out, catch her before she destroyed his railroad.

Later, when Fletcher heard Emily return, he called her into the parlor. He rose when she entered. She took off her straw bonnet and brown cloak and laid them on the sofa. Smoothing her hair, Emily joined him by the fireplace. The firelight made her purple dress look almost black.

She held out her hands to the warmth of the fire. "What is it, Fletcher?" The flickering flames deepened the lines of fatigue etched on her features.

For a moment, he wondered if he should pursue his concerns about Penny Barton now. "You look tired. Perhaps you should give up this tutoring."

His aunt snorted in a most unladylike way. "Fiddlesticks. I'm fit, and these people need my help. How else will they ever rise above being common laborers? No, I need someone to help me that is all. I thought to ask Penny."

Leaning against the side of the mantel, Fletcher frowned. "I'm not sure that would be wise." He stared at the blue-eyed porcelain shepherdess, seeing again the hot blue of Penny's eyes. He clenched his fist. "Besides, I doubt Miss Barton will be with us for long."

Emily looked up at him, a question in her eyes. "Why? Have you two quarreled?"

Hands clasped behind his back, Fletcher paced from the fireplace toward the window. "I spoke with Miss Barton this evening. She said some quite extraordinary things." He stopped and faced his aunt. "How much do you know about her?"

Emily studied him before replying. "She appears a sensible young woman who may have had a spot of bad luck."

"Such as?"

Looking down at her folded hands, Emily glanced at him from the corner of her eye. "The loss of her valise and all her clothing and money." His eyes widened at that. "I believe her intelligent, capable, and spunky. I quite like her."

Fletcher sighed. "She may be all those things, but she is first and foremost an adventuress." He studied the shiny toes of his boots.

"An adventuress?" Emily laughed.

"You have not heard the tall tale she spun tonight." Fletcher could not restrain the bitterness from his voice. "Worse, I think she may be involved in a plot against the railroad."

"What? Why?" She stared at him as if he had taken leave of his senses.

"I think you had best sit down."

Emily sank onto her rocker and waited for him to continue.

"She—" Fletcher struggled for words. "She says she comes from—the future. She claims to have been born in 1980."

"I see your point." Emily pursed her lips and leaned back in her rocker. "Yes, that must seem illogical to you."

"Indeed, no one can travel in time." He lifted the curtain edge and peered out the window.

"Don't be so quick to say that. Why only last month, I read a story posing that very thing."

Doubting his own ears and her words, Fletcher stared at her. "What? What do you mean?"

"Yes, it appeared in a literary journal from a few years back, but you know how tardy overseas mails can be. It turned up in the belongings of one of the Irish families. Let me see . . ." She paused a moment, her finger alongside her cheek. "Ah, yes, an anonymous piece and that Irish journal. The title was . . . *Missing One's Coach*. Yes, that was it."

"A scientific journal?"

"No, as I recall a literary journal."

"There, you see? Fiction not fact."

"Perhaps, but I have noticed a number of strange things about Penny." His aunt studied his face for a moment before continuing. "For one, she is a strong-minded young woman. After I found her in front of your store, we confronted Dan Hudson. Let me tell you, she did not let his arrogance pass unchallenged. Put him in his place she did."

"So? What has that to do with her lies?"

Emily stiffened. "Fletcher, you go too far in saying that. Penny may have perhaps shaded the truth for reasons of her own, but you should consider her situation."

"She can offer no proof to support her wild assertions. If she really believes what she says, perhaps we should worry about her sanity." He stared at his aunt.

Searching his face for a moment, Emily then shook her head.

"No, I do not believe that for a moment. Have you examined that book of hers?"

"Yes, I saw it." He stopped in front of the fireplace and fingered the dainty porcelain shepherdess. "A clever forgery, just like her card with all those strange numbers and an address that does not exist."

"Has it occurred to you that if she wanted you to accept her story, if she had planned all this in advance, that she would have used something you could identify? When you first met, she had no way of knowing how well you knew Columbus. She impressed you enough for you to try and find her again. That should tell you something."

"Yes, what a complete fool I was to accept her at face value. A benighted simpleton." He hit the mantel with his fist and made the shepherdess rock.

His denial brought a smile from Emily. "But not in the way you think. Now, what is this about a plot against the railroad?"

"She claims someone will try to derail the train on its inaugural run."

"Um, do you think there is any truth in it?"

Frowning, Fletcher pondered the matter. "I think there must be, and she is trying to mislead me about it."

"But why tell you about it then?"

"I . . . I don't know." He stared down into the fire, more perplexed than ever.

"Well, what did she tell you?"

"She said she had come from the future with no explanation of why or how. She spoke about a war over slavery and about the train derailment, that is the sum total."

"How interesting, but of course we won't know about those until or unless the war and the derailment happens." Frowning, Emily fingered her skirt.

Straightening the little shepherdess, Fletcher said nothing for a moment. Then he looked to his aunt, unable to suppress his doubts. "She mentioned Dan Hudson and said he was married."

Emily looked puzzled. "Dan, married? Um, must be that Irish lass who lives with him."

"Miss Barton," Fletcher said, arching an eyebrow, "had the temerity to claim Dan will die to save the train. I cannot see him in the role of a hero, especially as regards the train."

Nodding, Emily half smiled. "Oh, I see. So you immediately assume she is conspiring with Dan Hudson."

"Well," he said, facing his aunt, "what else can I think? Her story about coming from the future is too preposterous."

"Is it? Perhaps so, but you prefer to believe the worst of her without considering she might have good reasons for not explaining how she knows about Dan." Emily sought his eyes, but he turned away. "I have spent more time with Penny than you have and have grown to like her a great deal. I think I know her character. She may be impetuous, but she has integrity. Why not wait a bit?"

Fletcher resumed his restless pacing. His aunt's staunch support of Penny Barton both surprised and troubled him. It fueled his own ambivalence towards her. He wanted to believe her, but that made him distrust his ability to view her and her story objectively.

"What do you suggest I do?"

"Nothing for the moment. Let her stay with us. Here, you can watch and observe her. If you believe she is involved in some scheme, surely you have a better chance to prevent any action by keeping her with us?"

He mulled over his aunt's proposal, which agreed with his own thinking. "Um. Yes, it makes sense, but it means you must keep her under watch."

"Fletcher, be sensible. What is she likely to do? I cannot see her prying up railroad track, and she knows no one in town except us."

"That is what she told you. How do we know it for the truth?"

Emily sighed. "Unlike you, I trust Penny. Listen to what she tells you about the future. You will have plenty opportunity to verify her predictions. If she has lied, I suspect she has done it only to protect someone else."

Fletcher snorted. "The only things she has predicted so far concern a war in five years and the train sabotage."

"Well, I presume the latter is soon, so you will have proof one way or the other shortly."

"April eleventh, she said."

"Well then, let us wait and see what happens."

Clenching and unclenching his fists, he stared at his aunt. "Neither she nor anyone else will interfere with the opening of the railroad."

"Of course." Emily leaned forward and touched his arm. "Please, give Penny a chance. Don't condemn her without proof."

Fletcher stared down at his aunt's hand. "I'll wait, but once I find proof of her involvement, I shall ensure the law takes a hand." He gave her a hard look.

Nodding, Emily sighed. "All right. That is fair enough. But until then, we must treat her as the guest she is."

Fletcher snorted and stalked from the room. He would allow the deceitful and enigmatic Miss Barton to stay, but neither she nor anyone else would destroy his railroad. As for Dan Hudson, he would more likely destroy the train rather than save it. Fletcher would have to watch Dan and his cronies.

CHAPTER 8

His back to the fireplace of the Union School, Fletcher watched Penny Barton from the corner of his eye across the main room. Her animated conversation and the broad smile on her face attested to how much she enjoyed Dan Hudson's company.

The student tables had been pushed to the far wall, while the wooden chairs and benches had been pulled forward to provide seating for the crowd. Men in frock coats and white, stiff-collared shirts conferred while they waited for the speakers to take their places on the platform at one end of the room. Only a scattered sprinkling of women accompanied the men.

To improve his view of Penny and Dan Hudson, Fletcher shifted around and leaned his elbow on the broad oak mantel. Whatever could Miss Barton, a supposed newcomer to town, have to discuss with Hudson? Aunt Emily's explanation had not set any of his fears to rest.

Uneasy about Penny, her interest in Dan Hudson and the canals and locks only strengthened his certainty of her dubious intentions. But his unease came not entirely from his worry over possible harm to the railroad. Hudson appeared altogether too familiar as he leaned close to her.

Fletcher shrugged and jammed both hands in his pockets. A splinter of irritation poked him as he watched her basking under Hudson's attentions. Too attractive for her own good, she must realize the impression she created on Hudson and every other man in the room—behavior all too typical of an adventuress or a loose woman. He still could not sort out his feelings toward her. Such boldness, and yet she also had an openness and firmness so like Aunt Emily.

"So then, we have a deal?" Mr. Johnson, the portly banker extended his hand.

"A deal?" Flushing, Fletcher realized he had not heard a word of what Johnson had said.

"Look, Dawe, only two thousand more and we will hit a hundred and eighty thousand. That is a lot of stock to sell in support of the railroad and all of it well spent. You know that yourself. We have bought superior materials and hired skilled labor." Johnson's hand remained extended. "Well?"

"Yes, yes. Two thousand dollars then. You know you can count on me. The railroad is inevitable. We all know that. And from my point of view, it represents the best possible investment. That is one more reason for my attendance this evening." Fletcher shifted his gaze back to Penny as he grasped Johnson's hand.

"What do you mean that is why you are here this evening? Do you expect this political debate to differ from any of the others?" The banker grimaced as he gazed about at the crowd.

Fletcher shook his head and gave Johnson his full attention. "Some would spare no effort to stir up trouble among the rail crews and might view this forum as an opportunity to raise side issues against the railroad. The Know-Nothings want to talk antislavery or anti-Catholicism. The rail crews are Catholic, so a discussion could create some problems. However, you know yourself most of the people here are more concerned with their economic welfare than the railroad inaugural. Look at this crowd." In a sweeping motion with his hand, Fletcher indicated the fifty or more participants packed into the small schoolroom.

"Humph." Johnson surveyed the room. "Surely they have no cause to attack your workers. The only lost jobs will be those of the lock workers and bargemen, and most of them will find new work with the railroad. Shortsighted if they cannot see that we will all be better off."

"Well, not everyone sees the future quite as clearly as we do." Fletcher's attention returned to Penny Barton and then focused on Dan Hudson. Hudson had offered her his arm, and she rested her hand upon it.

"Excuse me. I fear I have been remiss in leaving our houseguest alone too long. Perhaps we should finish this conversation later. I need to talk with you about details regarding the inaugural festivities, but those will have to wait until later." Keeping his eye on Penny Barton all the while, Fletcher began to move away.

Johnson waved a hand in the air. "Plenty of time for that later. And when you get a chance, I too would appreciate an introduction to your pretty little guest." He winked and smiled.

Fletcher's eyes widened, but he nodded, slipping into the crowd and wending his way across the floor to Miss Barton and Hudson. He shook his head. Johnson's comments only confirmed his fears of the view others would take of her bold behavior.

The throng in the room jabbered at a frenzied pace. A blue-gray cloud of cigar smoke hung thick near the ceiling. Business and professional men or laborers in mud-spattered work pants filled most of the benches.

Someone at the front of the room banged on the lectern. "Gentlemen—and ladies—please take your seats." A few ladies took their places next to husbands or fathers.

Reaching his quarry at last, Fletcher grasped Penny's elbow. "Miss Barton, I apologize for spending so much time with Mr. Johnson. I hope you were, shall we say, entertained." He bristled as he glared at Dan Hudson.

"She was well cared for, if I do say so." Hudson gave him a

crooked grin and then turned a dazzling smile on Penny.

"Mr. Hudson has just been telling me about the canals." Her shining eyes reflected an excitement Fletcher wanted to deny.

"Well," he said, starting to move forward, almost pulling her with him, "that will have to wait. We must take our seats. And I see Aunt Emily is holding two for us on the other side of the room."

He guided Miss Barton away from Hudson, who called after them., "Wednesday, then, as soon as I can get away."

She smiled back.

"Wednesday?" Fletcher spoke through clenched teeth.

"Yes, Mr. Hudson invited Emily and me on a tour of the locks. I can hardly wait. I want to see them in use. In my time . . ." She did not finish her sentence, but instead directed her eyes to her feet.

"Hush." Fletcher tightened his grip on her arm as he hissed the warning. "Remember you are the niece of my aunt's friend, and you must act and speak accordingly. The fewer questions you encourage in others about you and your affairs, the better, unless you wish to be thought mad or suffer arrest."

He guided her to a seat next to Aunt Emily on a long, narrow bench facing the front of the room, and sat on the other side of her. Exhaling, Fletcher compressed his lips together. Sandwiched between them, Miss Barton could not cause further trouble or say something to create suspicion about her visit. He settled onto the low bench and watched the proceedings.

The moderator, Jonas Whelks, introduced first himself; then William Morris, the member of the American party; and lastly, Elias Pentegrass, the member of the Free Democrat party. All three men shook hands, and the moderator read the rules of the debate. First, a short statement from each man, to be followed by a list of prearranged questions. An open forum with questions from the audience would round out the discussion. The crowd, with eyes on the men in front of them, whispered among themselves. The room reeked of smoke, and someone in the back coughed.

Mr. Morris, a prosperous grain merchant Fletcher knew well, cleared his throat and straightened his cravat. "Gentlemen and, ahem, ladies, it is a pleasure to speak to you this evening and clarify for you some of the gross misunderstandings and outright lies our opponents persist in spreading regarding our efforts to adhere to the principles of our founding fathers and the U.S. Constitution. We believe only those native-born sons should hold elected office. The present Locofoco government is rife with graft and waste. We must turn the rascals out."

"Hear, hear!" someone yelled.

"You wanna elect the Injuns?" another shouted. Catcalls and jeers followed. Men at the back stamped their feet and thumped their benches.

The moderator banged for order. "Please, please, gentlemen, there are ladies present. We must have quiet." He turned to the Free Democrat. "Mr. Pentegrass."

The black-coated man stood and grabbed his lapels. Fletcher knew him to be a sharp dealer and a crony of Denton Jackson's, an influential member of the Board of Public Works.

"Now, gentlemen and ladies, we all know the reputation of our esteemed colleague, Mr. Morris. But we must also question those who belong to certain secret societies and claim to 'know nothing.' We have a progressive Board of Public Works. They have overseen the construction of the canal and now we shall soon have a railroad link as well. What more can we ask than for the continuing economic well-being of our community? If that is Locofoco, well then, I say, I, for one, am glad to have such a group looking out for the local welfare."

"You tell 'em," a man called, followed by a general uproar, even louder than before.

The moderator banged his gavel. "Order! Order! We are here to debate, not to name call. Perhaps we had best move on to the questions."

The first two questions related to school reform and the role of the church. Fletcher held his breath at first, but they concerned the proposed Methodist Seminary for young women and not the Catholic Church so dear to the Irish.

The third inquiry, directed to the American delegate first, pertained to antislavery. At least the debate progressed in the direction Fletcher had hoped. Any questions concerning the railroad would best be answered in a small group. With some luck, maybe there would be no questions about the increased cost of building the railroad line or the frequent labor problems. No need to stir up any more animosity between the laborers and lockmen.

The anti-Catholicism of the Know-Nothings made them opposed to the Irish workers used on the railroad. Some of them feared efforts by the workmen and their families to settle in the area. To Fletcher's knowledge, Morris had never objected to that, merely to them running for office. He eased to the edge of his seat, propped his elbows on his knees, and leaned forward to listen.

As he glanced around the room of mostly men, he saw Sarah Jamison by the window. Somehow she always came to the public gatherings he attended. He suspected his aunt kept her well informed. Despite Aunt Emily's encouragement, he found it difficult to view Sarah as a suitable marriage partner. He turned and looked at his aunt, who was intent on the debate. Since Penny Barton had arrived, Aunt Emily had spoken less of Sarah Jamison. Fletcher smiled.

Leaning back on the bench, he studied Penny. Her eyes sparkled, and she leaned forward, focusing on the speaker's every word. From time to time she bit at her lower lip and clasped and unclasped her hands. Other than his aunt, Fletcher had never known a woman so interested in politics and business. Penny and Emily had more in common than not, and both appeared equally happy with the three-month companionship trial Emily had proposed. If only he could resolve his many doubts. Fletcher rolled his head and stretched his neck to loosen tight muscles.

"If you relaxed and enjoyed the debate, your neck might not feel so tense." Penny whispered in Fletcher's ear. Her warm breath caressed his neck and sent a shiver through him. So close, she smelled like Aunt Emily's garden in full bloom. He detected a hint of gardenia. Or jasmine? The warmth of her cheek raised his temperature as she leaned closer.

"You're going to ask them some questions, aren't you?" She placed her hand on his arm, then cocked her head, and waited for his reply. The heat of her hand penetrated his coat sleeve.

"In time," he replied, careful to keep his voice low. "But as in most situations, one learns more by listening and patience." He looked straight into the deep blue of her eyes. He resisted saying, "As I do with you, Miss Barton." She nodded.

Fletcher continued to watch her. His eyes followed the curve of her soft lips and traced the outline of her slender neck. He hesitated as he studied her dress where the deep purple fabric pulled taut against the gentle swell of her breasts. If she were not the adventuress he knew her to be, he would almost be tempted to—to what? Flushing, he cleared his throat. Such thoughts would only cause them both trouble. He turned his attention to the men at the front of the room.

After an hour, the moderator invited the audience to ask questions from the floor. He called on one man, then another. A third withdrew his question and rephrased it, and a fourth summarily accused both parties of skirting the real issues involving antislavery. The moderator tried to quiet the crowd as they grew louder and more excited. Antislavery, anti-Catholicism. Fletcher glanced from the crowd to the participants at the lectern. An Irish laborer from O'Brien's crew yelled something from the back of the chamber. Fletcher winced. Just stay with the topics.

Suddenly Penny Barton's arm shot up; Fletcher saw his aunt nudge her, and for several seconds she whispered to her young houseguest. The moderator spotted Miss Barton, but hesitated.

Fletcher swiftly grabbed her arm and pulled it down. "What," he hissed into her ear, "are you doing?"

Penny turned in her seat and faced him. "I have a question. How will the railroad and increased trade with the East affect funding for the schools and employment opportunities?" Her steely eyes bored through him.

"Did Hudson put you up to this? Besides, I thought you already knew the answers to such questions. From what you told me earlier, you know most everything that is to happen here in town and elsewhere." Fletcher lowered his voice, as his face grew hot.

His aunt as a widow had earned her right to speak so boldly, but most would hold it unseemly for an unmarried woman to do so. With her mouth set in a tight pout, Miss Barton swiveled in her seat and faced the front of the room again.

"Let her ask the question, Fletcher!" a strong voice whispered from the bench behind them. Then the man laughed.

Fletcher turned to confront the portly man behind him. "Denton Jackson, ask for yourself, if you want to debate the virtues of rail travel." He struggled to speak in a whisper as a man addressed the moderator.

"It would make for an interesting evening. But as a member of the Board of Public Works, I must share my loyalty between the railroad and the canals. Wouldn't want to show favoritism, even though the canals haven't suffered the problems the railroad has. Time is passing, Dawe. Can you still make the April opening date?" Jackson crossed one leg over the other and leaned forward. "But enough of the railroads." He spoke louder than necessary. "I have yet to make the acquaintance of your guest." He snickered as he pulled a large cigar out of his pocket and cut off the end.

"Miss Barton is my aunt's guest and has come for an . . . extended visit." Fletcher pitched his voice just above a whisper.

Jackson raised a bushy eyebrow. "If she's just a houseguest, then I don't suppose you would mind if I called upon Miss Barron?" He cocked his head toward Fletcher as he surveyed him, a sardonic glint in his eyes.

"Barton. Penelope Barton. And you must ask Miss Barton herself." Fletcher followed Jackson's glance, which rested on Penny's tight-waisted dress and ample bosom. "And," he quickly added, "at present I prefer to attend to the debate, as should you." He turned, leaving Jackson still ogling Penny while she remained focused on the debate.

The discussion at the front of the room failed to hold Fletcher's attention. His eyes strayed to Penny Barton's hands, neatly folded in her lap. She had long, slender fingers. For a moment he studied her face and then glanced sidelong at Sarah Jamison who sat across the room on a chair near a window. What Sarah lacked in beauty she compensated for with the stylish clothes she wore, but her virtues didn't end there. She might have limited interests, yet she demonstrated responsibility and honesty. No one had ever questioned her integrity. Everyone spoke of her as a marriageable miss.

Even Aunt Emily had encouraged his interest in Sarah. Fletcher straightened and turned to his aunt, now whispering in Penny Barton's ear. Until this young woman had arrived, Aunt Emily had done all she could to bring Sarah to his attention, but that had changed.

Sarah, whom he had begun to regard as the most suitable of the local ladies, now appeared more boring and lackluster than ever when compared to Penny. Fletcher's collar constricted his neck, and he tugged at it. But he preferred an honest and responsible woman to a devious adventuress any day. And soon he would solve the mystery of Penny Barton. Even if he had to befriend her to do it.

Penny stared straight ahead as she listened to the men debate the issues. She tried to focus, but as the name-calling continued, her thoughts wandered to Fletcher sitting beside her. He looked much too tense. He fidgeted, twisted, and turned in his seat, and observed everything around him except this debate. Whatever his thoughts, they had significance for him. But then, the nasty business with the laborers on the railroad would disrupt anyone's concentration. In the short time she had known him, she could not remember him acting so distracted or out of humor except when she had told him she came from the far future.

For a brief moment, Penny glanced to the seat by the window where a prim and proper Sarah Jamison sat, back straight and attention focused on the speakers. Her pale cheeks and chapped lips did nothing to enhance her appearance, although her gray silk dress with its Belgian lace collar looked especially neat and feminine. Ah, she must be the reason for Fletcher's distraction. Of course, he would feel uncomfortable seated next to her while Sarah, perched nearby, observed his every move.

Penny twitched her nose almost imperceptibly. Sarah Jamison didn't seem Fletcher's type at all. Penny studied first him, then Sarah, for several long moments. To her, Sarah appeared pleasant, but no beauty and with too little spirit. Why would he waste his time and attention on her? Fletcher really needed someone like his Aunt Emily. An attractive, strong woman with an interest in business or maybe current events, or surely something other than the myriad of methods for catching a man or the latest hairstyle. Penny suppressed a giggle, and Fletcher turned in her direction, a scowl on his face.

Shifting on the hard bench, she thought of all she had learned in her research on Coshocton and the railroads. She had learned a lot in planning the commemorative train trip, but not so much about Fletcher, despite orders from her boss to find him. She had found him all right, but had no way to tell Whalen that. Now Fletcher, who had fascinated her from the first, only intensified her interest, but he continued to doubt her. At least Emily had accepted her.

Fletcher needed a woman like Emily. He admired and respected his aunt—even though he didn't always agree with her progressive views or share her liberal ideas. He depended on her pragmatic advice. She and Emily had so much in common.

Penny sighed and stared down at her folded hands. Regardless of how much alike Emily and she might or might not be, Fletcher showed no romantic interest in her. He considered her a scheming threat to the security of his railroad investment. He even accused her of conspiring with Dan Hudson, of all people! Okay, so Dan had a certain attractiveness and clearly showed interest in her, but he didn't appeal to her. Her only interest in him remained in preventing his death. No one deserved such an awful fate.

Clearing her throat, Penny tried to follow the debate. If only she could convince Fletcher that Dan Hudson really had the best interest of the railroad at heart despite what he might think. Ryan O'Connor's newspaper clippings reported the facts. Convincing Fletcher of that had proved harder than she had expected. Maybe the promised tour on Wednesday would give her something to use. Only a short time remained before Dan's death, but Fletcher's feelings toward him grew more bitter every day.

"Well, Miss Barton?" The raspy voice behind Penny startled her and drew her attention from her thoughts of Fletcher and Dan Hudson. Blinking, she turned to face the speaker on the bench behind. She had not listened to Fletcher's whispered conversation with Denton Jackson although she had recognized the name. Now Fletcher gave her an icy stare.

"Apparently Fletcher has no intention of extending the courtesy of an introduction. I'm Denton Jackson." The unctuous man grinned broadly, exposing a mouthful of tobacco-stained teeth.

Penny nodded politely. "Penelope Barton."

She eyed the man's thick, unkempt hair, but his bold stare at her breasts annoyed her. Somehow she had expected manners more like Fletcher's instead of such rough and ready ones. She scolded herself, but then thought just because she disliked him didn't mean he wasn't an effective politician. She never expected much from politicians, anyway. As a member of the Board of Public Works, he must have political power. That explained Fletcher's tolerance of his behavior. He might have substantial authority over the railroad.

Swallowing hard, Penny pulled her shawl over her shoulders and across her breasts. She offered Jackson a weak smile. If Fletcher tolerated him for the sake of the railroad, she had better follow his lead. Tonight she would be pleasant to Jackson; being polite wouldn't hurt her. She sighed and faced forward.

Wednesday she would discover Dan Hudson's true feelings about the railroad. At their first meeting Hudson had come on a bit strong, but he'd been pleasant this evening and anxious to please. In any event, Emily would chaperone them. If only she could discover something that would help her convince Fletcher of the truth of her story.

His distrust exasperated her. Maybe she shouldn't have told him the truth, but she hadn't any other explanation for her presence in his life. He had caught her off guard, and she, like an idiot, had blurted out the truth. So far, she had found no way to reverse the process. Thank heavens for Emily. In time Fletcher would see. If only she could be patient. With a little luck, the visit to the canal with Dan would do it.

CHAPTER 9

Emily Dawe sat at the desk in her room and sharpened her pen. She had managed to carve out a little time to catch up on her correspondence. Picking up Amelia Bloomer's last letter, Emily sighed. A month had passed and she had yet to reply. She dipped her pen into the inkwell.

My Dearest Amelia:

My apologies for such a tardy response to your last missive. I continue to tutor the Irish children and some of the young wives. They want so much to learn, but time is a problem. I exert all my ingenuity to acquire, beg, borrow, or create tools and materials for them. It saddens me so. My greatest hope is to promote a scholarship for my best pupil, Kathleen O'Brien. With an education, she could become a teacher and assist others among her kind.

Pausing, Emily reread what she had written. Excuses, nothing but excuses, but true nonetheless. At times the task overwhelmed her. By comparison, carrying water in a sieve appeared easy. If she could but change things for the children. Yet she knew once the workers completed the rail line, they and their families would move to the next job. She wanted more for Kathleen, but her mother Brigid needed her help with the younger ones.

Emily sighed again and decided to turn to more cheerful

matters. She picked up her pen.

> I always find your news of Susan Anthony and Mrs.
> Stanton exciting and try in my small way to further our
> cause. Our own "Aunt Fanny" keeps us on our mettle. We
> are lucky to have women like Frances Gage to lead us. I
> have more reason than ever to believe we will succeed in
> our efforts to free the Negroes and our sisters. I fear times
> of trial face us all, but we shall triumph.

Emily paused again and pondered how much she should tell
Amelia. Even if she revealed the entire truth, would Amelia accept Penny Barton as a visitor from the distant future? Emily
had to admit she too found Penny's story difficult to accept, but
Penny . . . how could she reject her? Amelia, as a religious
woman and a strong supporter of the Temperance Movement,
would consider Penny a miracle from God, a charlatan, or a
madwoman. Emily snorted. Some people would not accept the
truth despite the veracity of the teller—her nephew, for one.

Nibbling the end of her pen, Emily sought the best words to
convey to Amelia her views on Penny. She sighed and again put
pen to paper.

> I have a houseguest, my new companion, an intelligent
> young woman of sturdy character. I am rapidly coming to
> regard her as a daughter. She shares our views and
> concerns and will be a great asset to our movement. I have
> some hopes that she and my nephew may find mutual
> interests. Penelope Barton is what I wish my own beloved
> daughter might have become had she not, alas, preferred
> to follow fashion's dictates and cared naught for the world
> of letters and intellect.

She reread her words, frowning. It was true. Despite the short time she had known Penny Barton, she regarded her as the daughter she had always wanted Mary to become. Mary had been such a sad disappointment—so narrow in her views and only interested in finding a husband and raising a brood. However, Emily had loved her despite such limited interests, and to have a life cut short hurt. She had not expected to bury her daughter, not after Mary survived birth and had thrived so well as a child. One never knew. Emily shrugged. She could only accept what Fate had dealt and try to make things better for others.

After Mary's death, she had thrown herself into her work with the Irish with renewed energy. With no child of her own and now no prospect of any grandchildren, the time spent with the Irish workers' families helped dull her grief. Fletcher, too, had filled a part of the void, and she had encouraged him to consider Sarah Jamison, although she had to admit she felt little kinship with the girl. Still, Sarah came from a good family and would make a suitable wife and mother, but with Penny Barton's arrival, he had a better choice.

Amelia would find Penny a kindred soul. Perhaps she should arrange a visit.

I am anxious for you and Miss Barton to meet and hope we may find a mutually convenient opportunity. We must plan a visit, either to you or from you. I know how busy *The Lily* keeps you, but hope you may find a little time for yourself. Please let me know your wishes in this matter.

I sometimes wonder how we all continue to work so hard for such small results. I know Mrs. Stanton felt most discouraged over last year's failure to obtain passage of the New York bill guaranteeing property rights for women. We are both more and less fortunate here. My own situation is satisfactory, but that of the workmen's wives is not.

In addition to my teaching efforts, I wear my Turkish pantaloons, popularly known as "Bloomers." I agree with your sentiments on their practical nature. Some of the ladies and gentlemen do stare now and then, but I am known locally as an original, and they would expect no less from me.

Do write soon and let me know about a visit. I long to see you and even more to bring you and Penelope Barton together. She attended our most recent local political meeting and asked an intelligent and penetrating question, one I'm sure Fletcher wished he had asked instead. She set a good example for the others, but no other woman had the courage to follow her lead.

Emily laughed as she remembered Fletcher's discomfort and his efforts to silence or distract Penny at the debate. But she had also seen him stiffen when Denton Jackson, that unmitigated rake, had attempted to flirt with Penny. As if Penny would even notice such a rodent. No, she could not tell those things to Amelia. She had better sign off and get on with dinner.

Your Friend as Always,
Emily Garrett Dawe

Emily folded and sealed her letter. Fletcher would post it for her tomorrow. Carrying the sealed letter, she went downstairs to prepare dinner.

From the parlor, Penny heard a bold knock on the front door. The echoing thump set her heart to pounding and for a moment she paused, one hand to her throat. Then she set Emily's mending aside and rose to answer the door.

Through the window she saw Dan Hudson, twirling his cap and glancing first in one direction and then another. As lockmaster, he wore a navy double-breasted coat slightly shorter than the normal frock coat. The navy cravat offset by the high, stiff collar of his white shirt looked suitably nautical and, along with his dark, sparkling eyes, presented a pleasant picture.

"Good day, Miss Barton." Dan inclined his head to Penny as she opened the front door and smiled at him. "I came like I promised to take you and Miz Dawe for a little tour of the locks." He continued to twirl his cap, but now his dark eyes focused on Penny with a grin.

"Come in." Penny held the door open and glanced at the clock in the hall. He had come early, and Emily still worked in the kitchen. "Please take a seat in the parlor while I call Mrs. Dawe."

Flashing her a lopsided grin, Dan nodded. He sidled past her and into the parlor, but said nothing in response. Instead, he surveyed the furnishings.

Penny hurried down the hall to the kitchen where Emily sat at the table and peeled potatoes for supper. Bending, Penny picked up a stray peel from the floor.

"Emily, Dan Hudson's here; too early. You're busy, so I'll ask him to come back later."

Sighing, Emily set down the knife and picked up the pot of potatoes. "No, no. But I suppose he is in a hurry. Men always are." She set the pan on the counter and washed her hands in the sink. "These will be just fine covered with water, and it will not hurt them to sit until we return."

She dried her hands and removed her calico apron, tossing it on a hook near the door. "At least we have a nice, sunny day. Not much fun treading around those canal paths in the wet. Still and all, we had better wear our boots. It is much too wet for slippers or pumps. Those horses and mules churn up plenty of mud, and," she said, lowering her voice to barely a whisper as if conspiring with Penny, "manure." She scrunched up her nose and chuckled.

Emily's reticence over manure amused Penny. At least in the Dawe household, she never heard profanity. Her mood improved, Penny swung about on her toes and admired the flowered skirt of her borrowed dress as it flared outward. The dress, courtesy of Mary Dawe, suited the season with its pale pink blossoms against a dark green background. As Penny finished her pirouette she caught the dancing sparkle in Emily's glance.

"It's spring, Emily, and we're going to see the canal."

"Indeed, we have both spent far too many hours inside. Getting out of this stuffy house and taking some exercise will do us good. Spring always stirs my blood. Even my daffodils have peeked forth this morning. Soon you'll see the lovely garden we have." Emily smiled her satisfaction and led the way toward the foyer.

"You're a gardener, too?" Penny wondered what Emily's interests didn't include. Was there anything she couldn't do or didn't have interest in?

"Heavens no, a few of my students wanted some way to thank me, so they come by now and again and plant things or weed. I merely enjoy the fruits of their labor. To tell you the truth, I would be more likely to pull up a flowering plant than a weed. I love dandelions and they make a healthful wine, too." Emily took Penny by the arm. "We had best hurry or Dan will grow impatient."

They scurried upstairs and gathered coats, bonnets and reticules. Penny slipped into the dark green jacket that matched her flowered dress while Emily, gowned in a more subdued brown print with sprigs of soft lavender flowers, wore a longer brown wool coat. After fastening their bonnets, they joined Dan in the parlor.

Rising, he smiled at their entrance. "I am lucky today with

two such lovely ladies to escort." He offered Penny his right arm and Emily his left. "Every gentleman in town will envy me."

"Go on, Dan," Emily chided him, "with Penny perhaps, but not with a matron like me." Playfully she poked Dan's rib with her elbow.

"Now, Miz Dawe, you're a right handsome woman. Everyone says so. But we all know there isn't a man within fifty miles who could keep pace with you."

"Right you are, Dan, and just remember that." Emily smiled as if well pleased at the compliment and proud of her reputation as an independent woman.

Together the threesome moved out the door and down the walk. Dan had clearly set out to be agreeable today. Penny noticed his smile, no longer even reminiscent of his leering grin when she had first met him. Maybe his suspicion of her had faded. His flattering attention at the debate had angered Fletcher.

She studied Dan's face as he and Emily traded quips and gossip about the community and its leading citizens. Not bad-looking at all, but he had a wife according to the newspaper report of his death. Pity tugged at her as she remembered that. Such a short time to live and he had no inkling. She should warn him. Then the unpleasant thought struck her if she warned him, would that change the future? Would the train derail and injure or hurt people? Just because she had somehow traveled to the Coshocton of 1855 didn't mean she could alter history, and, if she did, the consequences might prove catastrophic. Some of those weird science fiction stories said exactly that. But why had she come, if she couldn't change anything?

Fletcher Dawe had dismissed her warning as a lie. Instead, he believed her to be a part of some conspiracy against him. She sighed and shook her head at the hopelessness of the situation. Shades of *Hamlet*. No wonder Shakespeare had depicted the fellow as paralyzed and unable to act. She found herself in accord with the Danish prince and sighed.

Dan glanced in her direction. "Pretty big sigh, Miss Barton. I hope we have not tired you so soon?" He cocked his head and smiled a quizzical smile that made his dark eyes twinkle.

Flushing, she tried to brush his concern aside. "No, not at all. So early on such a sunny day, how could anyone be tired?" Seeking to distract him, she fastened on the blooming garden ahead. "Oh, look over there." She pointed to the front of a tall frame house where beds of crocuses and daffodils bloomed in bright profusion.

"It'll soon be like that all over town. Won't it, Miz Dawe?"

"Yes, any time now. Coshocton is so pretty in the spring, that is, provided the floods don't wash us away."

"Shouldn't this year. The thaw has passed, and we weathered that fine. Canal's open so we should be safe until the August thunder moon."

"Thunder moon?" Penny stared at Dan, mouthing the words a second time, unable to imagine what he meant.

"Yep, that's what the Indians call it, 'cause we get lots of thunder and heavy rains in August." Dan looked pleased to be able to impart a bit of Indian lore.

As the trio neared the river, the buildings no longer sat on spacious lots, but huddled together, leaning one against the other, as if dependent on each other for support. Most had peeling paint, shuttered windows, and other signs of poor maintenance. A few log cabins, remnants from the first settlers, stood among the cluster. Down the street a little farther along, a street sign offered whiskey and hot meals at Kitty's Ale House.

Men in grubby pants and muddy wool jackets lounged about on boxes and crates smoking pipes or whittling at sticks with shiny-bladed knives. Most wore unkempt beards or hadn't yet shaved yesterday's whiskers.

"Morn'n, Dan," the men called as the three passed, eyeing the ladies with special interest.

Dan grunted in reply, until they had moved beyond the next building and safely out of earshot. "Lazy louts," he muttered, "they should be loading cargo, not idling about."

"Oh, do those men work for you?" Penny looked back a moment at the men and then turned to Dan.

"Me?" Dan raised his eyebrows. "No, they work on hire to the boat captains or to one of the lines running freight. Sometimes one of them signs on as an extra hand if one is needed. Mostly they just lay about. Lazy buggers."

"They could always find work on the railroad." Emily smiled across Dan at Penny.

He curled his lip. "Not that lot. If they did, the boat captains wouldn't hire 'em back. The captains are mad enough already over lost business to that Cleveland-Columbus-Cincinnati Railroad. Not as much through business from Lake Erie as there used to be. A lot of 'em don't like the new line, either."

"You mean the Steubenville and Indiana Railroad?" Penny watched for his reaction. The bitterness in his tone supported Fletcher's view of Dan. "The railroads increase business, not lessen it."

"Not to the canals. All them rich merchants in Steubenville want cheap transport to Columbus and west. The canals and the Ohio River aren't good enough for 'em." He snorted loudly and straightened his shoulders defiantly.

"But Dan," Emily interjected, "to use the Ohio and Erie Canal they have go north to Lake Erie or south to the Ohio River and the Ohio Central Railroad first to reach Coshocton and Columbus. It adds delay, and the canals cannot operate in the winter. Even in the spring sometimes there's too much ice to navigate the river."

"That may be, but the southern canals run most of the time and trains can't run when snow buries the tracks," he growled in a loud voice. His face had turned brick red.

"That only happens in a blizzard. When is the last time we had snow that deep? Most of the time, it doesn't matter."

"Miz Dawe, you haven't been through those hills in the winter or you wouldn't say that."

"But they drove tunnels through the hills," Emily reminded him.

"Not the whole length of the track. You just wait and see. Besides, them steam engines ain't safe. Those engines blow up and look what happens then. And, the speed some travel—I heard twenty miles an hour—it's not safe. Not safe at all." He paused to catch his breath after his impassioned speech.

"Now, our packets provide comfort and travel day and night. Folks have time to see the countryside and get to know their fellow passengers. And we feed them—none of this stopping at some inn and such for a meal and then having to gulp your food 'cause the engineer's blowing the whistle."

Emily pursed her lips in disapproval. "I see this is one area where we disagree, Dan. And perhaps the less we discuss it, the better. Now why don't you show Penny where the boats stay until they can pass through the locks?"

"To the right, Miz Barton," Dan pointed to a large pond to the right of the path, "this holding basin lets the captains stop to unload freight or make repairs. We can hold some thirty boats here."

Dan's voice carried a note of pride, but Penny saw only a few derelict hulls with peeling paint and cracked boards lying next to the shore in the basin. The rest of the pond reflected the spring sunshine, and slight ripples crossed the smooth surface of water.

"It's empty now," she said.

"Just the lull before the season starts in earnest. Just wait till June. It'll be crammed then. You'll see."

"Oh, there's Kathleen O'Brien." Emily pointed to a girl of ten or eleven ahead on the path. "I must inquire about her mother. Please excuse me. I'll be right back." Emily hurried off to catch the child, leaving Penny and Dan standing by the holding basin.

As Penny watched Emily hurry toward the girl, she had a momentary impulse to follow. When she looked toward Dan Hudson, she found him studying her with a quizzical grin on his face.

"Well, Miss Barton, how do you like our little town? Are you planning to stay long?"

Reminding herself to say as little as possible, Penny wondered why he had bothered to ask. "I find the town pretty, but it's much smaller than Philadelphia or Cincinnati. The length of my visit really depends on Mrs. Dawe."

Dan raised an eyebrow and pulled a stem of new grass from the path. He studied it for a moment and then stripped the stem. "Any word on your lost valise?"

Sighing, she looked down at her reticule, and tried to muster a genuine tone of regret. "No, and Mrs. Dawe says some thief must have taken it. I had just gotten a new one for this trip, too. But it doesn't matter." She waved her hand in the air as if to dismiss the problem. "Mrs. Dawe has seen to that, and my father has been informed, so no damage has been done."

Dan tossed the grass stem away. "It's not like the folks hereabouts to steal. We get an occasional runaway slave, but the sheriff or the bounty hunters soon take care of that." He fixed her with a steady stare. "Most likely you'll see some black gal parading around in your clothes."

Penny looked back toward the holding basin, as if not much interested in lost clothes. "Really?"

He nodded and then followed her gaze toward the decaying hulls. "You're not afraid to ride this new machine, this steam engine?"

She swung toward him, causing her skirts to swirl against her legs. "Of course not. They're safer to ride than a wagon. Trains will carry passengers and freight to St. Louis and beyond one day and unite this country from coast to coast. They'll be known as the engines of progress."

"Humph." Dan kicked a pebble from the path. "Not the way I hear it." Animated again, his tone sharpened. "They're ornery machines, and them boilers can let go and kill a man. Like as not, they'll blow up the whole kit and caboodle."

"No." Annoyed by his attack on railroads, Penny raised an eyebrow and tried to look down her nose at Dan. "Sabotage by rivals might wreck a train." His eyes widened. She paused as she studied his face with care. What might he know? "Or an untrained engineer who doesn't understand the equipment."

He rubbed his chin and pursed his lips. "Sab-o-tage? Now what makes you say that?" He focused unwavering eyes on her.

Aware of his role in averting exactly such an event, she flushed. "Surely you've read the newspaper accounts?"

Dan's black eyes bored into her again. "I read the newspaper, but I recall no such story."

Penny grappled furiously trying to concoct a believable story. Such accidents had happened, but she couldn't recall any specifics. In any case, the rapid pace of the railroad expansion made it unlikely Dan could know about every accident. "Well, it happened in New York, about five years ago."

"Oh, hmm, well, that may be. Can't say as I heard tell of it." Dan looked doubtful.

"Yes," she rushed on, pushing her words out as fast as she could, "some men piled tree limbs on the track to derail the

149

train, but an alert engineer saw the debris and stopped the train in time."

"Oh." Dan said nothing further for a moment, mulling over what she had said. "What would have happened if he hadn't?"

Penny shrugged. "I don't know, but most likely the locomotive would have derailed and pulled the rest of the carriages with it. People would have been injured or killed. It's even possible the locomotive would have blown up."

"Sounds horrible. We sure wouldn't want that to happen here." Dan's words sent a chill through Penny. "It would turn people off the railroad altogether, and Mr. Dawe would lose all that money he's invested."

To Penny, his words held an implied threat. Did they also have a touch of personal jealousy at Fletcher's wealth? It would only be natural.

"Penny!" Emily called and waved from where she stood talking with the young girl with the red pigtails. "Come here."

Penny and Dan hurried forward to join Emily. As they approached, the solemn-faced child smiled at Dan and nervously twisted the sash of her drab, threadbare dress.

"Morning, Mr. Hudson."

"Hello, Kathleen." Dan nodded to her.

"Kathleen," Emily said, "this is Penny Barton, the daughter of a . . . dear friend. Penny, Kathleen O'Brien is one of my best pupils."

"Hello, Kathleen." Bending forward to better see the petite girl, Penny extended her hand. For a moment the girl appeared to consider whether or not to accept the hand. Then she shyly offered her own.

Penny smiled at her, enchanted by the clear green eyes in the small freckled face. "Shouldn't you be in school?"

Kathleen screwed up her face in a frown. "Da can't pay them school fees so Miz Dawe teaches us instead." Eyes glowing, she smiled up at Emily. "She's a good teacher, too, better than that Miss Favham at the school."

Blushing, Emily patted Kathleen on the shoulder. "Kathleen helps me with the younger children. Her father heads up one of Fletcher's work crews."

Suddenly the child tossed her pigtails and shifted from one foot to the other. "I gotta go, Miz Dawe. If'n I don't hurry, Ma will worry."

"Of course, Kathleen." Emily reached into her reticule and pulled out a bright, shiny penny. "Why don't you get some candy and share it with your brothers and sisters?"

With a broad smile on her elfin face, Kathleen took the penny and bobbed a curtsy. "Thank'ee, Miz Dawe. Thank'ee." She hurried off down the path, pigtails flying.

"They are a needy family. Seven children and the youngest still a babe." Emily watched as the child rounded the corner of a nearby building and they could no longer see her.

Dan snorted. "The shanty Irish, white niggers, they breed like spring rabbits. It's no wonder they can't feed 'em all."

Emily sighed, hands folded over her stomach. "You have no need to speak so, Dan. Their religion teaches them to 'be fruitful and multiply.' I'm not one to dispute religion, but it would be better if they multiplied a little less frequently."

Penny grimaced. The same cycle of pregnancy and poverty continued in her own time, too, despite options for family planning. The inevitable course of poverty led to a downward spiral for too many. Why did some problems, in her time or at the moment, seem to have no solution? Squaring her shoulders, Penny pushed those grim thoughts aside. Instead, she savored the warm sun and sparkling water.

Then her own problems bobbed up again. Somehow she must convince Fletcher Dawe of her genuine interest in the completion of the railroad and its survival. Dan chatted with Emily as they strolled along the towpath. He talked of the operation of the locks and the traffic up and down the canal as Emily removed her bonnet and fluffed her hair. And he even told a story or two about this captain or that crew. His enthusiasm made his face glow.

Dan's attitude toward the railroad annoyed her, but she needed his assistance. He would save the train; therefore, he would be present when the "accident" took place. Stopping his death would prove her a liar, but letting him die, if she could prevent it, would make her no better than a murderer.

CHAPTER 10

Fletcher recorded the week's progress on laying track and then dropped his pen in disgust. Compared to reports from Izzy Dille, working from the Newark end, the Coshocton crew had bogged down. The bridge work and the line from Newark remained on schedule, but the connection at Coshocton had slipped, and unless work progressed at a faster pace, the project would not be completed on time.

Compressing his mouth in a thin line, he pulled on his coat, left his store, and walked at a brisk pace toward the proposed depot site. From a distance as he approached the work area, he saw towheaded Jamie Matthews perched atop a pile of rails, chewing a stalk of grass.

He cupped his hands and yelled in Jamie's direction, "Where are the work crews?"

"Down by the river, I guess. They been grumbling about the rails." The boy resumed chewing and shrugged his shoulders.

"The rails? Why?" Fletcher stared at him. No one had said anything about problems with the rails.

Jamie spat the grass aside and rolled his eyes skyward. "Don't know, but Carmody sez they're no good. Sez they won't last a season."

Fletcher frowned. One more nuisance to sort out with Carmody. "Where did you say they are?"

"Down by the river."

Fletcher left Jamie sitting on the rails and walked, at an even brisker pace, toward the work site on the river. He balled his hands into fists and plunged them into his pockets.

With all the problems he'd had to deal with over the past several weeks, at least the weather had cooperated. It had warmed a few degrees, and the afternoon spring sun made the landscape glow. The flowers had taken full advantage of the warm sun and bloomed in bright rainbows of color. The magnolias in velvety soft white and pink vied with the first of the flowering trees—white apple and purplish-pink redbud. While Fletcher sensed the fragrance and beauty of the spring flowers, the potential problems with the rails pushed everything else aside.

What could have happened this time? An earlier shipment of rails had been too brittle to use, and getting a replacement shipment had taken a month. He had shifted the crews to grading the right-of-way. But now, at this point in the construction, procuring new rails would cause serious delay. The rate of new railroad construction in Ohio and throughout the nation had forced some mills to work overtime, strained coal and ore supplies, and only complicated matters.

When Fletcher reached the river site, he grimaced as he glimpsed the crews lolling about smoking and talking. Two men lounged under a tree and shared a flask. He saw Carmody off to one side with a tin cup in his hand.

Fletcher stalked toward the crew boss. "Carmody, what's this about the rails? Jamie Matthews said you had a problem."

Carmody nodded, drops of ale glistening on his bushy mustache. "Well, it's a wee one. They're not all bad like that one lot last year, but I'd say maybe a third can't be used." He sipped from his cup.

"So what are you doing about them?"

Licking a thin white line of foam from his upper lip, Carmody shifted from one foot to the other. "I told Mr. Foster, and he's ordered more. We're doing what we can with what we got."

"We're running out of time." Fletcher couldn't keep the exasperation from his tone. "We have to finish this link, and soon, or we won't meet the opening date."

One eyebrow raised, Carmody then quickly smoothed his face. "You want I should use those rails, anyway?"

Fletcher stared at his crew leader as he tried to assess the risks. "What would happen if you did?"

Carmody rubbed his bristled chin. "Well, now, I can't rightly say. When the weight of the locomotive or a heavy freight car hits them, they'll most likely break up. Sometimes, you can still run, sometimes not. I've seen more than one derailment over bad track."

"I see." Fletcher straightened his cravat. The last thing he could afford was a derailment on the new line. "We might be all right and, then again, we might lose a train."

"That's about it. No way t' tell for sure. Rails can be funny, but when you hit one with a sledge and it cracks, it ain't a good sign."

With a deep sigh, Fletcher stared at the crew boss. "How short of rails will this make us?"

Twisting his mouth from side to side, Carmody pulled at his mustache. "Can't rightly say, but we always have some rails left over. Keep 'em as spares and for repairs. But I think we'd need some more. A third is a lot to put aside."

Fletcher nodded. He would have to get rails from somewhere. "All right, I'll telegraph to Dille in Newark and see if he can spare us some. I'm not sure a new shipment will reach us in time."

Carmody arched his left eyebrow again. "That mean you want us to put the bad ones aside?"

"Of course, there is no point in wasting labor laying bad track or risking a derailment later. I'll find some way to get the replacement rails; just get your crews back to work."

Nodding, Carmody turned his now empty cup upside down and shook the remaining moisture from it. "Right you are, Mr. Dawe. Come on boyos, off yer duffs. We've work to do."

With obvious reluctance, the men emptied their pipes and drained cups as they stood up and moved toward the pile of rails stacked at Carmody's feet. Fletcher watched for a moment and then turned back toward town.

Why had Carmody himself not come to report the shipment of inferior rails? Fletcher shook his head. At times, Carmody behaved just like the rest of the crew, careless and lazy. If only they would work just a while longer or work a bit faster.

At the telegraph office, Fletcher sent telegrams to both Izzy Dille in Newark and to Israel Pemberton in Steubenville. One or the other might have some good rails to spare. In the telegram Fletcher stressed the need to maintain the construction schedule. Maybe, if both men knew just how desperate he was, they would send the shipment today. Fletcher grimaced. No doubt they were both busy with their own problems. One could only hope for the best.

He walked toward home reviewing one plan or another in his mind. What else could go wrong?

Miss Barton had warned him about a derailment, but he hadn't really given her warning much credence. Could she somehow have known about the bad rails? Did she have some link to the mills? No, that seemed too outrageous to believe. Nonetheless, she had specifically mentioned a derailment and so had Carmody. Fletcher ran his fingers through his hair. Was there no one he could trust?

So far, he had been unable to determine Miss Barton's motives and exactly what she wanted. But surely, she had some reason for her actions and her stories. He thought again of the colorful tale she had concocted. He simply could not accept her story about the future. Either she lied for some personal gain—what that could possibly be, he couldn't fathom—or she suffered mental delusions.

Fletcher pondered the implications of either cause, and he found himself unable to decide which he preferred. He abhorred deceit; it implied a character defect and a lack of integrity. But delusions meant derangement, and otherwise Penny Barton appeared so normal. Aunt Emily liked her. He had always trusted his aunt's judgment in the past. He knew her to be impulsive at times, but his aunt understood people—sometimes much better than he did—and he had never known her to misjudge anyone's character.

Penny Barton remained a puzzle he had not solved, and he had no means to do so. If she engaged in deceit, surely over time her perfidy must stand revealed. Her cohorts must contact her at some point. So far, she had done nothing he could fault except perhaps allowing Dan Hudson and Denton Jackson to pay her too much attention. She had acted a trifle forward, but then, so did Aunt Emily.

Having reached home without having resolved anything, Fletcher climbed the front steps and entered. He shut the door and started to hang his overcoat on a peg in the hall when Aunt Emily called to him from the kitchen doorway.

"Fletcher, I need to talk with you. Now." Her voice, hardly more than whisper, just reached his ears.

She rarely asked him to do anything unless she had a good reason, so he hurried to join her in the kitchen. She shut the door to the hall behind him and wiped her hands, which already appeared to be dry, on her apron. Her face, flushed with heat from cooking, looked grave.

"I wanted to tell you Penny and I went with Dan Hudson to look at the locks today."

Fletcher frowned and started, but his aunt held up one hand.

"I know how you feel about Dan, but I was with them the entire time and it was all quite innocent. Penny had never seen the locks, and the walk did us all good. Dan did all in his power to make it a pleasant tour."

Raising a doubtful eyebrow, Fletcher stood with his arms crossed. "Somehow I can hardly believe that."

"I wanted you to know in the event Penny said anything at dinner. Please don't badger her about it. Nothing happened."

"Perhaps, but no good can come of Miss Barton spending time with Dan Hudson. If they are in league, it will only give them more time to plot." He pressed his mouth into a thin, bitter line.

Giving a loud sniff, Emily reached for a wooden spoon. She stirred a pot on the stove with more vigor than he thought necessary. "Fletcher, sometimes you infuriate me. Why can't you accept Penny as she is?"

His eyes widened as he pondered how to make his aunt accept the simple facts. He fussed with his cravat as he sought the proper words. "Because, her story is physically impossible. No one has ever traveled in time. Rudolf Clausius's Principle of Entropy proves it impossible. No sane person can accept such an event." Fletcher considered his words and then added, "With all due respect, how can you possibly believe this tale she tells?"

Snorting, Emily banged the spoon on the side of the pan. "Well, I have an open mind, and I consider myself as sane as anyone."

Fletcher gave her a fond smile. "Yes, I'll grant you that, but in this case, don't you think perhaps you want to believe Penny Barton because she reminds you of Mary?"

Flinching, his aunt stared at him for a moment, her face devoid of color, before turning away. "I grieved over Mary. That is past. Mary died, and Penny is alive, very much alive." She shook her head and set the spoon down with a *thunk*. "No, it is not because she reminds me of Mary. It's because she reminds me of myself. She's the woman I might be if I had been born a hundred years from now. I love Penny, but I also believe in her and in what I see and think."

"What do you see and think?" Fletcher splayed his hands in front of him, palms up.

"Her book, all the things she knows: James Buchanan will be the next President, we're going to have a civil war, women will vote, she graduated from William and Mary."

Fletcher laughed. "The last is patently false. They don't accept women. The things you mention haven't happened yet and may well never happen. In fact, I wager they do not. Nothing she has said proves anything. They are delusions, no more than lies or, at best, guesses. As for the book, anyone can print a fake. Such things are done all the time."

Removing her apron, Emily then folded it with care and laid it on the table. "What about the railroad run on April eleventh?"

He said nothing for a moment, thinking about the brittle rails and the possible delay they might cause. "Again, the derailment has not happened. We are so close. It will be any time now. But I am not convinced the actual date is to be the eleventh."

"I see nothing will convince you. Please, even so, do not harass Penny over dinner. It will not help her digestion or my own."

Studying his aunt's set face for a moment, Fletcher no more relished such a discussion over dinner than did she. He had no interest in harassing Penny Barton. He would, however, talk with Miss Barton another time. He made a slight bow. "I shall accede to your wishes."

Dinner passed peacefully without discussion of work on the railroad, problems with the crew, shortage of rail ties, or the canal. After washing the dishes and restoring the kitchen to order, Emily left to visit the O'Briens.

Fletcher and Penny retired to the parlor to pass the rest of the evening. She picked up the basket of Emily's mending while Fletcher made several attempts to read the current issue of *The Coshocton Age*. Finally, he cleared his throat, folded the paper into a neat rectangle, and placed it on the table adjacent to his chair.

He skewered Penny with his dark eyes. "So, my aunt said you visited the locks today."

Penny nodded from the chair closest to the fire. "Yes. Dan Hudson took us on a brief tour. Very impressive."

Raising an eyebrow, Fletcher struggled to curb his distrust. "Oh? Hudson or the canals?"

She continued to concentrate on making neat, small stitches on the shirt cuff in her hands. "I had no idea the canals carried so much traffic, although we saw only a few boats today."

He suppressed a smile of amusement when she refused to respond to his taunt about her impression of Hudson. "The northern locks are getting ready to open. The canals up there freeze over in the winter, so it will be a few weeks before we see much traffic here."

Nodding, Penny bit off a piece of thread. "Yes, Dan said that. He knows everything about the canals and the economics of water transport."

"As lockmaster, he should."

She searched Fletcher's face for a moment. "I know the canal and railroads are rivals, but you don't like him, do you?"

Without comment, Fletcher returned her gaze until she looked down at her mending. "Let us say I have my reasons for not trusting Dan Hudson, and I'd prefer that you, especially under the present circumstances, did not consort with him."

A small smile tugged at the corners of her mouth. "Really? The present circumstances?" Penny put her mending aside.

"Hudson opposes the railroad and takes every opportunity to stir up trouble. He spreads rumors and provokes my work crews."

Quiet filled the room. The silence stretched, demanding something.

Finally, Fletcher spoke. "You've told me of an impending plot to derail a train. Hudson is the most likely candidate to instigate such a plot. Consequently, I see any association with him as likely to further such activity."

Jumping up from her chair, Penny almost knocked it over. "You've got it all wrong! Dan Hudson isn't going to sabotage the train. He's going to die trying to stop a derailment."

Fletcher's eyes flashed. "I find that almost as hard to believe, Miss Barton, as your 'story' of coming from the future. Hudson hates the railroad. Therefore, he is least likely to give his life to save it."

"I know that." Penny sank back into the chair, a deep frown furrowing her forehead, and leaned forward toward Fletcher. "But it's one thing to destroy equipment and quite another to deliberately injure or murder people. Dan might have no hesitation about wrecking rail cars or stirring up trouble with the crews, but killing people is another matter altogether." Her eyes reflected her horror at the thought.

"Humph." Fletcher gave her an exasperated frown. "Look, where do you think these little fights among the Irish lead?" He ran a hand through his hair. "Last year near Steubenville, such a feud killed a man. I am not saying Hudson would set out to murder anyone, but when you stir up trouble among the Farups and Fardowns, that is almost a given. An excitable lot, they are prone to violence when angered, especially when they drink to excess."

Silent for a moment as if weighing his words, Penny then sighed. "I understand your reasoning about the potential danger.

However, I won't be rude to him if I meet him."

Fletcher preferred she snub the man at any opportunity rather than extend courtesy, but knew he could not win such an argument. He sighed. Easing back in his chair, he tried to accept her decision with good grace.

"I cannot see Hudson in the role of savior, however. Therefore, I doubt your story can be true. It goes against everything I know about him."

Her bottom lip took on a stubborn set. "Well, you'll see. Just wait until April eleventh."

"Since that is only days away, we will all see very soon. Meanwhile, I have doubled our security guard. Nothing will disrupt our inaugural run."

"Well, you can be sure I won't. Good night, Mr. Dawe." She rose and swept from the room without finishing her mending.

Her rapid and noisy ascent of the stairs underscored her anger with him. Well, he had a right to his doubts and distrust of her. Somehow Penny Barton had a decided talent for raising his ire. Knowing how he felt about Dan Hudson, she had still accepted an invitation from him. Yes, Aunt Emily had accompanied her and had not left them alone. But given Hudson's attitude toward the railroad, neither woman should have gone.

Pacing in front of the fire, Fletcher mulled over their exchange. Aside from everything else, he did not trust Dan Hudson, nor did he like the way Dan ogled Penny at every opportunity. Fletcher had bristled at the insult to her, but Miss Barton had paid no attention. A man like Hudson would consider that encouragement.

Shaking his head, Fletcher leaned back to relieve his tight muscles. Penny Barton understood so little of the situation. She knew nothing about the Farups and the Fardowns, let alone Dan Hudson. She persisted in her ridiculous story about coming from the future.

So far, he had found no one who knew anything about her, and, besides himself, no one acknowledged ever having met her before she arrived in Coshocton. As far as he could determine, she had suddenly appeared descending from a rail carriage parked on the tracks. He had talked with several workmen there at the time, but they hadn't known where she had come from, just that she had appeared there.

Returning to his chair, he sat in silence. He had exercised care in his questions to the townspeople because he did not want to stir up doubts in the minds of others. His inquiries of the conductor and the engineer had also revealed nothing. John Waterson, the conductor, swore Penny Barton had never ridden on his train. Fletcher wondered if she had traveled in disguise, come by wagon, or canal packet. But if by packet, then Dan would know her. Either she had not, or he pretended to not know her and they conspired together.

It appeared Miss Penny Barton had arrived suddenly, coming from nowhere in particular and oblivious to everyone in the community. That she was an adventuress, he did not doubt. But what she hoped to gain from her charade, he could not decipher. Living in his home gave her access to him, but also meant he and Aunt Emily had her under close watch.

Fletcher rested his head in his hands, lost in thought, until the clock, chiming in the hall, woke him with a start. He rose to inspect the fire, stoked it, and then sat again.

Why did Aunt Emily persist in her belief Penny Barton had traveled through time? Sometimes his aunt had too much imagination and too little common sense. She liked Penny and let her feelings for the young woman get in the way of her rational judgment. For a long time, Fletcher sat as he pondered his aunt and her reaction to Penny. It was not like Aunt Emily to let herself be swayed that way. What power did this young woman have over his aunt?

Once the inaugural train run was completed, he would find some way to make Miss Barton tell him the truth. Then there would be no good reason for her not to tell him who she really was and from whence she had come.

He crossed the room to the writing desk in the corner. From the center drawer he removed a letter with an ornate seal at the top. *William and Mary College, Williamsburg, Virginia.* The reply to his inquiry had come back as expected. The college had no record of a Penelope Barton. She could not have enrolled at the college because they did not admit women. Neither had she been employed there or associated with the institution in any manner. Perhaps, Mr. Sawyer, the author of the letter, suggested Mr. Dawe should inquire nearer to home since Oberlin College of Ohio had taken the questionable position of admitting females and people of color to its programs.

Refolding the letter, Fletcher returned it to the drawer. Of course there had never been a Penelope Barton at William and Mary. Neither had there been a woman who resembled the young lady upstairs. No such woman existed. But she did, as he knew only too well. He could not ignore the reality of her, as much as he tried. Nor had he discovered any way to ascertain her real identity. If she continued to conspire with Hudson, Fletcher would have proof of her guilt. He clenched his fists. He wanted that, and yet he dreaded it. He must put the safety of the railroad first and protect it, no matter what the personal costs.

CHAPTER 11

Leaving the Dawe home for Grange's Emporium, Penny carried a small willow basket to hold her purchases. Emily had asked her to pick up cinnamon—the longest sticks Mr. Grange carried—some buttons Fletcher had forgotten to bring home from his store, and one other item. What was it? Penny scolded herself as she tried to recall what.

Whistling, she strolled along enjoying the spring sun. Her warm woolen shawl protected her from the slight breeze. Sooner or later she would remember the third item. Looking up at the bright azure sky, she marveled at a solid blue undimmed by a hint of a cloud anywhere. Inhaling a deep breath of sweet spring air, she savored the scents of magnolia and crab apple.

The trees carried a pale fringe of green, harbingers of the lush foliage and warmer weather ahead. Penny paused a moment and leaned her head back to savor the warmth of the sun on her face. Business and the rush of daily life had consumed her life in her own time and left no space for such simple pleasures. Too much time had passed since she had basked in the sun and enjoyed the coming of spring. The days now stretched longer and longer, obliterating the chill of a cold, wet March. In some ways, this enforced holiday had brought unexpected benefits. Without work to fill her time, she intended to enjoy every hour of leisure.

Too busy for even a Florida vacation, she regretted her winter-white skin. The warmth of the sun energized her. She wanted to soak it up and store it for later. Later? She had no idea what later meant anymore. She sighed, resumed whistling, and strolled ahead.

A tall woman in a straw bonnet approached, frowned at Penny, then sniffed, and looked the other way. For a moment Penny puzzled over the woman's obvious displeasure and wondered what had caused it. Suddenly she smiled, amused. Of course, no respectable woman of 1855 whistled. Ceasing her whistling, she shrugged her shoulders. The beautiful day offered too much to dwell on such niceties.

Remembering all the *do*s and avoiding the *don't*s of the polite society of 1855 exhausted her. More frequently than not, she caught herself just in time before committing yet another error. She made a mental note to refrain from whistling, at least in public. Yeech. She had never fully appreciated the freedom of her own time, yet such restrictions never bothered Emily. If Emily paid no attention to them, she should do the same.

Straightening her shawl, she marched down the street, but gradually slowed her pace to a more ladylike walk as she neared the business district. At Walnut Street a familiar figure dressed in dark blue came striding her way, too near to avoid.

Dan Hudson tipped his captain's cap. "Hello, Miss Barton. Lovely weather." His generous smile and bright eyes implied pleasure at seeing her.

"Yes, wonderful, Mr. Hudson. How are you?" She smiled, but as Fletcher's words, "I prefer you not see him," echoed through her mind, her smile faded. "I can't chat today. Emily—Mrs. Dawe—needs some cinnamon for a pie."

Dan raised an eyebrow at that. "I hear tell she's one of the best cooks in the area." He paused and rocked back on his heels. "Although I have not had much occasion to taste her pies. Fletcher Dawe has taken an active dislike to me." He gave her a quizzical look. "I hope he hasn't influenced you against me, too."

"What?" Penny stared at him for a moment. Courtesy demanded a polite denial. "No, of course not." She flushed at the lie. "Mr. Dawe doesn't choose my friends." Chin forward, she stepped ahead, determined to complete her errands.

Falling into step beside her, Dan shortened his stride to match hers. "Glad I am to hear that. I enjoyed your visit to the locks." He gave her a sideways glance, but Penny ignored it.

She walked a bit faster. "So did Emily and I. They're fascinating."

"Then you must come again."

"When I have more time—Emily and I both will." Not wanting to be rude or to say too much, she remained silent for several moments. Snubbing overbearing men had always come easily to her, especially cutting them down to size, but Dan no longer fit that category. His diffident efforts at courtesy surprised her.

He swooped down and grabbed a stem of grass from in front of a house. He chewed on it thoughtfully. They soon reached Fletcher's store, but Penny walked past. If Fletcher saw her with Dan Hudson, who knew what he might do.

Dan twisted the grass in his fingers then threw it away. "Hmm, after losing your valise, I suppose you've grown cautious of trains."

Unease kept her silent.

After no response, he made a nervous cough. "I . . . would avoid travel by train for a while."

"What?" Stopping, Penny frowned and then stared at him with narrowed eyes. "Why? I'm not going anywhere."

She bit her lip, thinking again about the looming rail accident. The sudden image of his body, broken and bloody, his blue jacket splotched and torn, rose before her. Squeezing her eyes shut a moment, she pushed that ugly vision away. No one deserved such a fate. Being a hero came at too high a price.

"Cinnamon, I think you said." Dan stopped in front of Mr. Grange's Emporium.

"Um, yes, I did."

Distracted by her worry and the vision of a crushed Dan, she had nearly passed the Emporium altogether. Stepping in front of her, Dan reached for the door.

"Mr. Hudson." She gulped, but forged on as she placed a hand on his outstretched arm. "You ought to take your own advice. I'd hate to see you have an accident. Train derailments are horrific."

The muscles of Dan's arm tightened. He dropped his hand and stared at her, his dark eyes wide, then hastily looked away. "I don't ride the train, so I should be quite safe. The canals are good enough for me." He opened his mouth to speak, and then apparently thought better of it. Lifting his cap, he ran a hand through his hair. After replacing his cap, he gave her a puzzled, almost fearful look. His narrowed eyes glittered like points of black obsidian. "I . . . forgot; Denton Jackson wants to see me about improvements to the locks. Good day, Miss Barton." He tipped his cap and strode off, a man in a hurry to be elsewhere.

Staring at his retreating back, Penny wondered at his nervousness. Had she been wise to warn him about the future? Had he even understood her hint? Still shaken by that bloody vision and her confusion about Dan's heroics, she turned first one way, then the other, and finally just stood in the center of the walk. She couldn't do anything more.

Gaining Hudson's cooperation to convince Fletcher of her truthfulness wouldn't work. Maybe he had just happened to be in the wrong place at the wrong time. Damn!

Better she should consider her own future. If only she knew whether she was here to stay or might somehow find her way back to where she belonged. She couldn't stand still forever.

She'd better get a life and stop relying on someone else to take care of her. With a sigh, she pushed open the heavy door to Grange's Emporium. Head high, Penny straightened her shoulders and strode forward, fingers tightly clasped on the handle of her basket.

Mr. Grange's Emporium, a small-town general store, carried a limited selection of bottled and tinned goods on shelves that reached from floor to ceiling behind the counter. She brushed past neat rows of sacks near the door that held flour, sugar, and salt. Staples in barrels and boxes and sacks of foodstuffs filled most of the floor space.

She glanced toward wooden shelves with large scoops sticking from the metal bins Mr. Grange used for dry foods. For a moment, she savored the aroma of coffee, spices, and beeswax. Nearby, pots and pans in various sizes, graniteware coffeepots, and kitchen utensils hung from hooks on the wall. Her glance skipped over the stored hardware items, including hammers and nails and a miscellany of gadgets arranged in neat order under the counters at the back of the store.

Mr. Grange left fine fabrics and notions to Fletcher or one of the other stores featuring dry goods. Unlike Fletcher, he carried a select sampling of only the most requested notions and dry goods: mainly papers of pins, needles and thread, and the commonest of fabrics. Penny laughed to herself as she realized how the megastores of her time had come full circle to carry the same range of goods, but in a wider variety.

Balding and with gray muttonchop sideburns, Mr. Grange appeared every bit the prosperous small-town merchant. He stood behind a long wooden counter and gossiped while he served a stout woman. Penny assumed he hadn't seen her enter, so he surprised her when he stopped talking and turned in her direction.

"Good day, Miss Barton. Anything special for you today?"

He removed a pencil from behind his ear and quickly added a row of figures on a piece of brown paper before him.

"Yes, I need some cinnamon. When you have a minute. I'm in no hurry."

"Be through in just a moment. Miz Dawe's usual order?"

Penny nodded and browsed about the shop while Mr. Grange finished with his customer. Maybe Emily would like a packet of candy from the colorful display nestled in jars by the window. She busied herself examining one item after another. A bowl of brown eggs sat beside a wheel of yellow cheese. In her time, even villages had K-Mart, Wal-Mart, and Krogers, large, impersonal stores. The cozy feel of Grange's Emporium welcomed and reassured her.

"Good afternoon, Miss Barton," a soft female voice called from behind her.

Spinning on her heel, Penny saw Sarah Jamison, resplendent in a yellow cotton dress with black silk fringe and a lavender wool shawl. "Oh, hello." She had really not talked much with Sarah and had no idea what to say to her.

Sarah looked down at her spotless black boots and then up at Penny. "I saw you walking down the street a little earlier and hurried to catch you." She paused. "I have meant to ask you long before this, but would you and Mrs. Dawe come to tea? Perhaps tomorrow?"

Penny frowned. "Tomorrow?" Should she accept? What would the proper etiquette be? What would Emily do? "I'll have to consult Mrs. Dawe first. She often tutors her students in the afternoon, but thank you for inviting us."

Sarah edged closer. "I have been longing for a chance to talk with you." She wrung her hands and a crimson flush crept up her neck and into her face. "Coming from the East, Philadelphia as I remember, you must be acquainted with the latest fashions. Coshocton is so remote, you know."

With no desire to lie about something she knew nothing about, Penny interrupted, "Um, well, I can't say I've ever paid much attention. Mrs. Dawe has the right idea—practicality and comfort."

Sarah stared at Penny for a moment as if puzzled by her words, and then she laughed. "Oh, of course, you are referring to her 'Bloomers.' They may be practical, but surely you don't find them attractive? I really fail to understand how she can wear them."

Offended by the insult to Emily, Penny shifted her basket and stared back at Sarah. "I'm thinking of a pair for myself, better for horseback riding than a dress and for getting in and out of a carriage." Penny cringed, debating how to end the conversation without offending Sarah.

"Yes, I . . . I see what you mean." Sarah fingered the fringe on her dress and then looked up with a shy appeal in her brown eyes. "Miss Barton, I wonder, could we start over?"

"Start over?" Penny frowned. What the hell did she want?

"Yes, you see . . ." Sarah twisted the fringe around one finger and glanced toward the jars of candy. "Well, once I had . . . hoped that . . . Fletcher and I might . . . well, that we might marry."

"Oh?" Penny struggled to keep her face neutral. Why did Sarah feel the need to share this with her?

"Well, yes, and I think . . ." Sarah scuffed the toe of her shoe against the rough, hand-hewn boards. "That is his aunt . . . well, she encouraged me you see." She looked up at Penny, seeking reassurance. "That was before you came. But now, well, now I think she prefers you."

"Me?" Penny's eyes widened in genuine disbelief. She had sensed no change in Emily's behavior. "What do you mean?"

Sarah took a deep breath and plunged forward. "I believe she has come to prefer a match between Fletcher and you. But I speak to you to assure you it is of no matter to me now because . . . You see . . . well . . ." She smiled up at Penny and raised her shoulders. "Mr. Meeks has asked me to marry him and . . . I know he truly loves me." She took another deep breath. "So I'm going to marry him." Her eyes sparkled, and her cheeks glowed a becoming rose.

"Congratulations, Sarah." Penny smiled, happy to see such joy and feeling a bit guilty for her earlier thoughts about Sarah. "How nice for you both. Does Fletcher know?"

Sarah shook her head. "You are the very first to know. Besides Mama and Papa, of course. We are planning an engagement party in a few weeks, and I want you and the Dawes to come and share in my happiness. You will?" Sarah smiled and looked almost beautiful in her delight. Obviously, she had been anxious to share the news with someone, anyone.

Penny wondered if she had been this excited when Gerald had asked her to marry him. If she had, the anger and disappointment that followed had overshadowed any happy memories a long time ago. What would it feel like to have someone she truly loved ask her to marry him? Would she be so ready to say yes a second time?

Determined to shake off her own jaded thoughts, Penny focused on the beaming girl. "Of course, we'll be more than happy to come. A party sounds fun. When will you marry him?"

"Oh, not for a year. Papa says we must wait until Mr. Meeks has built us a new house. Papa is giving us the land as an engagement present."

"That's very generous of your father, and a year gives you plenty of time to prepare."

Penny could think of nothing more to say and wondered even whether she would be here in a year's time. The news of the engagement had knocked her off center, but then Sarah and Mr. Meeks, for all she knew about him, suited each other well.

"Yes, plenty of time, but I would prefer somewhat less." Sarah gave her a rueful smile. "Now, I must go. Please give my regards to Mrs. Dawe and convey to her my invitation to take tea with Mother and me. I hope we can be friends now, good friends."

"Of course, we are, Sarah."

Penny's cheeks grew warm at her weak attempt at enthusiasm. She and Sarah had so little in common. Somehow she couldn't see her as anything more than an acquaintance, but in a small town like Coshocton, she didn't need any enemies.

"Good luck to you and Mr. Meeks, and I will, if I may, tell Mrs. Dawe the good news." Penny tilted her head and gave Sarah a conspiratorial smile as she waited for Sarah's permission.

"Please do. I would appreciate it. Mrs. Dawe has always been kindness itself to me." Sarah backed up several steps and clutched her package to her bosom. "Until tomorrow, Miss Barton."

"Until tomorrow." Penny nodded and then grimaced as Sarah in her haste nearly upset a stack of bagged onions and potatoes.

Sarah hurried out the door and closed it tight behind her before Penny heard Mr. Grange's call.

"Miz Barton? Here's the cinnamon for Miz Dawe." He slid a small packet across the worn counter. "I've put it on her account. Can I get you anything else?" He dusted his hands on the sides of his apron.

"Uh, yes. Some lemon drops, too."

Mr. Granger placed a small scoopful into a paper cone and twisted it neatly, then handed the packet to Penny.

"Thank you." She glanced at the clock on the shelf behind him. "It's later than I thought. Good day, Mr. Grange." She tucked the packet into her basket and turned toward the door.

Outside the store, staring at nothing in particular, she digested Sarah's news. A twinge of guilt poked at her conscience as she remembered her judgment of Sarah at the political rally. That evening Sarah had looked birdlike and fragile. A spinster overdressed for the occasion. Penny had assumed she had primped and preened to capture Fletcher's attention. She smiled. So much for jumping to conclusions. Instead, Mr. Meeks had been the object of Sarah's interest, not Fletcher.

Taking several steps away from the store, Penny remained lost in thought. Sarah would be happy as the new Mrs. Meeks. Even the name, Sarah Meeks, suited her. It also removed Penny's only known rival for Fletcher's affections.

Smiling to herself, Penny straightened her shawl and strolled toward Fletcher Dawe's store. Once there, however, she shifted her basket on her arm and studied her feet for a moment. Waiting on customers in his store, he always looked capable and professional. Probably half his customers, especially the young, unmarried ones, fantasized about the handsome owner. His store thrived because so many of the ladies enjoyed basking in his smile. Penny knew only too well how devastating his brown eyes could be. Despite his annoying distrust of her, he still attracted her like a bear to honey. The image made her laugh. Logic had nothing to do with it.

Shifting from one foot to the other, she peered through the large front windows of the store. Near the back, along the wall, two women she did not know appeared to be completing a purchase with the slick-haired Mr. Meeks. She saw no sign of Fletcher or anyone else.

Pushing open the door, Penny entered. The heavy door slipped from her grasp and slammed shut. Both the women and Mr. Meeks raised their heads and stared toward her.

She smiled and shrugged. "Sorry, it slipped."

"Ah, Miss Barton," Mr. Meeks greeted her. "Pay no attention to the door. I have meant to oil that hinge for several days." He returned to wrapping a piece of cloth for the two ladies.

Meandering through the store, Penny smoothed her hand over bolts of fine cotton and fingered shiny satin and soft silk. She bent to examine a box of wooden buttons and debated which size Emily wanted. The large ones? She should have paid more attention as Emily described the buttons she needed. Perhaps she would have to take both large and small.

"Miss Barton," Mr. Meeks greeted her. "How may I assist you?"

Penny jumped, momentarily startled. "Oh, I've come for some buttons for Mrs. Dawe. Flet . . . uh, Mr. Dawe forgot them when he came home for lunch. But now I'm not certain which size she wants." With one finger Penny slid all the large buttons to one side of the box, the small ones to another.

"Um." Mr. Meeks pursed his lips. "Let me ask. Mr. Dawe is in his office at the moment." Turning briskly, Mr. Meeks marched the length of the room and then disappeared though a door behind the long counter.

Waiting, Penny glanced around the store. While Fletcher's shop met the needs of the Coshocton ladies, to her it appeared limited and understocked. The merchandise suited the time, but looked old-fashioned. Compared to the fabric stores of her time, Fletcher's store looked sparse. He offered fewer choices and less color. While he carried a variety of fabrics—gingham and calico, muslins, cottons, linens, woolens, and even silks— most were in a limited range of colors. She didn't see the colorful neon hues, fuchsias, and teals so popular in her time.

Fletcher's stock of ribbons and laces attracted her. The laces had to be hand made, so the variety of patterns amazed her. Reels and hanks of thread, but no spools hung from pegs. She saw needles and scissors, but no sewing machines. The absence of the latter reminded her that families either made their own clothes or employed seamstresses or tailors. Penny glanced down at the dress she wore. All the more reason to take special care of

Mary's carefully sewn garments.

"Miss Barton." Fletcher approached her with Mr. Meeks on his heels.

At the sound of the familiar voice, an odd twinge of expectation struck Penny. His slate gray frock coat contrasted nicely with his blue trousers and vest. As always, he wore his silk cravat neatly knotted. She raised her eyes to his face and those intriguing brown eyes.

"I planned to bring the buttons home this evening." He surveyed her with a look of surprise that made her blush. "You had no need to make a special trip."

Flustered, she brushed away his concern with a wave of one hand. "No special trip, really. I had to stop at Grange's for some cinnamon, so I told Emily I'd pick up the buttons. Actually, I would have been by earlier except I . . ."

Penny caught herself before mentioning Dan Hudson. Fletcher would surely be angry if he knew she had talked with Dan and, with Mr. Meeks standing near, she felt it unwise to mention Sarah. "I'm afraid I enjoyed the beautiful day a bit too much."

Fletcher gave her a rueful smile. "I am sorry my forgetfulness has brought you out."

Penny clutched her basket tighter. "I needed the exercise. Besides, Emily wanted to use the buttons this afternoon."

He looked about and seemed suddenly aware of Mr. Meeks hovering in the background. "Would you care for some refreshment? I have just brewed a pot of tea."

She smiled as thirst assailed her. "Tea? That sounds wonderful."

"This way," He led the way behind the counter into his office and held the door open for her. "You have not visited here before. May I take your basket?"

"Oh, of course." She relinquished the basket to him,

conscious of the brush of his fingers as he reached for the handle. Even such a slight touch exhilarated her. Breathing deeply, she steadied herself and perched on the wooden chair facing his desk.

His office, small and neat with nothing out of place, reflected his inclination for order and purpose. Emily had said he spent much of each day here on his accounts and orders. A quill pen lay next to the inkwell. A lamp, almost identical to the one in the Dawe parlor, illuminated one corner of the desk, and a brown leather ledger lay open near the lamp. A steaming teapot rested on a small tray opposite.

Fletcher placed the basket on a cabinet against the wall and picked up a china cup and saucer. "Milk? Sugar?"

"Only a little sugar, please." Penny cupped her hands in her lap and leaned forward. She watched, entranced, as he poured the steaming liquid into the translucent white cup and added a spoonful of sugar. Not since the train reenactment had she noticed his muscular hands and his long, capable fingers. She caught herself staring.

His intense scrutiny over the rim of the cup caused her cheeks to flush. Her palms suddenly grew moist. Had he somehow learned about her encounter with Dan Hudson? She shifted in her chair and unconsciously cleared her throat. Even if he did, she hadn't done anything. She had no cause for guilt. Raising her chin, Penny smiled back.

He handed her the cup and then poured one for himself. "Well, how was Mr. Grange?"

"Mr. Grange?" Penny stirred her tea and set the spoon in the saucer. "Helpful as always." She stirred the tea and considered what to say. Small talk never had appealed to her. "I met Sarah Jamison there. She said she's engaged."

Surprise painted Fletcher's face as he turned to face her. "Sarah? Engaged? Whomever to?"

Penny smiled; evidently neither Mr. Meeks nor Sarah had told Fletcher. "Mr. Meeks."

"Mr. Meeks? Ah, that sly devil. Well, I wish them good luck. Sarah is a nice person and deserves better than Clarence Meeks, to be sure. But then again, Coshocton is a small town and offers little choice for either men or women. I hope she will be happy with him."

Penny studied Fletcher's face for any sign of regret. His expression registered nothing.

"Sarah says so. They won't marry for a year, though. Her father wants Mr. Meeks to build a home for them first." She stirred her tea to cool it and then sipped. She longed to know how Fletcher really felt about the engagement. "I thought you and Sarah would eventually . . . I mean Emily said Sarah liked you."

His eyes twinkled. "Sarah and I have known each other since childhood. Of course, we are friends, but we have never been more than that. To tell the truth, Sarah's interests seem so narrow. And although her attraction to me was quite obvious, I cannot say I reciprocated. One could never have a philosophical or political discussion with her."

He reached for the teapot and raised it. "More tea?"

Relief flooded Penny. "Uh, no, actually, I should go. Emily is waiting on the cinnamon—and the buttons."

"Oh, yes, the buttons." Fletcher opened the drawer of his desk and took out a small packet. "Perhaps, you will come again for tea?"

"Yes, I'd like that." Penny set her cup on the desk and rose.

He tucked the packet in her basket and handed it to her. Again his hand brushed hers and a sharp spark of static electricity jumped between them.

"Oooh!" Penny lost her grip on the basket and it started to fall.

He snatched at the basket, closing his hands over hers. "Are you all right, Miss Barton?" He stared down at her with concern and took her arm.

The quick snap of static electricity now forgotten, a surge of excitement coursed through Penny. A titillating mixture of Bay Rum and herbal soap assailed her senses from Fletcher's body. She lost herself in his worried gaze.

"Yes," she stammered, "yes. Just the shock."

She clutched the basket to her chest, much too conscious of his nearness. She looked up at him and then down. His dark eyes intimidated her, and she couldn't decide if he liked her, or his intense scrutiny represented his continuing distrust of her.

"I . . . really must go."

She moved as though to leave, but Fletcher still held her arm and partially blocked her way. Looking up, she found herself mesmerized by his searching eyes. She hung suspended and the moment stretched between them, demanding something, anything, to release the tension. Paralyzed like a rabbit caught in an open field, she could not move. She could barely breathe.

He leaned closer; his dark eyes, immense pools of uncertain depth, pulled her inward. Down, down into the core of his being. "Miss Barton, I—"

A loud knock sounded on the door. "Mr. Dawe," Mr. Meeks called out, "Mrs. Jackson wants to know about that shipment of paisley shawls."

Fletcher drew back and released Penny's arm. "Oh, one moment. I'll be right there."

Taking a deep breath, Penny, adrift, blinked to clear her vision. For a moment, she heartily wished both Mrs. Jackson and Mr. Meeks far away. She very much wanted to know what Fletcher had started to say to her.

"I'll see you at home this evening. I must attend to Mrs. Jackson." Fletcher straightened his cravat and opened the door for Penny.

Nodding, she clutched her basket close. "Thank you for the tea." She sailed out the door, acknowledged Mrs. Jackson, smiled absently at Mr. Meeks, and found her way to the store entrance. The sooner she returned home, the better.

"Ah, Mrs. Jackson," she heard Fletcher greet the woman, "Mr. Meeks said you were inquiring about our shipment of paisley shawls."

Fletcher smiled at Mrs. Jackson, but his eyes followed Penny Barton as she closed the door behind her. What had possessed him to forget himself so? The nearness of that woman did strange things to him, and he found himself contemplating actions he knew he would regret later.

"A lovely lass, that friend of your aunt's. Will she be staying long?" Mrs. Jackson studied him with avid curiosity.

"What? Miss Barton? I am not certain. I believe Aunt Emily indicated Miss Barton had come for an extended visit. Perhaps you should call upon Aunt Emily and ask her." He smiled, attempting to take the edge off his implied criticism.

"Yes, yes, I have been meaning to do that, but with the children and all, I hardly have time." She placed a finger alongside her chin and gave him a coquettish smile. "I hear Sarah Jamison has become engaged. Perhaps we can look forward to a similar announcement for Miss Barton?"

Fletcher stared at Mrs. Jackson unable to suppress his surprise. "Miss Barton? Engaged?"

"Oh, well, perhaps I read too much into what I saw. She and Dan Hudson looked so intimate, walking arm and arm on the street."

Fletcher turned to straighten a bolt of fabric. He did not want Mrs. Jackson to read any further emotions from his face or mien. "I am sure when and if Miss Barton accepts a suitor, she will ensure it is properly announced. Miss Barton comes from the East, and ladies there are perhaps a little more independent and forward in their manners than are Coshocton ladies. Now, about those paisley shawls—"

Inwardly Fletcher seethed. Penny Barton had not mentioned Dan Hudson. He had been right about them conspiring against him. He would confront Miss Barton about that and also to warn her further about her unseemly behavior. She had to be made to understand that her free manners gave others the wrong impression.

He stopped a moment and stared at the box of shawls. No, perhaps he was wrong, and they had the right impression. After all, an adventuress would behave exactly as she had. He had no intention of becoming a victim of her all too attractive charms.

CHAPTER 12

Dan walked with his head down and his shoulders hunched forward, oblivious of any passersby. He shoved his clenched fists into his trouser pockets. Twice now that Barton busybody had talked about "accidents." How had she learned of his plans? He had told no one except Billy O'Brien. The railroad would be opening any day now, and he hadn't succeeded in stopping Dawe. Oh, he had managed to delay the schedule a bit, but somehow Dawe always managed to get the laborers back to work. According to Billy, today would pretty well complete the track-laying with only a few rails to be replaced.

He needed something spectacular, something that would frighten the farmers and merchants so badly they would refuse to use the railroad. He remembered the conversation with that Barton wench about derailments and had decided then to plan one for the opening run. But today, she spoke of an accident to him along with a train derailment. What had she meant? Was she threatening him?

If she said anything to Dawe, the sheriff would come for him and then he would have no chance to carry out his plan. Somehow he had to get her out of the way, but how? He had no money to bribe her. It took every cent he could scrounge up to pay off O'Brien. Lucky, too, O'Brien had no way to know he would get no further money after the derailment.

Dan chuckled to himself. Once O'Brien derailed the train, he could do nothing to Dan because if he said anything, his own role would stand revealed and Dawe would prosecute him for loss of property and any injuries. No, O'Brien could not afford to say anything.

That left the Barton wench. He had to find some way to keep her from reporting to Dawe or to the sheriff. Dan considered his choices. Muzzle her or kill her. Somehow killing a woman held little appeal. But killing a whore was another matter. He might do that, but then he would have a body to dump or hide. And if anyone tied the crime to him, he might hang. He shook his head. No, murder would only be a last choice.

He had already rejected bribery, although perhaps he could lead her on and make her believe he had money. Women like her would do anything for money. After all, she had agreed to work for Dawe, hadn't she?

Getting her out of the way for a few days until after the deed was done would do it. He puzzled over various ways to abduct and hide her. He needed a place no one would go and yet one where his presence would not be questioned. He couldn't keep her at his house. Maeve would be onto that for sure, and then there was no telling what that woman would do. She could raise a ruckus, all right.

Never should have married an Irish lass. Pretty enough, but hot tempered as hell. She near killed him the night she threw the cast iron frying pan at him. He smiled a wolfish grin. But she brought that same fire to his bed, and he didn't mind that at all, not at all. She had also brought him a place with the Irish workers. A clannish group, they wanted little to do with the Lutheran Germans and the other townspeople. No, he couldn't bring himself to regret Maeve, despite the brat she had brought with her.

He sighed. The lockmaster's office and the warehouses had too many other people coming and going. He wanted somewhere isolated and private. Dan scratched his chin. There had to be a suitable place. Hmm, why not his old boat at the holding basin? Yes, that would do nicely. No one ever went there, especially not Maeve. If he gagged and bound Penny Barton, she couldn't summon help.

But how could he lure her there and overpower her before she called for help? She had plenty of spirit, and he suspected she would put up a struggle. Maeve had shown him just how much strength a female could wield. He needed some way to knock her out. There had to be a way.

Knock her out? That sounded familiar. Why did those words strike him so? Something about that doctor fellow, Dr. Wes—Wescott. Then Dan remembered the slim brown bottle he had filched from the doctor. The bottle of Chloro—chloroform. The doc had said it would render a person unconscious. All he had to do was saturate his handkerchief with it and hold the handkerchief to her nose. She would be helpless. Um, yes, the very thing.

Dan straightened his shoulders and whistled as he strolled toward his office. Yes, siree, he had the means to remove the Barton wench as a threat. Nothing could stop him now. Not her or Fletcher Dawe. The canals would survive and the railroad would be disgraced. He smiled with narrowed eyes.

Fletcher's silence during dinner disturbed Penny. He had said little. Mostly he responded in monosyllables to Emily's observations. Once or twice she had caught him watching her, but when she looked toward him he had glanced down at his plate.

Maybe her visit had disturbed him as much as it had her. Her arm still tingled where his hand had rested. But she might have read more into his manner and his words than he meant. What else had they talked about? Sarah. Sarah Jamison's engagement.

The thought that Sarah's engagement depressed Fletcher

startled and disturbed her. His response when she told him the news had pleased her. He had responded as if he had no serious feelings for Sarah. But tonight she began to wonder if she had misread him.

"I must say, Penny, you took me quite by surprise with the news of Sarah Jamison's engagement." Emily passed a dish of hot biscuits to her.

"Not knowing Sarah well, I didn't know she had any interest in Mr. Meeks." Penny turned to Fletcher. "Had you?"

"What? Had I what?" He looked up, confusion on his face.

"Sarah's engagement surprised Emily and me. Neither of us remembers seeing her with Mr. Meeks."

"Oh, Mr. Meeks. They saw each other at the store. He always made it a point to serve Sarah." Fletcher stared down at his plate. He had eaten only a little of the ham and almost none of the rutabaga.

Penny laughed. "Love in a dry goods store. That's rich, Fletcher. Very rich." Emily joined her laughter.

"And why not? It is as good a place as any other." His face flushed and Penny reddened as she remembered his nearness this afternoon.

"Now, now, Fletcher. I am sure Penny meant nothing improper. How is the railroad coming?"

"I think I can at last say we have finished. Carmody and O'Brien have their crews completing the final cleanup. Carmody wants to replace some questionable rails in one section, but that's all."

"So when will the first train run? Remember, I said I wanted to ride the train to Columbus." Emily's eyes sparkled as she glanced at Penny.

"Um, I am not quite certain. Any day now. It really is up to the Steubenville directors to decide. They have been advertising schedules in the newspaper for months now, but we have still had to use the canal packets for the link from here to Newark."

"April eleventh. I told you, you'll see." Penny couldn't keep a note of triumph from her voice.

Fletcher tossed his napkin alongside his plate and stood up, almost knocking his chair over. "Humph, perhaps. But I expect it a day or two sooner. I see no reason for any further delay. Now, if you ladies will excuse me, I have some papers to read."

Watching him stride from the room, Penny wondered what had made him so angry. She turned to Emily, seeking an answer.

"Don't worry, Penny. It is just that things have been difficult lately. That bad shipment of rails upset him, and he finds it hard to realize his troubles are at an end." Emily rose and began to remove the serving dishes.

Penny sat for a moment longer and then joined Emily. Something clearly had disturbed Fletcher, but what? Did he resent his attraction to her? That is, if he felt one. Or had something else happened? She had said almost nothing to Dan Hudson and, while Fletcher had urged her not to speak with him at all, she had said no more than she would say to any other man. In a small town one had to be polite. Penny shook her head. Well, too bad. Fletcher's bad humor was his problem, not hers. She piled up the plates and followed Emily to the kitchen.

After washing and drying the supper dishes, Emily and Penny joined Fletcher in the parlor. He sat barricaded behind his paper and ignored both of them. Emily picked up her mending and worked on turning the cuffs of one of Fletcher's shirts. Penny stoked the fire and then lit the lamp next to the sofa.

After taking a seat there, she picked up one of Mary's dresses and began taking up the hem. Sewing had never been her favorite task, but without the money to pay someone else, she had to do it. The good fortune of meeting Emily still amazed her; it had given her the space to work out a future. If she had confronted Fletcher that day, he would probably have called the sheriff, and she shuddered to think what might have happened. From what she remembered reading about nineteenth-century jails and asylums, she wanted none of them.

She still hoped Fletcher would accept her story, but he showed no sign of changing his mind. Earlier today, she thought she had made some progress in gaining his trust, but tonight his behavior had reverted. He wanted nothing to do with her. Why?

Penny's frustration grew. Why had she been pushed back in time if she couldn't change the future? Why torture herself with might-have-beens when they could never be? She'd better go to Columbus or some other city and make a new life for herself. She had promised Emily three months. Somehow she would last those three months, but then she would go. No matter what, she still had a life, intelligence, and energy. She only had to identify the opportunities and convince someone to fund a start-up.

Trying to be rational and sensible had no effect on her emotions. She hurt. No man had ever hurt her this way. She had made a mistake with Gerald, but his behavior had made it easier to leave. If only she and Fletcher could wipe out the past and start again. If only she really was Clotilde von Wahl's niece, but she wasn't, and she couldn't be.

The clock in the hall struck nine. Penny folded the dress on which she had been working and rose. "Good night, Emily, Fletcher. My head aches, so I think I'll go up now and try to sleep."

Emily looked up, an anxious look on her face. "Would you like some willow bark tea or a laudanum powder?"

"No, I'm sure a little sleep will set me right." Penny turned the lamp down, lit a candle from the fire, and made her way to her room.

Fletcher's behavior rankled. If he wanted her to leave, all he had to do was say so. She clenched her fists, and two large tears rolled down her face. How could she possibly love any man as stubborn and inflexible as Fletcher Dawe?

CHAPTER 13

Dan Hudson chewed on the soggy end of a cigar as he leaned against the side of the apothecary just out of sight of anyone passing. From behind a pile of old boards, if he angled his neck just so, he could see both sides of the street.

"Whaddaya doin', Hudson?" The slurred voice came from behind.

Dan reeled. "None o' yer business. And git away. Here." He flipped a coin at the old drunk. "Go git yerself a drink. I'm too busy to talk to yo' now."

Silently the drunk scrambled for the coin and stumbled toward Bailey's.

Peering from behind the boards, Dan slumped against the building. By this time most days, foot traffic dwindled to an occasional shopkeeper closing up, but today he saw too many people out and about. At least, too many for his liking. Two carriages passed, and he listened for others. A man walked across the street, whistling. Two dogs snarled over an old piece of bone they had found somewhere. A rhythmic *clang-clang-clang* came from the other end of town, as the blacksmith's hammer struck his anvil.

Dan cocked his head and listened for solitary footsteps. Sooner or later Penny Barton would pass this way. He smiled with narrowed eyes. Who did she think she was, anyway? Come here from out of nowhere pretending to be so interested in the canals and locks. No woman he knew, except maybe Miz Dawe, asked more than an occasional question about the boats or the locks.

"Hmph. Bitch ain't as smart as she thinks she is! She can't fool me," Dan hissed from between clenched teeth. "And Fletcher Dawe put her up to it."

His eyes narrowed as he thought of Fletcher. He might be able to fool some folks, but it would take more than a fancy city girl to fool Dan Hudson. No doubt Dawe had hired the Barton wench from one of the houses in Columbus where fancy women made twice as much as any of Kitty's girls. Dan pulled his cap lower on his head. Probably told her to cozy up to the important men in town to find out who supported the railroad and who fought it.

That Dawe! If he could, he would destroy the canals. Anything to get business for the railroad. Just wait until the "accident." It would fix Dawe and ruin his railroad.

Crossing his arms over his chest, Dan glanced up and down the street again. At least the wench hadn't been smart enough to get much information. He struggled to remember the questions she had asked the day he had shown her and Miz Dawe the locks. He screwed up his brow. Near as he could figure, in spite of asking about his work at the canals and pretending to be interested in the locks themselves, she hadn't asked anything Dawe could use against him. But then all that talk about train accidents. Worry pecked at Dan. Just couldn't trust women no how.

He kicked at a stone and sent it reeling halfway into the street. Well, that Barton wench certainly took her time to get down to business. Not that he wouldn't mind sampling a few favors, but he'd give nothing away. Nothing. He smiled at the thought of such favors. Forward and outspoken enough, she didn't act quite like Kitty's girls. Nice figure she had, but she covered herself up a little too much. Kitty's girls sure didn't do that. He'd take care of Penny Barton. Teach her a lesson about asking questions and making a man look a fool.

Gazing up the street, Dan took a long, deep breath. She had to come this way. He pulled his watch from his pocket. Where could she be? When he last saw her, coming out of Sally's Millinery Shop, she already had an armload of packages and had started toward Dawe's house. Where else could she have gone? She had to pass the apothecary to take the most direct route home and, with teatime so near, she would be unlikely to dilly-dally much longer. Women! They had no proper sense of time.

The western sun turned the low-lying clouds shades of pinkish orange. If Penny Barton really sought information for Dawe or any of the other railroad investors, somebody had to get rid of her. Dan licked his lips. But why not have a little fun with her first?

Stretching his neck, he rose on his toes. He didn't want her to think he had been waiting just for her. No sense in giving her that satisfaction. From his perch behind the boards, he would see her before she saw him. Unless, somehow, he had already missed her. He frowned. Catch her off guard, that's what he would have to do. No, she might scream or run.

If anyone saw them, he wanted this to look like a friendly little visit. He spat a piece of cigar into the dirt and then reached into his coat to pat the flat brown bottle, safely hidden inside his shirt. His fingers fumbled for the cork while his eyes searched both sides of the street. The cork of the bottle reassured him, and he withdrew his hand.

Dan slipped out from behind the pile of boards and ambled slow and easy, toward the front of the store. He had to be careful. Depending on who saw him, he might need to give good account of why he had left the locks. Since the weather had turned, business had picked up and he needed every hand available. For now, the locks had plenty of work, but after Dawe's train began running, then what? Then maybe they would all be looking for work. Dan spat again. No way would he work for Dawe. Never!

He thought of Maeve, and his shoulders slumped. Maeve and her brat. If she had another one in the hatch, he would need work. Dan clenched his fist and then forced himself to relax. A man did what he had to do to support his family. He grimaced and walked a little faster.

Suddenly Penny Barton appeared from around the corner of the post office and came toward him, no more than thirty feet away. Her eyes widened a moment as if surprised to see him, and then she smiled at him.

"Why, Dan, what are you still doing here? I would've thought you'd be busy." She approached him, drawing her brown shawl tight around her. "Or that you'd be down at the docks working on that old boat you showed us."

She stopped, close enough for Dan to smell a flowery, feminine scent. For a moment he felt snared. He didn't know enough about ladies' scents to tell what it might be, but just the fragrance of Penny Barton made his thoughts wander.

"Oh, uh, had some errands to run, but I need to get back to the locks." He hesitated and buried his hands in his pockets. "Want to get that old thing in the water by next week." He eyed the pale skin of her delicate neck and slowly rolled his tongue around the wet end of his cigar.

"Oh, by the way, if you're going back to the Dawes'," he said, nodding in the direction of the Dawe house, "if you stopped in at my office you could take a package come today on one of the boats for Mr. Dawe. Looks kind of important, but I didn't get the chance to deliver it. Been awful busy. Usually I deliver goods myself or have one of the hands do it." He noticed Penny direct a questioning glance at the packages in her arms.

"It's just a wee parcel. You could tuck it in there somewhere.

You wouldn't mind?" He couldn't let her get away. Not now.

"No. If I can fit it in here." Penny shifted her bundles from one arm to the other.

"Very well. Shall we?" Dan extended his arm for Penny's hand.

Looking over her shoulder, Penny let her fingers slip from Dan's arm. Fletcher would be furious if he saw her with Dan. Their last conversation made his distrust of Dan clear. If he saw her walking toward the locks with Dan, he would surely suspect her of plotting some scheme.

"So, you and the Dawes plannin' anything special for the opening of the railroad?" Dan turned and studied her face.

"Special?" She blinked and paused. "No one mentioned anything special. There's the fair in town that day, but it doesn't have anything to do with the train."

Dan's question puzzled her. Why would he want to know whether the Dawes planned anything special? According to Fletcher, if the crew didn't finish the cleanup work on the rails today, the train might not run for another week.

"Why do you ask?"

Dan shrugged. "Curious, I 'spose. Hear tell there's been more trouble with the work crews again." His laugh sounded gleeful.

Penny focused on the curl of his upper lip. So that's it. Dan wanted to know whether the train would be running at all. She studied his face and pondered what to say. She had already tried to warn him, and the last time he had rushed off. Lately, she had trouble seeing him as a hero. The rivalry between the canals and railroad could only grow worse.

As they approached the locks and Dan's office, he moved closer and grasped her elbow a little tighter than Penny considered necessary. "Before we get that package in my office, let me show you how the work on the boat's coming. It's slow goin', but I'm making progress."

With his free hand, Dan touched his cap, then turned around and looked in the direction from which they had come. Something about his voice and the way he kept looking over his shoulder made her hesitate.

"Another time. It's late, and the Dawes probably already wonder where I am." She wriggled her arm free from his firm grip.

"Aw, come on. You said you liked boats." He grasped her arm again and began to guide her toward the decrepit boat in the holding pond.

Penny's heart beat faster. Dryness filled her mouth. Something niggled her. Dan had never seemed so assertive or insistent before. If anything, he had always reminded her more of a follower than a leader. Now, he loomed over her, almost pushing her toward the boat.

"Really, Dan, Emily's waiting." Penny clutched her packages as she glanced toward his office then back to him. Her stomach knotted. A gust of cool air brought a shiver.

Dan mumbled a muffled response as he pulled her nearer the water. Under his viselike grip, her steps followed his. Not wanting to make a scene, she sighed. A look at Dan's boat would satisfy him and then she could say good-bye. Let Fletcher retrieve his own package. A long walk just might do him good.

Dan guided the Barton wench across a broad plank stretching from the oozing black mud of the shore to the dilapidated deck of the boat. "Look. Right through there. Closer. I've just about finished the hull. See." He leaned into the darkening hull where a dusky, pre-evening gloom already filled the corners.

She peered into the murky darkness. "I can't see much now, Dan. Maybe in the morning I could see better." She started to pull back, but he stood behind her, almost on top of her. She drew in a deep breath.

"No, no. Too busy in the mornin.' Can't you see?" Dan pointed into the hull.

A shroud of wet fog floated just above the water and the listing boat creaked against its mooring. Behind her, Dan edged farther and farther forward as he fumbled in his coat to loosen the cork on the bottle. He pulled a ragged handkerchief from his pocket and slapped the rag over the bottle.

"So, what do you think?" The heat of her body reached him as he stood behind her. He smelled that flowery, feminine scent again.

"It doesn't look any different than when you showed it to Emily and me the other—"

In one deft movement, Dan wet the rag and slapped it over the bitch's mouth and nose.

Her arms thrashed wildly and her packages flew in all directions. Dan stepped this way and that to avoid her frantic kicks. With his left hand he grabbed a fistful of her hair and jerked her head back.

"Bitch. Now what are you and Dawe gonna do?" Dan held the chloroform-soaked rag over her mouth and nose for several seconds. As she slumped to the deck, he slid one arm around her waist and slipped the other behind her legs, scooping her up like a small child. Her arms hung limp, and her head flopped backward.

Dan carried her onto the dank hull and dropped her to the deck like a useless sack of garbage. Her body sprawled across the floor. A small cut on her head wept beads of red. He ducked back up and took a quick look around. No one. He scooped up the scattered parcels. Kicking open the door, Dan dropped the parcels inside and then dragged Penny through it.

"There. Nobody'll think to look for you here. This thing'll

sink before anybody comes lookin'. Besides, nobody would expect a prissy thing like you to wander off around old boats." Dan snorted as he kicked Penny's parcels into a pile next to her body.

"But we'll make sure you can't get too far when yo' wake up."

He jerked a wad of thick twine from his pocket and looped it around her ankles first, then her wrists. He drew the cord tight and knotted her hands behind her back. Wadding up a rag, he stuffed it in her mouth and fastened his handkerchief over her eyes. He pulled the material as tight as he could. His eyes traveled the length of her body as she lay prone on the floor. He stared for several seconds at a rip in her dress.

"Maybe later, when you're feelin' a little more lively, you and me can have a little fun."

He laughed a deep, throaty laugh, then ran a grimy hand across her breast. He left a muddy mark on the bodice. As he left the hull, he locked the door behind him and whistled his way back to his office.

CHAPTER 14

Over the top of his newspaper, Fletcher watched Emily part the parlor curtains from the tall front window and peer out. He pulled his watch from its pocket and checked the time once again. Six thirty-five. Within the last twenty minutes Emily had gone to the parlor window four times. He set the paper aside and studied her worried expression. Her eyes darted over the cold, empty grate of the fireplace then to the shepherdess on the mantel, and finally back out the window.

"Is dinner ready?" Fletcher stirred in his chair, but continued to watch his aunt.

Although she rarely let a clock or a schedule dictate most of her actions, she had always served dinner promptly at 6:15 each evening. Tonight, however, she had not even mentioned dinner.

"Yes." She spoke with her back toward him.

"Well, then, shall I call Miss Barton? Possibly she is engrossed in a book upstairs and has simply overlooked the time." Fletcher rose from his chair and began to make his way to the stairs in the main hallway.

"She left to do an errand hours ago. She said she would be back no later than four. Now it's approaching seven." Emily marched to another window and peered out.

Fletcher moved back to his seat and picked up the paper, flattening the pages methodically with smooth, even brushes of his hand. He made an effort to read, but the words on the page became a jumble of senseless symbols. What type of errand required so much of Penny Barton's attention?

Clenching his fingers, Fletcher crimped the edge of his paper. "Perhaps she found something more interesting to occupy her time. She hasn't found much excitement here, and I cannot imagine she has enjoyed herself." Most likely she had met a man of interest—Dan Hudson, no doubt.

Emily frowned, pleating the front of her white apron. "Penny loves it here. We have talked often. She intends to make Coshocton her home. She would like to open a bookstore." Edged with frustration, her voice sounded choppy. Fletcher strained to hear her words.

"A bookstore?" He lowered the paper and gazed at his aunt. He couldn't decide what bothered him most—that Penny planned to stay, or the thought of her engaging in commerce. Involuntarily he raised his eyebrows. "Where would she find the capital?"

Emily straightened a pillow resting on the divan. "I plan to fund it. Coshocton needs a bookstore. If the town grows, as you say it will, then it can surely support such an enterprise."

"I'm sure it can, but Miss Barton as the proprietress of such an establishment strains the imagination."

"And why is that? Because she is a woman?" Emily snorted. "Penny's business acumen exceeds yours, if I say so myself."

"Um." He gave her an indulgent smile and wondered at her agitated state. "While I do not agree, I am sure you are prepared to argue the issue."

Sighing loudly, Emily made no answer but peered out the window again. "I cannot imagine where she can be. She is always so punctual. I fear something dreadful has happened, Fletcher."

He raised an eyebrow at his aunt's words and then turned back to his paper. "I surmise Miss Barton returned from whence she came, and high time it is. The line opens in two days, so any work she had to do here should already be done. She has probably collected a good fee and gone home."

Emily shook her head. "I don't believe that, Fletcher, and I do not believe you do, either. Penny Barton is far above any covert activity for financial gain. Anyway, she would not have left without telling me good-bye."

"How can you be sure?"

"Because I know Penny. Something has happened, something bad." Her worried frown carried a touch of panic.

"Rubbish. She tired of the masquerade. That is all." He folded his paper neatly and laid it on the table next to the reading lamp.

"Fletcher, there are times when I wish I could still turn you over my knee. Your attitude of unrelenting suspicion does you no credit. In fact, it speaks of your unwillingness to attempt any level of understanding or compassion. Penny has given you no reason to distrust her."

"Oh? She hasn't given me any reason to trust her. All her talk of a derailment! Humph!" Rays of sunshine had long since withdrawn their warmth from the room, and now it appeared gloomy and cold.

"Well, just suppose that Penny is correct and someone here in town plans to disrupt the inaugural run of the train to destroy confidence in the railroad. If such a person heard Penny mention this impending 'accident,' would they not wonder how she had learned of it? Would they not suspect her of knowing what they planned? Such knowledge could put her in grave danger."

"What?" Fletcher sat bolt upright as his aunt's words penetrated. "That is a lot of supposition. Surely it makes more sense to assume she finished her work and has left."

"For you, I'm sure it does." Emily faced him, her face serious and her lips compressed in a thin gray line. "But what if I'm right? Then Penny may be in deadly peril. A number of folks here in town might benefit from a derailment. You know that better than anyone else. Think of all the problems at the work sites." She marched to his chair and stared down at him, hands on her hips.

"If . . ." Fletcher found it hard to answer the accusation in his aunt's eyes. ". . . mind you, I say *if* you are right . . ." Growing waves of unease percolated upward from his gut, even though his common sense insisted he had Miss Barton pegged. ". . . then who would be behind this alleged plot, and where might they hide Miss Barton?"

"I don't know." Emily wrung her hands. She wadded her apron into a tight ball and began to pace. "We must start with those who have a motive to stop the railroad."

Fletcher snorted. "We would have to include every canal boat captain and crewman, Dan Hudson, any of his cronies, Denton Jackson, anyone who hates me. For all I know, we could be talking of half of Coshocton."

Emily's eyes widened. "Surely not. Rather, we are speaking of someone of questionable integrity. That should narrow the list a lot."

Rising, Fletcher walked toward the window and then turned to face his aunt. "And again, there are a number of scoundrels in this town. With the canal traffic, scum arrive every day. Furthermore, still seemingly respectable citizens, whose integrity," he said, thumping his chest with a finger for emphasis, "I question, seek to disrupt the railroad. As to where Miss Barton could be—she could be on a canal boat on the way to Columbus or Cincinnati."

"No, Fletcher. I don't believe she would go without saying farewell." Emily shook her head. "Absolutely not, not of her own free will."

Arms behind his back, Fletcher paced the length of the room and back to stop before his aunt. "Well, then, if we accept your hypothesis, these . . . these villains would want to get her out of the way. The possibilities are endless."

"Oh, Fletcher. No!" His aunt looked horrified.

His forehead a mass of frown lines, he traced that thread of logic and stared at his aunt. "She might be down a well, in a derelict building. She could be anywhere. She could be . . . dead." His words hung in the air like a judge's dread pronouncement. Fletcher shuddered. "No. On second thought, I don't believe anyone would kill her."

The thought of injury or harm to Penny jolted him. Images of Penny unconscious, with blood on her forehead, or a blackened eye, reeled through his mind. His gut cramped. Despite his distrust of her, he would do anything to save her from hurt.

"Fletcher, I'm worried. If something should happen to her . . . We must do something."

He dragged his watch from his pocket. "Yes, we must. It is now seven-fifteen." He started for the door. "I'll talk with Sheriff Seton."

"I'm coming, too."

Emily followed him from the room, untying her apron as she went. As Fletcher buttoned his coat, she plucked her cape from the hook by the door and tossed it over her shoulders. He held the door for her and then closed it.

Together they hurried around the corner and down several short blocks to the sheriff's home. To Fletcher, with his aunt struggling to maintain his gait, it seemed they walked too slowly—as though thick, unyielding mud sucked at his feet. But despite the chill of darkening evening that made him draw his coat tighter, the weather remained clear and dry. In ten minutes he bounded up the steps of the sheriff's clapboard house. Breathing hard, he rapped sharply on the door. Beside him, Aunt Emily struggled to catch her breath.

John Seton, a large man with a red face and a prominent graying mustache answered the door himself. His fierce eyes scrutinized Fletcher, but softened when they reached Emily.

"Fletcher," Seton's voice boomed. "This is certainly a surprise—"

Fletcher held up his hand before Seton could continue. "I'm sorry to bother you, John, but our houseguest, Miss Barton, has not returned from an early afternoon errand, and my aunt and I are quite worried."

He could not remember ever having to seek the sheriff at his home on such a matter. He wanted to impress Seton with a need to act, yet the added worry that questions now might arise about Penny and her mysterious origins only increased his confusion and unease.

"Evening, Miz Dawe."

Emily acknowledged Seton's greeting with a mechanical nod. "It is as I told my nephew. Penny—Miss Barton—went to do some errands on Second Street this afternoon. She left about two and promised to be back by four. She has yet to return."

Seton smiled at her. "Perhaps she was delayed. Some young women have no sense of time. Take our Martha, for instance. She never—"

Emily shook her head. "No, I am sure she would have sent a message."

"Maybe a young man distracted her." Seton winked at Fletcher, who flushed. "Must have had one or two come courting."

Before Fletcher could speak, Emily responded. "No," she snapped, "not courting. Although Penny is a lovely woman, she is anything but a flirt. I cannot say that any attention paid her would have been considered courting."

"Well, perhaps not," Fletcher felt compelled to add, "but Dan Hudson and Denton Jackson both seemed quite taken with Miss Barton. In fairness to her, however, I cannot say she paid them much mind."

The sheriff smiled. "Have you talked with either of them?"

Fletcher looked down at his boots. He had not considered going to speak with either Jackson or Hudson directly.

"No, we haven't. My aunt fears some accident or misadventure has befallen Miss Barton. She—Miss Barton, that is—has been an exemplary houseguest since coming to visit us. I am quite certain had she been delayed, she would have sent some communication to us. She is well over three hours late."

Seton pulled on the ends of his mustache. He drew his shoulders back and sucked in his gut. "Maybe she got a telegram summoning her home."

Fletcher looked at Emily and then back to John Seton. "I really do not think so. Surely it would have come to her at our house. Besides, she would at least have gathered her belongings and said good-bye to Aunt Emily."

As Fletcher considered this option, he stared into his aunt's worried eyes. Penny Barton had few belongings with which to concern herself. Aunt Emily had not convinced him Penny had not decided in haste to leave. To go as she had come: from seemingly out of nowhere to nowhere again.

"Yes," Seton said, grooming his mustache, "I suppose she would. Well, I'll ask about and see what I can learn." He patted Emily's arm. "It's a mite early, Miz Dawe, to get so het up though. This evening I'll check the taverns and the docks."

Fletcher stood motionless and said nothing while Emily stared up at Seton.

"The worst we get is a crewman who drinks a little too much and starts a fight. Nothing more serious than that around here. So, I'm sure she'll turn up."

Emily surveyed Seton with raised eyebrows that served to say she had not found his words reassuring. "You will let us know if you hear anything?'"

"Of course, Miz Dawe. Now don't you worry. Coshocton's a peaceable town with a lot of real nice folks. I'm sure your guest will be found safe and sound. You leave it with me. I'll find her. You go on home now and don't be fretting. Besides, she might be there waiting on you." Seton laughed at his feeble joke before he looked to Fletcher. "You let me know as soon as she comes back." He stared at Fletcher, his eyes doubtful.

"Yes, yes, of course." Fletcher took his aunt's arm. "We had best let John get on with . . . with whatever he was doing." Supper, for most folks, was long over. "Good evening, John."

Fletcher led his aunt away from the house and down the street in silence.

"I know something has happened to her." Emily withdrew her arm from Fletcher's gentle grip. "She would not go without saying good-bye."

"If she could. Remember, if you really believe she came from the future, is it not just as likely she has returned there? Unexpectedly? Maybe without warning?"

"I suppose so, but I don't know how. She seemed so unsure about how she had arrived here. She said she just stepped out of the rail carriage. She seemed equally unsure of how to go back. And, I, for one, am not convinced she really desires to leave us."

Frowning as he hurried his aunt along, Fletcher pondered what he could do. "I'll ask after her at the depot and see if anyone saw her today." He patted her arm, now genuinely concerned about both Penny and his aunt. "Why don't you go home and wait? She may already have returned like Seton said. If she comes home, someone should be there." Cold, Fletcher hunched his shoulders up and plunged his fists into his coat pockets.

Emily studied his face for a moment. "Yes, I guess you're

right. I'll go home, but please check the depot, and maybe you should talk with Dan Hudson, too."

"If it will make you feel better, I will. Now, hurry home. It's almost dark." Fletcher frowned as his aunt walked off.

Her unease and Penny Barton's absence weighed heavily. Tired, helplessness overwhelmed him as he hurried to the depot site. Most likely, John Seton would prove to be little help. While he did not trust Penny, she and his aunt had become good friends and he—he felt a responsibility for finding her. He agreed it seemed unlikely she would leave without at least some sort of farewell to Aunt Emily.

Fletcher turned in the direction of the depot. He walked at a rapid pace, trying to warm his cold, tight muscles and racing against time and impending darkness. While part of him wished Penny gone, another part yearned for her return. He had grown used to her presence in the house, and he would miss her, in an odd, unaccountable way, if she left. If anything happened to her, he would blame himself.

At the next cross street he turned to his right and quickened his pace. Aunt Emily was wrong. He did have compassion and understanding of others. But how could anyone, with a degree of rational thought, believe Penny's tale? Her story could not possibly be true. Then, too, saying she had been at William and Mary College. He had known that for a lie, too, but nonetheless he had written the College and received the expected reply. Therefore, how could he believe anything she said?

When Fletcher reached the depot, only a thin, weak light stretched across the horizon, shrouding piles of rails in semidarkness. At the depot itself—he called it that despite the absence of a building—he saw no one and no evidence of any problem. He stumbled around rails and ties, tripped over a sledge hammer carelessly left by some workman, but could discern no sign of Penny Barton or anything or anyone else in the growing darkness.

"That you, Mr. Dawe?" The high, thin voice of a boy came from a smallish blob of blackness.

"Jamie?" Fletcher strained to see the boy's features through the opaque gloom. "What are you doing here? You should be home."

"I'm goin'. Just been running an errand for Ma."

"A little late to be running errands, Jamie."

The hair on the back of Fletcher's neck stood stiff. He had begun to suspect everyone. Could Jamie Matthews possibly be a pawn in the evil plan Penny had described? Could he have some part in causing a train derailment? A young boy out in the dark at a deserted work site raised more questions for him.

Fletcher cleared his already clear throat. "Jamie, did you see Miss Barton today?"

He could barely make out Jamie's nod in the gloom. "Earlier I did."

"Here?"

Jamie took a moment before answering. "No. It was up on . . ." The boy hesitated. "Second Street. Yes, Second Street. That's it. She had some parcels."

"Did she come by the depot today at all?" Fletcher rushed his words, anxious for more information.

"I didn't see her, but then I wasn't here the whole time, neither."

"When did you see her on Second Street?" Fletcher leaned closer to the boy.

Jamie screwed up his face. "Um, after three I think. I remember the church bell rang. It was after that."

"Which way was she going?"

"North."

"North? You're sure? And did you see anyone with her?"

"She was goin' north for sure, and I saw Mr. Jackson talk to her for a moment, but then he tipped his hat and walked off. She went on, like she was heading home."

Fletcher chewed over Jamie's words. They confirmed what his aunt had said about Penny's plans, but something had happened after she talked with Denton. Might he have suggested she meet him somewhere later? He sighed.

"Jamie, if you see Miss Barton or hear anything about her, come to me at once."

"Has somethin' happened, Mr. Dawe?"

"I don't know, Jamie. We can't find her."

"Is Miz Emily gonna make her go to bed without supper?"

Fletcher stifled a chuckle. "No. My Aunt Emily is very worried and so am I. You had best get home, Jamie, but come to me if you see or hear of Miss Barton."

"Yes, sir, I'll do that. I'll ask if any of the other boys have seen her. Good night, Mr. Dawe." The boy jumped to the ground with a dull thud.

"Good night, Jamie."

Fletcher rubbed his chin. Jamie placed Penny on Second Street with parcels. Just where she had told Aunt Emily she planned to go. So what could have happened to her after talking with Jackson? Jamie said Jackson had gone his way and Penny hers. Perhaps she had said something to Jackson about what she expected to do next. It wouldn't hurt to ask him, even at this hour.

Crossing the rail yard, Fletcher turned down an alley behind the feed store and headed in the direction of Denton Jackson's home. Jackson would not expect him to call at night—unless he had harmed Penny. Fletcher grimaced. Better to surprise Jackson. If he had anything to hide, Fletcher would have the advantage of surprise and Jackson might let something drop.

As he walked, he thought about the oily man. Jackson's hair always looked so slick, a tad too much pomade, and he wore his clothes too tight. His wife must feed him exceedingly well. Fletcher detested the frequent stains on Denton's clothing, and his slovenly appearance suggested the Jacksons had no laundress, or a very inept one. A man of his position should certainly look better groomed. An appearance like Jackson's made one question the man's character and intelligence.

Considering Jackson's position on the railroad, Fletcher clenched his fists. His jaw tightened in anger and frustration. Still, while he knew Denton to be sly and underhanded, he had never appeared the vicious type. Fletcher couldn't imagine him resorting to violence with Penny or anyone else.

By the time he arrived at Jackson's home, Fletcher had nearly convinced himself that Penny had some assignation with the oily snake. Another part of him argued that she had better taste than to stoop to someone like Jackson. His rap on the door sounded louder and harder than he intended.

Mrs. Jackson, a plump sparrow of a woman with wide, excitable eyes, opened the door with a startled look on her homely face. "Why good evening, Mr. Dawe. What brings you calling so late?"

"I'd like a few words with Denton for a moment."

"I shall just fetch him. Please, take a seat in the parlor." Mrs. Jackson opened the double doors to the parlor and hurried off, leaving Fletcher to sit on the edge of the hard divan. He glanced around the room, noting a few prints of hunting scenes and dark mahogany furniture, heavily carved and ornamented.

Before Fletcher finished his appraisal, Denton Jackson entered, puffing on a long, black cigar. He removed it from his mouth and licked round the edge before speaking. "Fletcher, good to see you. How's the railroad these days?" Jackson rocked on his heels, evaluating his cigar.

"Fine, just fine. We should be finished soon. Denton, I understand you spoke with Miss Barton this afternoon."

"This afternoon?" Denton took a long drag on his cigar and blew out a cloud of blue smoke. "Um, yes, I believe I did. We exchanged the usual pleasantries."

"Did she say where she intended to go?"

Denton studied Fletcher, then the tip of his cheroot. "Why, I assume she was going home. She had some bundles under her arm. Shopping, I suppose." He narrowed his eyes and studied Fletcher. "Has something happened to her?"

"We're not certain, but my aunt is concerned. She expected Miss Barton back by four, but she has not returned yet. We've been to John Seton, and he has gone out looking for her as we speak. Meanwhile, I thought I would see if I could learn anything. Aunt Emily is quite worried."

Jackson laughed. "Well, with an attractive filly like Miss Barton, who knows?" He lifted his brows and cocked his head toward Fletcher, questions filling his dark eyes.

Angry at the slight, Fletcher narrowed his eyes and skewered Denton with his gaze. "Attractive filly?"

Denton looked away. "Well, a poor choice of words, perhaps. But she is, you know. Dan Hudson certainly noticed, and I'm sure others did as well. She is a little forward, don't you agree? Doesn't know her place, if you know what I mean."

"No, I do not. Miss Barton emulates my aunt. Are you implying that my aunt's behavior is improper?"

"No. No, of course not, but—" Denton took a long puff on his cigar. "Well, some men might be offended by—Miss—uh, Barton's manners or some might assume she meant more than she did." Denton winked. "Um, you see what I mean?"

Fletcher frowned. "If any harm has come to Miss Barton—" He clenched his fists.

"Now, I didn't say that. Besides, I don't know anyone in Coshocton who would harm a woman unless it was one of them Irish. You know them better'n anyone, since most of 'em have worked for you at one time or another. They beat their women, I hear. I'd ask among them."

"I intend to, but I doubt any of my workmen would be foolish enough to interfere with a guest of mine." Fletcher walked toward the door, determined to be polite and not vent his ire on Jackson, despite the unctuous nature of the man. It would do neither Penny nor his position with the Board of Public Works any good. "If you hear anything, let me know at once."

"Of course. I hope you have news of her when you reach home. Good night." Denton stood at the door looking after Fletcher as he walked away.

Fletcher resented the things Denton said or implied about Penny. While he knew her to be forward, she appeared open and had shown herself able to cut off both Dan and Denton. He could not imagine she would not set any man straight if he overstepped the boundaries of good taste. She, like Aunt Emily, enjoyed a good argument and would not be inclined to avoid one.

Stopping, he took a deep breath of the crisp night air. He had found her intelligent and capable. Still, something had clearly happened to her, or he or Emily would have heard from her long before this. His aunt had asked him to talk with Dan Hudson. Denton Jackson, too, had mentioned Dan's interest in Penny.

Drawing his coat tighter around him, Fletcher hurried off toward the canal and the lockmaster's house. He hoped he could find Dan as easily as he had found Jackson.

Walking up to the neat stone cottage with its low windows and narrow strip of lawn, Fletcher heard loud voices. Angry voices, and one of them a woman, indicated some sort of argument. He strained to listen, but the thick walls and the heavy door muffled the voices and they faded in and out. From what he could tell, neither the tone nor the words sounded like they came from Penny.

He knocked on the door. The voices suddenly quieted, and he heard only footsteps approach on the other side of the door. It opened a crack and Dan Hudson peered out with fox-like eyes.

"Mr. Dawe. What do you want?" Dan opened the door wider, holding a lantern high in his right hand to throw more light upon his caller.

"I came to ask if you have seen Miss Barton. She has not returned home from an afternoon of shopping, and my aunt is afraid some accident may have befallen her."

"Miss Barton? No, can't say I've seen her recently," Dan answered quickly and turned for a moment to glance behind him.

In the light of the lantern, despite Dan's heavy shadow, Fletcher saw an angry red scratch on one side of his face. "Been in a fight, Dan?"

"What?" Dan reached up and fingered the wound. "Oh, that. Just a little souvenir from one of Kitty's ladies." He grimaced. "Not much of a lady. Told Kitty she ought to get rid of that one. Not good for business." He turned his cheek away, shielding the scratch from view.

Fletcher shifted from one foot to the other, uncertain what more to ask. He pulled his collar tighter against the chill. He studied Dan for a moment more and then sighed. "Well, if you see Miss Barton or hear anything of her, please let me know at once. My aunt is quite distraught."

"I'll do that, Mr. Dawe. Good night."

Dan shut the door with a greater hurry than Fletcher thought necessary. For a moment he faced the wooden door and pondered what to do next. He could think of nothing else at this late hour. He had already checked the rail yard, spoken with Denton Jackson and Dan Hudson, and called upon Sheriff

Seton for help. What more could he do?

He turned his steps toward home. At daylight he would assign Carmody and O'Brien and their crews to help look for Penny. Those two knew every alley and corner of town, and they would welcome a day away from the track cleanup. He jammed his hands in his pockets. With their help, she would be found, or she would have returned from whence she had come.

Once he had devoutly hoped she would go. Now he found himself feeling bereft, as if he had lost something or someone important to him. Logic dictated he should have no such concerns, but his emotions refused to obey logic. Something about her persisted in disturbing his thoughts and wouldn't surrender to mere logic. He had to find her, if only to convince himself she meant nothing to him.

CHAPTER 15

When Fletcher stepped onto the porch, Emily flung the door wide. Her eyes shone dark with worry, but now she looked to him with hopeful eyes.

He shook his head. "No, I found no sign of her. Jamie Mathews said he saw her on Second Street shortly after three and Denton Jackson spoke to her at one point, but he could tell me nothing more. Jackson said they exchanged pleasantries, and Penny set out to return home. Dan Hudson says he has not seen her." Fletcher tried to keep the anxiety from his voice, but could not suppress a frown.

Emily rubbed her arms and then glanced over her shoulder at the tall clock at the end of the hall. "Where can she possibly be at this hour?"

"I cannot imagine. I asked Jamie to listen for any word of her, and I'll speak with the work crews first thing in the morning. You had best go to bed." He looked out the narrow window next to the door. "There is nothing more we can do now in the dark." He took his aunt's elbow and steered her toward the stairs.

"You must rest. I want to be up at first light." He watched a moment as she hesitated, then nodded, and slowly ascended the stairs, discouragement and concern evident in the set of her shoulders. He turned the lock and then followed her upstairs.

After undressing and donning his nightgown, Fletcher sat for a long time on the edge of his bed. That angry scratch on Dan

Hudson's cheek worried him. Could Penny have made it? He wished now he had forced his way into the lockmaster's house, but reminded himself the woman's voice had not sounded at all like Penny. Loud and strident, with no evidence of careful grammar or education, it resembled the voice of no woman he knew, but came closest to one or two of the workmen's wives.

Hudson had a reputation for liking the ladies and spent more time with Kitty's girls than he should. Fletcher vaguely recalled some fight over a workman's wife, not Carmody's or O'Brien's, but Fitzgerald's or Brennan's.

Blowing out the candle, Fletcher then tried to settle down. His pillow felt lumpy and he shook it out, but it made no difference. He tried first to rest on his left side and then his right. Images of Penny as he had first seen her rose unbidden. Her oval face framed by smooth waves of auburn hair, her blue eyes sparkling as she gazed up at him, lips slightly parted. He had wanted to search those eyes, to plunder their depths, and savor the intelligence and humor in them. Fletcher clenched his fists.

Despite her fantastic story, he wished her no ill. Far from it. If only she were not part of the plot to sabotage his railroad, he might—Might what? Seek her friendship? Act as her guardian? Those sounded so tepid somehow, less than adequate to what he wanted. He balled his fists. But he couldn't let anyone, especially scum like Jackson or Hudson, hurt her.

The mixture of feelings he held for Penny confused him. He liked her, but didn't trust her. Yet the strength of his attraction overwhelmed him. Love? No. No, he could not love someone of questionable integrity. Beautiful, Penny Barton might be, but he would not let that sway him.

He would find her—tomorrow—and then resolve all this. He pulled the covers up and closed his eyes.

Penny woke with a throbbing headache. Her temples pulsed.

Her stomach pitched and rolled, but she no longer smelled the sickening-sweet scent she remembered inhaling just before losing consciousness. Now, as she lay facedown, the fetid, sour air smelled of musty, rotting wood. She turned her head and tried to open her eyes. Something blocked her vision. She could see nothing but a thick, menacing blackness. Struggling to blink, she grew aware of some fabric against her face. Dan must have blindfolded her. The fabric stretched tight across the bridge of her nose and pinched both ears.

Her hands, pulled behind her and bound, palms out, felt like huge, stiff paddles. With each writhing movement, her arms ached anew, and the rope chafed her already raw wrists. She tried to kick with her left leg, then her right. Tied together with a heavy, wet rope, they held her down like sodden logs.

Penny grunted and strained against her bond. The coarse hemp of her ankle bindings tightened with every movement and made even the smallest motion more uncomfortable than the last. Nevertheless, she wrestled and arched her body, squirming in one direction then another, and struggled to free herself.

A thick wad of dirty cotton stuffed in her mouth tasted oily and rancid. Her stomach lurched. *Please, don't let me be sick.* Hot tears soaked into her blindfold. Her mind raced like a rabbit from a pack of beagles. How could she free herself? She tried to scream for help, but the cottony mass in her mouth reduced her yells to a muted whine.

Tears wouldn't help. She sniffed at the cold, damp air. Where had Dan left her? Why had he attacked her? A wave of pain pounded in her head and obscured her attempts to reason. Her temples throbbed again. A giddy sensation skidded through her, and she feared losing consciousness again. She tried to brace herself.

When Penny shifted her position, wetness seeped through the fabric of her gown, soaking her dress and saturating her stockings. Cold water. Icy cold. Penny stiffened and gasped. Memories of darkness and rising water flooded her mind. She pulled at the bindings on her wrists, whined into the gag in her mouth, and then kicked with her feet. Her limbs grew numb, paralyzed.

The wretched memory of Trotman's Cave assailed her again. Cold, deep water. Rising fast. Black. So black it encased her like a smothering velvet drape, admitting no glimmer of light, no reflection of hope. The water crept higher. Up her legs, past her thighs to where the coldness sucked at her groin and threatened to invade her. To pull her down, down, down.

"Umph, umph." Her muffled screams sounded thin, feeble. She struggled for air, yet feared to breathe. Feared to feel the water creep into her burning lungs and force the life-giving air out. Her thoughts raced through frightening passages of awakened memories.

Don't breathe the water. Black, cold water. Her body tensed with fear. If she couldn't breathe, she would drown. Air. Fresh air. Now.

Penny rolled her head from side to side, sickened by the flood of odors from her surroundings and gripped again by the horror of drowning.

In Trotman's Cave her head had bumped hard against the top of the rock passage. She couldn't find the opening, the way out. But there had to be an opening! She had come through one to enter the chamber. She pushed herself along, grabbing at the slippery wall, afraid to stop. She sought a crevice, a crack in the rock, any finger or toehold, as the water rose with unrelenting insistence. Then, it lapped her shoulders and gripped her neck with its icy fingers.

She slipped. Momentarily her head plunged below the surface and she reared up, making loud sucking noises, gasping for fresh air. If she didn't find the opening, she would die. Struggling for each breath, Penny forced herself forward, scraping her knuckles against the roof of the cave. She had to find the entrance. Stretching and pushing, her arms ached as she pushed her exhausted body further along the rough wall. Her numbed hands, slick with water and blood, no longer felt scrapes and bruises as they slipped off the rock wall.

Penny shrieked. She would die. Here. Now. Today. In a flash, she thought of all the things she hadn't done, all the things she still wanted to do. Why hadn't she taken the trip to Australia? For how long had she put off the visit to the Monet exhibit in Chicago? What about the Vivaldi concert next week?

She struggled onward, pushing forward. Got to keep going. Penny inched along the wall. No opening. No! She reached a corner. No! She must have turned the wrong way.

Exhausted, Penny debated the merits of retracing her path. No, better to go forward. Had the opening been to the left or right?

The water lapped at her chin. She tilted her head as high as possible. If she relaxed, she would breathe water. With stiff arms she struggled to move forward. Got to keep moving. She stretched out a flailing arm and felt—nothing. She drew her arm back, and her fingers scraped against a rocky edge. The opening! She had found the opening. Water sputtered from her mouth and nose. She lost her hold and faltered, slipping into the frigid water.

No.

Not now. Not when she was so close. Concentrate.

When she first entered the cave, she had placed her foot on a series of rocks and climbed down. Surely, she could find the rocks again. Taking a deep breath, she dove into the water. She groped along the wall for the projecting rocks. Her questing fingers met the rough, uneven surface of the wall, but nothing else. Her lungs burned. She had to surface. Gasping, she came up for air. Her head hit the roof of the cave where the rising water sloshed and splashed. Water had nearly reached the top.

Time had run out.

For a moment she floated on her back, one hand gripping the opening. Then, inhaling a deep breath, she submerged again and propelled herself toward the other side. She kicked out. Her foot hit something.

Penny swam toward it and grasped the projection with both hands. She levered herself upward on the rock, but her foot slipped. She tried again. And slipped again. Gritting her teeth, she forced her foot onto the projection and shoved downward to, propel her body upward. She prayed she stayed in the opening and didn't crack her head.

Feet kicking and arms above her head, her body shot upward. She broke through the water.

Air. Sweet air. Her head cleared the water and emerged into the chamber above. Thrusting both arms wide, she grasped for the sides of the opening, fearful of sinking back into the cave below. With trembling hands she pulled herself over the lip of the chamber and struggled to raise her body onto the rock. Desperation fueled her muscles, and she scrabbled up and forward to crawl from the lower cave. Gasping, she inched her way above the rising water.

Soaked and exhausted, a bone-chilling cold permeated Penny. Her teeth chattered. Deep shivers shook her body. She had to move forward. As she rested, the water had risen around her feet. Soon it would be to her knees. She forced herself up and began a slow ascent up the side of the larger chamber.

All sense of time disappeared. Scramble, rest, scramble again. She wanted to stop and sleep, but the water following her climb warned her of the futility of stopping. When at last she reached the outer cave, it took a moment for her to realize she had survived. Drenched, trembling with cold and too weak to move further, she had collapsed at the mouth of the cavern, unable to move or even call for help.

Penny moaned, rocking back and forth. She cried softly into her blindfold. Why did the memory always haunt her? Why, after so many years, couldn't she forget? As desperate now as she had been in Trotman's Cave, again she feared the sloshing water. But in the cave, at least, there had been a happy ending.

Gerald and the rangers had found her. They had bundled her up and fed her hot coffee until she began to recover. By the time they had taken her to the hospital, she had known she would live.

But now? Penny shuddered as the memories of Trotman's Cave ebbed. This wasn't a cave, and she hadn't been spelunking. Trapped, to be sure, but wood imprisoned her, not rock. She still had no control over the situation. She rubbed at the bindings on her wrists.

She had made it out of Trotman's Cave, and she would make it out of here. Somehow. She tried to spit the cotton gag from her mouth as she struggled to shift the rope at her ankles. Neither the bindings nor the gag yielded.

Penny lay still, thinking. Someone would be looking for her by now, wouldn't they? Surely Emily would realize something had happened to her to keep her from returning home. She clung to that thought, pushing away others that whispered Fletcher wouldn't care and would discourage Emily from pursuing her.

Chapter 16

Visions of Penny continued to haunt Fletcher, awake and in fitful dreams. She came to him, blue eyes shining in the firelight, clad in a fine, translucent cotton nightgown. He watched her from his chair as she crossed before him and stood with the firelight behind her. Her long legs, the swell of her hips, her narrow waist, and broad shoulders appeared as a dark form outlined against the filmy cotton.

"Fletcher, why don't you trust me?" Her red lips glowed and her dark blue eyes pleaded with him.

"Don't you think I want to trust you?" He looked away, unable to face the pleading in her eyes and clenched his fists. "I want that more than anything else, but how can I?"

"But I've told you the truth. Surely you know that." She stepped closer and raised his chin forcing him to face the penetrating gaze of her eyes. For a long moment he stared back. The symmetry of her features pleased him, but the honesty and the plea in her eyes frightened him. He brushed her hand away and looked downward.

"Fletcher . . ." She stretched out a slender hand and caressed the back of his clenched fist. The small hairs on his arm rose and heat raced through his veins. She leaned forward and the neck of her gown revealed a delicious glimpse of rounded flesh. The scent of gardenias embraced him. "Fletcher."

He sighed, unable to resist her plea or his own desire. He pulled her toward him and enfolded her body in his arms as he cradled her in his lap.

"Penny, Penny."

The warmth of her body created an answering heat in his. He buried his face in her hair and nibbled the tip of her tender ear. He trailed small kisses along her throat and over her smooth chin. With one finger he traced the generous outline of her lips then pressed it against her full bottom lip, opening her mouth slightly.

"Oh, Penny . . ."

Fletcher opened his eyes to the gray of a false dawn and a damp bed. He lay alone, his nightgown twisted around his chest, one pillow on the floor, and the covers in disarray. He sat up. Memories of Penny Barton's lush body still teased him, and his body stirred with desire.

He stared down at the bed. He had not engaged in such behavior since puberty. No woman had ever affected him in this way. He pulled his gown down and sat on the edge of the bed, his head in hands. He had dreamed the entire episode. Penny Barton had not come to him. What should he make of such an erotic dream? He blushed. How would he ever face Miss Barton and Aunt Emily? Then he laughed, a harsh, bitter sound in the still darkness. They could not know the treacherous trick his thoughts had played upon him. But he would know, and he would find it difficult to pretend innocence.

Tossing and turning, Fletcher finally threw back the coverlet at only four-thirty. He plumped his pillows and searched for a more comfortable position. His mind wandered to Dan Hudson. One could never quite tell about Hudson. At best, he frequently acted sly, not quite trustworthy. Fletcher pummeled the pillow. Just because Hudson had few redeeming qualities, did not mean he had or would cause Penny any harm. But that scratch? How had he gotten it?

Fletcher promised himself he would stop by Kitty's Ale

House and inquire about Hudson's scratch. Kitty Gottlieb would know if one of her girls had a problem with Hudson or any rowdy patron.

He gritted his teeth. If Dan had done anything to harm Penny, he would pay, one way or another. Fletcher clenched his fists. A good thrashing as a start. After a moment he relaxed his hands. He had no proof of any imagined misdeed.

Hudson had befriended Penny, and she had responded to his attentiveness despite Fletcher's admonitions and better judgment. The man, while coarse and too plebeian by far, had a certain attraction for women. Even Aunt Emily had remarked on it. Fletcher remembered how his aunt, despite her years, smiled at and joshed with Hudson.

The eerie light of the early-morning hour cast a chill gloom across the room. He jerked the coverlet back into position and pulled it snugly around him. Possibly Penny had gone off as mysteriously as she had come. It represented the most likely course of action. She had tired of his distrust and denial of her far-fetched claims. Fletcher raked his fingers through his tousled hair. He had been hard on her at times. But, under the same circumstance, would any other man be different?

Images of auburn silk against creamy flesh flashed through his mind and made sleep impossible. He remembered how the lamplight reflected in her eyes, made them shine green one minute and blue the next. The soft gardenia scent of her skin, so intoxicating and heady, when he chanced to move close to her. He laughed softly to himself. How could he forget the pleasant timbre of her voice when she talked with Emily? Or its defiant tone when she challenged him?

He hated to think of Hudson, or any other man for that matter, touching her either in pleasure or in anger. He tightened his jaw. When he found Penny, if he found her, he would—He would free her and ask her to return to his home and protection. He might even assist her with that bookstore Aunt Emily had mentioned, an advisor and a protector.

Since first meeting Penny, he had known how much she attracted him. Why had he been too stubborn to admit his feelings? On the train he had been surprised and shaken by the depth of his feelings. But he had never really doubted them. When the conductor called his station, he had hurried away clutching her card. He had not wanted to go, but had clung to the thought of soon seeing her again.

Pacing to the window, he then stared into the shadowy darkness. He remembered his bitter disappointment when he had failed to uncover any trace of her in Columbus. Shock and anger had overwhelmed his earlier feelings and only made his pain and despair more profound. He hated the thought she had manipulated him and played him for a fool. Then, when he found her in his own home, he had not known what her sudden appearance signified and had been both happy to see her, and still angry and resentful of her earlier behavior.

Fletcher crossed back to the bed and sank into its feathery comfort. Aunt Emily had told him, more than once, what a stubborn and suspicious man he had become. In shielding his heart, his own stubbornness and resolve had kept Penny at a distance. He had hoped to learn more about the alluring, mysterious woman who stirred his senses, but he had only succeeded in alienating her.

Had his heart through his dreams tried to outwit his head? Penny's preposterous story of coming from the future had sounded so unbelievable he had, like any rational man, dismissed it at once. And yet—yet Aunt Emily believed her and trusted her without question. Now it looked as though Penny had been right in her prediction of the date for the first train to pass through Coshocton. And if the train did run on the eleventh, would Dan Hudson avert a derailment? How could she know that?

No. Her story still made no sense. In his wildest imaginings, he could not envision Dan Hudson saving the railroad. Hudson hated the railroad, always had, and never hesitated to say so. He saw it as a threat to the canal. All his efforts to stir up trouble among the laborers showed his true feelings. Why had Penny been so persistent in her view of Dan? Had she been swayed by his coarse, good looks? His oily charm?

And now her sudden disappearance.

Fletcher leaped from his bed, grabbed a match and lit the lamp next to his bed. Suddenly everything fitted together, like a complicated, ominous puzzle. Penelope Barton was not the adventuress he had thought her to be. What if Aunt Emily's suspicions proved correct? What if someone else had heard Penny mention the train derailment? Fletcher shuddered. With livelihoods at stake and the potential loss of lucrative freight-hauling contracts, some men would stop at nothing to sabotage the railroad.

But would even the likes of Dan Hudson go so far? If Penny had been abducted—he refused to consider killed—who could have done it? Who would be most likely to harm her? Fletcher pounded the bedpost and turned down the lamp, unable to answer his own questions.

Sleep no longer mattered. He stared out the window waiting for the first light of dawn. At last, a thin stream of weak light seeped through the curtains. With his mind focused on the steps he must take, he washed, shaved, and dressed mechanically, without bothering to check his reflection in the mirror.

When he descended the stairs, he smelled hot coffee and frying bacon. A wry grin crossed his face. Aunt Emily had not slept, either. She seldom rose so early.

Downstairs, at the kitchen door, he leaned against the door-frame, arms crossed over his chest as he watched his aunt, busy at the stove. "Did you sleep?"

"Only an hour or two, at best. And you?" She transferred the bacon from the frying pan to a plate.

Fletcher grimaced. "I have not yet come to any conclusions on Miss Barton."

"Eat something first. You may find this a busy day." His aunt set a cup of steaming coffee on the kitchen table and gestured for him to sit. She quickly followed that with a plate of bacon, eggs, and toasted bread.

Ordinarily the aroma of a good breakfast tempted him. He enjoyed food, especially a hearty breakfast. Today the bacon smelled of old fat and the coffee tasted bitter.

After a few minutes, Fletcher pushed the half-eaten food away and rose. "I want to get to the site early and talk with Carmody and O'Brien."

Aunt Emily nodded. "You do that. I plan to visit some of my friends and see if anyone has seen Penny."

Emily cleared the table and began scraping leftover food from each of their plates. She had eaten even less than he had.

"I'm worried, Fletcher, but I believe Penny is sensible. Somehow she will survive this and come back."

Fletcher noted his aunt's questioning tone; she sought confirmation from him. He tried to wipe the doubt from his face. "Um, perhaps, but first we need to determine what has happened to her. I must double security along the track today and perhaps have some patrols to walk along it just to make sure nothing goes wrong."

Emily sighed and slumped onto one of the kitchen chairs. In her lap, she folded and refolded a tea towel. "As you think best. If trouble occurs, it won't come from Penny."

Fletcher made no response but hurried toward the front hall. He left the house at a brisk pace and within minutes reached the depot site. Two knots of workers clustered at opposite ends of the site.

"Morning, Mr. Dawe." Carmody greeted him with a wide grin on his face. "Not much to do today. We pounded in the last spike late yesterday." He rocked on his heels, hands in pockets.

"Good. Your men will have time then for two other tasks. I need one crew to patrol the tracks south, while O'Brien's men do the north sector. The rest of the men can help search for Miss Barton."

Carmody stopped rocking and raised an eyebrow. "Are ye expecting trouble now, Mr. Dawe?" His Irish brogue sounded especially thick.

"Considering all the trouble we have already had, who knows?"

"This Miz Barton, she the lass been staying with you?" Carmody readjusted his cap.

"That's right, as my aunt's guest. My aunt fears something may have happened to her. She failed to return home last evening and the sheriff has begun inquiries into her whereabouts. Meanwhile, I want you and some of your men, along with O'Brien's, searching the town. Ask anyone you see if they have any information. Maybe someone saw her last night."

Carmody pulled out his pipe and filled the bowl. He held a splint to the fire and lit his pipe. After a puff or two he looked back to Fletcher. "Sounds like you think someone done her in."

"Good God, Carmody, I am suggesting no such thing. And I sincerely hope not. But she may be lying somewhere injured or unable to seek help. That's why I want your men to look for her. So far, we only know she was last seen about three o'clock in the afternoon on Second Street. The crews should fan out from there. You and O'Brien must work it out among yourselves which areas to search. Please now, get your men moving, part to patrol the track from here south and west and the rest to look for Miss Barton. I'll send O'Brien over here to work out the details with you."

Fletcher hurried to the other end of the depot site and gave his instructions to O'Brien. O'Brien nodded his understanding and immediately directed half his crew north along the tracks. He strode over to Carmody to discuss the search plan. Fletcher left the two men talking and directing their men. He rushed on to tell Mr. Meeks to manage the store for the day. With Mr. Meeks in charge, Fletcher could continue his search for Penny.

Reviewing his plan of action, Fletcher decided to visit Kitty's Ale House and verify Dan's story. That might take a while. He should also call on Sheriff Seton again. No telling what developments might have surfaced since last evening. In spite of his haste and his focus on the next steps, visions of Penny as he had seen her in his dream tugged at Fletcher and urged him to hurry. Nothing must happen to her. Nothing.

Again Penny struggled to free her hands. Something creaked. She held her breath to listen. A footstep? She lifted her head to hear better.

Close by the low growl of a man's voice barely penetrated the wall, then another, slightly deeper voice. They talked in low tones, but one sounded familiar. Penny drew a soft breath and then held it, determined to learn what she could.

"Now, do you understand what has to be done?"

Penny's mind reeled as she recognized that voice as Dan Hudson's. Had he come back to dispose of her?

" 'Course I do," the other man muttered. "I know how to wreck a train. Done it a time or two, I can tell you. It's easy, if you know how."

Penny strained to listen. A train wreck? But the newspaper clipping said Dan died trying to the stop the derailment. Why were they discussing causing one?

"Remember, you won't get the rest of your money until it's done. No wreck, no money."

"I hear ya, but how do I know I'll get me money, once I done it?"

"Humph!" Dan snarled at the man, and then a harsh laugh echoed. "Have I ever failed you before?"

"No, but you never asked for such a big job, neither." The second man lowered his voice to barely a murmur.

"If you're as good as you claim you are, this job won't matter. So it's settled then. Today as the train pulls into town."

"It'll be slowing then," the second man interrupted. "Not the best time. To cause the most damage you want the engine to hit at full speed."

"Well, perhaps just before town then. I want it close, though, so people can see the wreck and know how dangerous trains are."

"They'll see all right." Penny heard a dark, sinister cackle. "Say, that Dawe's been about asking after that lady, that Miz Barton."

"He has, has he? Well, he'll be kept plenty busy then. Too busy to watch you."

"Maybe, but I ain't murdering a woman. She's a friend of Miz Dawe's, and Miz Dawe, she's been good to the younguns." The man's voice rose in volume and pitch. "You haven't already done anything?"

"Of course not." Dan's voice came out in a snarl. "But that old busybody has her long nose everywhere."

"Don't you talk like that about Miz Dawe." The man's voice rose sharply. "You show her respect, or get someone else to do your dirty work fer you."

"Now, now, I meant nothing by it. I know the good she does. I intend no harm to either Miz Dawe or her—friend." Dan's voice hardened. "You just do your job."

The man snorted. "You have me money ready."

"All right. Come to me right after the wreck, and I'll have your money. No more money, though, unless the job is finished."

Penny couldn't hear the second man's response, only hollow-sounding footsteps walking away. She listened more intently. The men must be walking on a wooden deck or dock. No other surface would produce such a hollow, empty sound.

Suddenly, a different pair of footsteps echoed. Close, closer, they paused and then moved forward again. A door opened and a cool breeze wafted past her forehead. Penny stayed motionless and quiet, feigning unconsciousness. A toe nudged her ribs. She forced herself to relax, unwilling to let Dan know she had awakened.

"Well." Dan's words came out as a soft sigh. "Still asleep. Thought sure by now you'd wake up. Too bad that old doctor didn't tell me how much to use. Anyway, it's best you sleep on, little lady. Can't have you interfering with my nicely laid plans, now can I? But I gotta decide what to do with you. Be a shame to kill you, but I can't have you tattling to Dawe." Dan snickered and moved to the other side of Penny.

"But we can have a little fun first, after you wake up. Yes, siree, we'll have us a hot ol' time." Dan grabbed Penny by the hair, lifted her head for a moment, and then dropped it.

Her head hit the deck with a thud that almost brought stars. She stifled a moan, glad now that the gag muffled any noise she made. Once she freed her hands, she'd fix that slime bag. She'd never let Dan Hudson or his ilk touch her. She bit the inside of her lip. Of all the gall! Some men couldn't get their mind above their zippers, or buttons, or whatever fasteners trousers these days used.

Footsteps walked away, and a door grated closed. Penny listened to fourteen or fifteen footsteps before she heard no more. His words made clear she had to escape.

How could she have misunderstood about the train wreck? Dan's conversation with the other man puzzled her. Dan and the man conspired to wreck the train, but Ryan and the newspaper story had insisted Dan Hudson died trying to stop the train wreck. He showed no inkling he would die in the act of stopping the derailment. And when he did, where would that leave her? He had told the other man nothing of her whereabouts. Her shoulders slumped against the floor.

No one knew where Dan had hidden her. It had to be somewhere close to the canal. The last she remembered had been stopping by his boat in the holding basin. Maybe he had hidden her in it or in one of those abandoned hulls she and Emily had seen moldering there. Penny shuddered. Of course. That explained the smell of stagnant water and rotting wood. She had to escape.

Once again she tried to loosen the taut ropes on her wrists, but the more she moved her hands, the tighter the knots grew. Only something sharp to cut the bindings would do it. She rolled to her side and drew her knees to her chest; she tried turning to a kneeling position, but fell. Finally, she scooted forward, shifted around, and managed to work herself into a sitting position. With her hands and ankles bound and nothing to brace against, she couldn't push herself to a standing position.

Scooting on her rump, she worked her way forward toward where she had first heard Dan's voice. The stinking water, lying in pools at the bottom of the boat, soaked her dress. She shivered with the cold, and sore muscles protested with every move. Her head throbbed, but she pushed on, snakelike, as she inched painfully ahead. As she crawled, she chewed and spit at the gag, pushing it sideways with her tongue. At last she managed to dislodge a part of it. Only half of the gag blocked her mouth now, but it was still sizable enough to muffle her voice.

Suddenly Penny jerked to a stop. If Dan Hudson had

lingered, would he hear her moving? Had she made that much noise? She strained to hear, but no voices, no horses, no sounds from the docks reached her. The boat held its silence and its secrets.

Cautiously she edged forward, careful to make as little sound as she could. Every few inches Penny stopped to listen. Still nothing.

After scooting across the deck, stopping to listen, and scooting some more, suddenly she encountered a wall. She held her breath and waited. If Hudson was around anywhere, at least he had not heard that. Using her hands and the corner of the wall, she inched herself upright. She had almost managed to stand when her foot slipped and she fell to the floor in a heavy heap.

She rested a moment and then began again. Almost upright, she took a deep breath. Then her foot slipped again.

"Damn." Penny gritted her teeth as she hit the deck. She landed with a thud and struck her cheek against the side of the boat. Damn and double damn. She had made it out of Trotman's Cave, and she would make it out of here, Dan Hudson or no Dan Hudson. She would try again, and again, and again. Somehow she must stand!

Resting for a moment, Penny gathered her strength for another attempt. At last she stood. She leaned against the splintery wall and rested. With her back against the wall she sidled along it and groped with her bound hands for the door she knew must be there.

"Ouch!" A splinter punctured one finger. As the stinging eased, she tried to reach for the handle but felt nothing. She struggled to remember what she could about canal boats.

Sometimes the handles of old doors were mounted higher up. She drew away from the wall, turned forty-five degrees and tried to raise her arms. Reaching and straining, her fingers touched metal. She tried pushing upward. Nothing happened.

She tried jerking downward. The lock clicked, and she pushed against the door. Nothing moved.

Had Dan locked the door? If he had, she didn't remember hearing a key. Stop; think. How had the door he showed her before opened? Inward! It had opened inward. She turned the handle and jerked the door toward her.

Still nothing.

She struggled to pull harder and the door yielded a fraction. A faint whisper of fresh air rewarded her.

Inching back, Penny pulled on the door, but overbalanced and fell. She landed facedown in the brackish water and inhaled a nose full of smelly water. For a moment her fears of Trotman's Cave assailed her again.

She rolled over and coughed against the gag partially blocking her mouth. She sputtered and choked as she tried to spit out the bilge water. The foul taste gagged her. For several moments her chest heaved as she fought for fresh air and to clear her mouth and nose of the vile water. She shook her head and drops of water sprayed her face.

Come on, Penny. You've got to get out of here. No time to rest. She worked her way back to the corner and again began the awkward process of getting on her feet. Once up, she maneuvered along the wall to the door. This time she moved past the door and hopped away one step. Again she inched her arms upward to reach the handle and pushed it downward, pulling it toward her. The door came forward, but just. Penny gave another hop, but wobbled a moment before regaining her balance. She repeated the process and moved the door another few inches.

This time she hopped back to the right and tried to force her bound hands into the opening. Leaning against her arms, she forced the stubborn door inward. At last Penny had created enough of a gap to push her body through.

She fell forward, landing with a thump against a short flight of steps. She turned over and struggled to push herself upward. Her bound hands banged on each next step with every move. She tried to raise her hands higher, but the strain became too much. Slumping down, she settled for inching up each step.

The cold wind rushed past, whipping her damp gown and tossing strands of snarled hair. Penny shivered and tiny bumps formed on her arms and legs. Her teeth chattered like hail on a tin roof and the harsh wind blew with hard, threatening gusts.

She had to find something to cut the ropes. If she didn't do it soon, she wouldn't have the strength left to escape Dan Hudson.

CHAPTER 17

As Fletcher neared the Tuscarawas River, the chill of the north wind made him huddle deeper into his coat. He pulled the collar up about his ears and walked with his head down, shoulders hunched. He did not want to admit to himself or to his aunt his growing unease over Penny's absence. Now, as he threaded his way among the crude jumble of cabins, shanties and sheds along the river, his mind wandered. Vivid fears loomed more likely now than they had only a few hours ago. By now someone should have seen or heard something.

Kitty Gottlieb's two-story tavern stood at the end of the street next to an empty lot. From his position several doors down, Fletcher eyed the building with suspicion. The drawn window curtains on the upper level implied the residents still lay abed, and he had seen no one enter through the front door. Had Kitty not opened yet? To his knowledge she opened early and closed late.

He crossed the street and pushed the heavy door open. Inside the dim room, the fetid air lay like a hot lead blanket. The odor of stale cigars, sweat, grease, and sickening-sweet perfume enveloped him. From upstairs someone laughed, and off to his right several boatmen huddled near the fireplace. Two of them held steins of ale while one struggled to light his pipe.

Fletcher ignored them, passed by the stairway to the upper level, and made his way toward the door at the far end of the room. He had almost reached it when a serving maid bolted through the door, balancing a breakfast tray on her hip.

She eyed his coat, boots, and his clean-shaven face. "Good day, sir. A meal or something to drink?"

"No, I'm looking for Mrs. Gottlieb."

For a moment, the frowning girl stared at him and then a smile creased her tired face. "Oh, you mean Kitty. She's in the kitchen." With a nod of her head, the maid motioned to the door behind her and then hastened toward the men by the fireplace.

Fletcher pushed open the door and walked into the large kitchen beyond. Pots and pans littered a long pine table, and a granite coffeepot steamed on the cast-iron stove. Kitty, a large woman, pushed a strand of fading red hair off her face as she looked up at him.

"Now," she said, moving forward and brandishing a large wooden spoon, "what does the likes of you be wanting? You've no cause to invade me kitchen. Out with ya!" Her brow furrowed in a deep frown.

Fletcher smiled as he watched her from the doorway. Hat in hand, he inclined his head in greeting. "I'm Fletcher Dawe, Mrs. Gottlieb, and I need a word with you." He looked over his shoulder. "If you prefer, we could return to the common room or step outside."

Kitty's anger, while legendary when given cause, was mostly for show. Fletcher never patronized the tavern, but he, along with the whole town, knew her reputation. She kept her girls in strict order, but took good care of them. With her thunderous voice and girth, she had no trouble quelling the rough Irishmen who drank there, using one of her heavy frying pans if all else failed. But she also tended bloody noses and listened to many a sad tale. Fletcher's own men spent time with Kitty or her girls and none had ever dared challenge her.

Her German husband had died ten years back, worn out

some said from trying to keep up with the bonny Irish lass he had married. From all reports, Kitty refused to take another husband and preferred instead to manage her own affairs.

"I've me work to do," she growled at Fletcher. "We had a late night. Them celebrating Irishmen wouldn't go. Speak your piece quick-like and git." She turned back to the stove and stirred a large pot.

"I came to ask you about Dan Hudson. He told me he had a . . . a scuffle with one of your girls last night."

"Dan?" Kitty snorted as she banged the spoon against the pot. "He can't leave nothing in petticoats alone. Guess that wife of his can't satisfy him."

"Wife?" Fletcher stared at her broad back. "Dan is married?"

Kitty wiped her hands on her apron. "Makes no never mind to me. But most other folks ain't heard of his wife, neither. He keeps her hid most of the time." She sniffed, her nose in the air. "An Irish lass's not good enough for him. She had the looks once, but he beat her up and wore her out, and now he seeks his fun elsewhere. She ain't educated, he sez."

Kitty shook her spoon at Fletcher. "Well, let me tell you, there ain't a sweeter lass about, or a better mother, either. She keeps her boy clean and out of trouble, not like some of these slatterns hereabouts." She rambled on, stirring the pot faster and faster.

"Please." Fletcher held up a hand. "I had no knowledge of Hudson's marriage, let alone of a son, too. But his marriage does not concern me. Did Hudson have a fight with one of your girls last night?"

"Dan Hudson never come near here last night. He knows I don't like him. He never comes alone, only when he's got one or more of the railroad gang with him. He figures I won't kick him out then." She sighed. "I don't like the skunk."

"Kitty, have you or any of your girls heard anything about

Penny Barton? Miss Barton is my aunt's guest, but she failed to return home yesterday, and we fear some accident may have befallen her."

Kitty looked up at the ceiling and then rubbed her nose. "Not so's I'd know, but I'll ask about her."

Fletcher nodded. "Please, and if you hear anything, send word to me at once. My aunt is very worried."

Kitty faced him, her expression solemn. "Miz Dawe is a fine lady. She treats us all like people, not like trash as some of those over-fine townsfolk do. I hope her friend is well. I'll ask me girls, and if they hear anything, you can be sure they'll tell me. If there's anything to tell, I'll send Deidre to you."

"Thank you, Mrs. Gottlieb." When Kitty turned back to her stove, Fletcher left by the kitchen door.

He hurried past the group clustered by the fire and into the street. Outside, the wind had not died down. He pulled his coat tight, glad for its woolen comfort.

Pondering the situation, Fletcher debated whether to speak with Hudson again. Maybe checking with John Seton would prove to be the best use of time.

Frightened and cold, Penny struggled to catch her breath. Her chest heaved as she gulped for air. Bound and unable to view her surroundings made her doubly vulnerable. If only she could see. She had to find a way to raise the blindfold. Seated upright on the deck, she scooted forward, her outstretched legs scraping and groping along the surface, leading the way. Determination overcame rising fear as she desperately wrestled the ropes that bound her. She stopped to listen.

Had she heard a voice? She sat stone still, without breathing. A hearty breeze stirred the trees along the bank in a soft sighing *swish*. No other sound reached her ears.

Ridding herself of the blindfold and the ropes had to come

first. She wouldn't stand a chance if Hudson came back again. No telling what he might do if he caught her on deck.

She scooted forward again. Something solid stopped her motion, and she scraped the toe of her boot. If she remembered correctly, most of the abandoned boats had gunwales running around their decks to keep cargo and passengers from sliding into the canal. She must have bumped it. Suddenly it occurred to her, she might be able to use it to raise the blindfold.

Inch by inch, she rocked around and pushed her forehead against the splintery wood. She tried to nudge the blindfold up. Dan Hudson had pulled it so tight it pinched her temples, but as she rubbed against the rotting wood she sensed movement, and she rubbed harder. Slowly, the edge of the blindfold started to slide. She pushed again.

"Ouch!" She stifled a yelp when a splinter pierced her forehead just above her right eye. A blast of cold air reached her eyes, and she blinked back tears. At least she could see now.

One obstacle overcome, she scanned the bow. If Dan worked on the boat, he must have used some tools. Perhaps he had left something she could use to cut the ropes binding her wrists and feet.

Penny stared about her. She sat at one end of the old canal boat with her back to the cabin near where Dan had hidden her. A heap of frayed rope lay coiled to one side; a stack of rotting wooden crates stood piled on the other. She saw nothing metallic, nothing that looked as though it might be sharp enough to cut the ropes.

Paint had peeled from the wooden planks and left them prey to the wind and rain, ice and frost, humidity and bright sun. All had conspired to weaken the wood and turn it to a soft, sponge-like mass, useless for abrading hemp rope. Despite that, for a while she tried rubbing the ropes against the gunwale, but only acquired more splinters.

Disgusted, she levered herself to her feet and tried to hop across the deck. As she turned toward the cabin and looked forward to the bow of the boat she saw a familiar figure clad in dark blue striding toward the boat basin. Squinting at the man, she thought the distant figure resembled Dan Hudson. If he caught her now, he would kill her.

Dan strode along the path to the holding basin, whistling a loud tune and looking over his shoulder every couple of minutes to insure no one observed him. The sun shone brightly, but the north wind made him fasten his jacket tightly. He hunched his shoulders against the wind and pulled his neck downward like a turtle into his stiff shirt collar.

He stopped whistling long enough to smile broadly. O'Brien would derail the train today; all he had to do was wait. At last, the months of worry done, he would finally see Fletcher Dawe ruined. He briefly considered staying to enjoy Dawe's downfall instead of leaving town for a few days. He had a canal boat to take him south to Portsmouth. Maybe he should stick with that after all.

Rubbing his chin, Dan relished the thought of Dawe's anger and frustration at seeing his railroad discredited and all his plans and hopes destroyed. Taking down the arrogant puke made him smile.

He'd take the Barton whore with him to provide a little diversion. That ought to add to Dawe's misery. He'd seen Dawe eye her and knew what that look meant. Yes, indeed. Dan rubbed his hands together.

Yes, that's what he'd do. He had the means to make the bitch cooperate. He patted the little brown bottle in his pocket and thanked the good fortune that had brought Dr. Edwin Westcott to his notice. Dr. Westcott had given him an effective tool to keep the fiery Barton wench under control.

Once they got to Portsmouth, he'd enjoy her to the fullest. Make her pay for all the trouble she had caused him. Just thinking of her full bosom aroused him. Yes, he and Penny Barton had a lot of fun ahead of them. Captain Gary's boat would leave at eleven, which gave him just enough time to retrieve and stow her safely away.

Penny shivered and her skin prickled. She darted glances from side to side seeking a place to hide. The boat offered nothing except the cabin where Dan had left her lying. With her feet still bound she couldn't run.

Frantic, Penny sidled along the gunwale to the stern of the boat. She looked down at the muddy water with its broken skin of half-melted ice lapping the sides of the boat. The bright sun promised warmth, but the icy wind made her shiver, and the water looked frigid.

With nowhere else to hide, the muddy water offered her only chance. Penny knew from Dan's tour that canal boats didn't draw much water, but she had no idea the depth of the water in the holding basin. So close to shore, it must be fairly shallow. She had little hope of swimming, but if she could stay afloat, she might—Might what? Surely Dan would find her as soon as he discovered the cabin empty. Even if he didn't, she could drown in the muddy water or die from the cold. At least with the sun shining, it wouldn't be a repeat of Trotman's Cave. Penny shuddered, but pushed those thoughts aside.

She stretched on tiptoe and craned her neck for another glimpse of Dan. He covered the distance between them at a brisk pace now. She stared into the dark water. She had to act. If she waited longer either Dan would see or hear her. Taking a deep breath, Penny squeezed her eyes shut as she leaned far over the side. She hopped upward to tip herself beyond the edge of the low gunwale. Her body slapped the surface of the icy water, and she splashed as she sank into the depths. She sloshed and sputtered for a moment before her feet settled into the soft silt of the bottom. At last, by pushing against the hull of the boat, she righted herself and drew in a needed breath of fresh air.

Her skirt swirled around her near the surface of the water, and she fought to force it down. She turned several times and beat at it with her bound arms as water penetrated the fabric. Keeping her head low to the water, Penny tried to move with only her nose and mouth exposed. At least in the water, the chill of the wind eased somewhat, but it would only be a matter of time before the almost Arctic temperature of the water sapped her strength. Already it had saturated her clothing.

She forced herself to stand still, barely daring to breathe. The sounds of a man's shrill whistle sounded closer. Footsteps echoed on the gangplank and then on deck directly above her head. Then, for a long moment, silence.

Dan grinned as he hurried over the worn plank and onto the deck of his old canal boat. Suddenly he stopped and stared, his eyes almost bulging out.

The door of the cabin gaped open on rusty hinges, a taunt to his hopes. He knew he had pulled it tight behind him when he had left. Tied up, Penny Barton could not have opened the door herself.

Fear and anger propelled his steps, and he crossed the deck at a full run. He poked his head through the doorway and then stopped. After the bright morning sun, the dim light of the cabin made it hard to see inside. It took a moment for his eyes to adjust, but Penny Barton no longer lay in the heap where he had left her.

"Miserable bitch!" He kicked at the door then ducked into the cabin and glanced around. Where could she have gone? The empty cabin offered no place to hide and the deck had even less shelter, yet he saw no sign of her anywhere.

"Damn! Where in tarnation could she have gotten to?" He scrambled out of the cabin and back onto the deck. He reviewed what he had done to her. He had tied those knots as tight as if securing a canal boat. His knots always held. No reason they would fail this time. Dan stamped his foot and spat into the water. Penny Barton could not have escaped by herself.

She had been unconscious last time he had seen her. No sign of loose ropes then. He walked across the deck and gazed down at the muddy water below. An icy blast of air swept across his exposed neck. Hudson shivered and then frowned. He quickly walked the length of the rotting deck, but saw nothing from the stern. He walked back to the bow, determined to survey the water again. Only a madwoman—or a desperate one—would brave the water this early in the season.

"Damn!"

Penny relished the fury in Dan's voice. Now if she could just keep quiet.

He must have discovered the open door to the cabin. The footsteps rushed forward toward the cabin. She held her breath. The footsteps returned and began walking along the side of the boat.

Penny crouched lower and closer to the hull. Fearing that might not be enough, she drew in a deep breath and dropped beneath the muddy water. *Please don't let him find me,* she prayed.

She lost all sense of time. Her heart pounded and the pressure to breathe grew more urgent. Her lungs burned as though they might burst. She didn't know how much longer she could hold her breath and stay submerged. Had Dan finished his search of the surface of the water? Maybe he would decide someone had rescued her. Sooner or later he would give up. He knew he had left her in no state to escape without help.

Penny tried not to breathe. *Hang on; hang on. Just give him enough time to go away; don't let him find me.* The pain in her chest grew. If she didn't breathe soon she would black out.

CHAPTER 18

"Mr. Hudson! Mr. Hudson!"

Dan whirled around as Tommy O'Brien clambered over the gangplank.

"Come quick! Da says he's gotta talk to you." The O'Brien boy, eight or so if he remembered right, pulled at the sleeve of Dan's jacket.

"Let go." Dan jerked his arm as he pried the boy's sticky fingers loose. "Now what does yer father want?"

The boy stared at him, his dark eyes large and round. "Don' know. Didn' ask. Da just said to get you and quick. He's at the ale house. Sez it's important."

Dan looked down at the boy and then to the open cabin door. His little pigeon had fled. No doubt she'd had help. He gnawed his lip. Would that endanger his schemes? She knew about his plans to wreck the train. She had said as much with all that talk of accidents and telling him to avoid the train. But what else might she have learned?

Tommy tugged again at Dan's jacket. "Please, Mr. Hudson. Da'll be awful mad if I don' bring you."

Dan nodded. He had to get away. If the whore escaped, she'd tell Dawe and the sheriff, and they'd both come looking for him.

"All right, Tommy. We'll go see your father."

Tommy ran ahead, and Dan followed at a swift walk, shaking

his head and glancing back to the boat. But the puzzle of the bitch's escape remained.

Finally, Penny could stay submerged no longer. She burst up through the water and gasped for fresh air. She dragged breath after deep breath into her lungs, and her chest heaved up and down. Coughing and sputtering, she tried to stifle the noise. She stayed as close to the hull as possible, hoping its curve would hide her. At last, when her breathing subsided into a more normal pattern, she strained to listen for sounds from Dan, but she heard nothing. She prayed he had gone.

Now she had to figure how to escape the water before she died of exposure. She tried to hop but the soft mud would not release her feet. She couldn't move. Dan might be gone, but somehow, and very soon, she had to escape the icy water. The fabric of her wet, thin dress clung to her skin, and the chill penetrated to her bones.

She slumped down into the water to ease the attack of the wind. Penny tried to float, to maneuver herself closer to the shore, but the clinging mud held her feet fast. The wind made ripples on the surface of the water, and rays of sunshine danced across its surface. The shimmering rays on the water sent glistening beams of light against the peeling hull of the decrepit boat. The combined light and motion made her dizzy. She closed her eyes for a moment to shut out the glare. She had to find warmth and soon. Think. Think.

Penny struggled forward, inch by inch, impeded by the muddy quagmire restraining her feet and layers of wet fabric tangled round her legs. She slumped back, supported by nothing but water. Her teeth chattered, and her numb limbs would not obey. Her heavy eyelids moved downward.

Aware of the signs of exhaustion and hypothermia, she shook her head and forced her eyes open. The battle to find her way out of the cabin and the coldness of the water had sapped her strength. She shivered and her head fell back, floating on the frigid water.

CHAPTER 19

Emily raced through the kitchen, leaving the dishes to soak in the sink. She snatched off her apron and gave her hands a quick dry. Still uncertain how she could best help Penny, she paced the kitchen. She would not sit idly at home so long as Penny's fate remained unknown. Yet Fletcher's plans seemed prudent, and she puzzled over what to do.

Not particularly religious, nonetheless Emily breathed an impassioned prayer. If harm had come to Penny, she would never forgive herself. Penny always appeared so strong and capable. Had some untrustworthy person taken advantage of her? Unlikely. She was much too intelligent for anything like that.

Emily tossed her cape over her shoulders, then locked the door behind her, and started off the porch. Surely someone would find her, and soon. Penny had come to seem like a second daughter, and she could not bear the thought of losing her. She stopped and stared at the door, troubled by the thought Penny might come home before either Fletcher or she returned. Penny would find the house locked and have nowhere to go. Emily turned, unlocked the door, and then hurried down the street toward the riverfront.

She wanted to talk with Brigid O'Brien or one of the other Irish women. One of them might have heard or seen something. Some of them worked as housemaids while others sewed or washed laundry for the wives of the merchants and tradesmen.

Their positions provided ample opportunity to learn the personal details of their employers' lives. Most of the women enjoyed a bit of idle chatter and gossip. None hesitated to discuss their observations or repeat snatches of intimate conversations not intended for their ears. Sometimes, in the close quarters of the Irish hovels, two-room shanties at best, though she tried not to listen, Emily could not avoid hearing their good-natured, but indelicate chatter.

Surely, one of them would have some news of Penny's disappearance. Emily pulled her woolen cape close around her. Despite the warm sunshine, a bitter wind blasted down from the north. She rubbed her cold hands together as she hurried toward the O'Briens'.

Because of Billy's position as head of one of the work gangs, the O'Briens occupied an old log cabin on a rise. Most of the Irish, housed on lower ground, had to contend with the frequent threat of an overflowing Muskingum River. She rapped loudly on the unpainted wooden door.

Brigid O'Brien opened the door a crack, just enough to recognize her caller. "Miz Dawe, come in out of that wind. What brings you to us so early in the day?" She flung the door wide and smoothed her unruly crop of dark hair.

"It is terribly cold for this late in the year, isn't it, Brigid?" Emily slipped into the cabin still rubbing her hands. The wind sucked the door shut behind her.

Emily squinted into the dark room. Thick, greased paper covered the two front windows and admitted little light. Despite the window coverings, a frigid draft seeped into the room and made the flour-sack curtains, looped back and tied with broad strips of coarse cloth, flutter with each blast.

A rush lamp flickered on the table. The O'Brien children, all jabbering at once, huddled under a blanket by the fire. Kathleen smiled shyly at Emily as she tried to quiet them.

"Please, sit down." Brigid dragged a rough pine chair from its position at the head of the table. "And you'll be havin' a cup o' tea to warm your insides, you will. A hot cup o' tea will set you right in no time."

"Yes, Brigid, that would ward off the chill nicely." Emily unfastened her cape and let it fall over the back of the chair.

From a shelf over the fireplace, Brigid lifted down a china teapot and then a canister of tea. She rinsed the pot with hot water from a kettle on the hob, measured in some tea, and filled the pot with hot water.

"Pleased I am to see you, but you don't often come so early. Could you be needing some help from Kathleen?" She glanced at Emily as she unwrapped a loaf of rye bread. She had already cut several slices before Emily could reach out a hand to stop her.

"No, Brigid, I have just had breakfast. The tea is sufficient."

Emily glanced again at the dark bread. Feeding a family of eight took every loaf Brigid could make. No need to waste good bread on guests. Suddenly uncertain and hesitant about how to approach Brigid for news of Penny, Emily studied her work-worn hands. She needed to ask, but feared to stir unnecessary gossip and speculation about Penny's absence.

Brigid stopped slicing and looked up with an anxious smile. "Are you sure, Miz Dawe? I baked it fresh this morning."

"I'm sure, but have some yourself."

Brigid sighed. "No, I'll save it for later." She rewrapped the bread and selected two china cups from the mantel. "Glad I am you've come to visit. I don't often have much chance to sit for a bit. And even less often do I get to use Granny Larkin's china."

She gently fingered the handle of a delicate cup trimmed with pink rosebuds round the rim. So thin and fragile, the shadow of strong tea showed dark through the cup.

Emily's face sobered as Brigid set a cup of steaming tea

before her. "It's one of the pleasures I anticipate when I visit you, Brigid. But no, I have not come for Kathleen. Quite another matter brings me here. I have come seeking news of my . . . my young friend."

Emily looked at the dark, strong tea and stirred in a little milk and one spoonful of sugar instead of her customary two. She must bring Brigid a sack of sugar on her next visit. She sighed. No clever words had come to her. She had best ask straight out.

"I came to ask you for news of my companion, Penny Barton."

Brigid's face brightened. "Ah, that pretty lady what's been visiting you. Kathleen was quite taken with her."

"Yes, and she with Kathleen." Emily bit her lower lip. "I fear something has happened to her. She failed to return last evening, and my nephew and I seek news of her. We fear she may have met with some accident. I wondered if perhaps you or one of the other women may have heard or seen something that would help us find her." Emily pushed her cup away and leaned forward.

As Brigid stirred her tea, a frown darkened her face. "Last night? No, I've heard naught, Miz Dawe, but I will ask about for you. Like as not, somebody's heard something."

"Thank you, Brigid. I so fear some ill has come her way." Emily stared into her cup, hardly noticing the thread of steam rising from the dark surface.

Brigid stretched out a callused hand and patted Emily's arm. "Don't fret, Miz Dawe. I'm sure Mr. Dawe and all our men will find her safe."

"Ma?" Kathleen, listening by the fireplace, came and stood at her mother's elbow. "I saw the lady yesterday."

"What?" Emily turned in her seat and stared at Kathleen.

The girl, wide-eyed, answered in a quiet voice. "I was coming back from the church and saw the pretty lady. She looked sick, her face so white. Mr. Hudson held her up, helping her walk."

Emily grasped Kathleen's hands. "When? Kathleen when was this?"

"I'm not sure exactly." She paused, her brow wrinkled. "But late afternoon sometime. Maybe toward dinner." She looked to her mother.

Brigid nodded her head slowly. "Yes, that would be about right. You came home to set the table."

Emily frowned and rubbed her forehead. Penny had been the picture of health before leaving the house. Why was she with Dan Hudson? For a moment, Emily feared Fletcher had been right. She shook her head. But no, Kathleen had said Penny looked ill. Why hadn't Dan brought her home?

"Where did Mr. Hudson take her?"

"I saw them near them old boats."

Emily rolled her eyes then frowned again, unable to grasp why, if Penny were ill, Dan would take her there. "Did you see anything else?"

Kathleen shook her head. "No, I was late, so I hurried on home. I knew Mr. Hudson would take care of her."

"Yes, I see." Emily stood up abruptly and pulled on her cape. "I must go, Brigid. Thank you for the tea, and thank you, Kathleen. You have been a great deal of help."

The wind, blowing less hard, still felt bitter against her face as Emily stood outside the O'Brien cabin. She debated whether to seek Fletcher's help first or go herself to look for Penny.

The holding basin lay only a short distance away. She jerked her cape firmly about her and strode in the direction of the boat basin.

CHAPTER 20

As Fletcher turned his steps to head back toward town, he glimpsed a familiar figure hurrying toward the holding basin. Aunt Emily. What could she be doing at the basin so early and in such chill weather? He changed his course to follow his aunt as she scurried toward the derelict boats lying on the far side of the basin.

"Aunt Emily!" Fletcher ran toward his aunt. "Aunt Emily!"

For a moment the woman ahead continued her brisk pace and then she turned. "What? Who's calling?"

She stared at him for a moment and then smiled in recognition. "Fletcher, have you heard anything more about Penny? Anything at all?" Her voice sounded desperate.

He shook his head. "No, nothing. I've sent crews to search the town for her. But Hudson may have had something to do with her disappearance. He lied to me about the scratch on his face."

"Scratch? What scratch?" His aunt stared at him with a puzzled look on her face. "What?" She waved his words away. "Oh, forget that for now. Kathleen O'Brien said she saw Penny with Dan yesterday. She said Penny looked pale, perhaps ill."

"Ill? What do you mean? Why did no one tell us?" Fletcher almost missed his footing.

"Kathleen did—as soon as I asked Brigid about Penny. She told me she saw both Penny and Dan Hudson near the old boats in the holding basin. It would be just like Dan to hide her there."

Fletcher took her arm and began striding toward the holding basin, pulling her along. "We had best hurry then. No telling what he might have done to Penny."

"She was alive yesterday, and I really cannot see Dan Hudson as a killer." Emily wrenched her arm from his grasp. "I'm walking as fast as I can, Fletcher."

"I know, I know." He tried to rein in his impatience. "It's just that she may be in pain."

"Um, so now you agree with me that Penny is in danger?" Emily trotted alongside Fletcher as she retied the strings of her bonnet.

"I—I'm not sure, but the scratch on Dan's cheek could have been inflicted by her. If it was, it bodes ill for her welfare. Let us say I'm trying to keep an open mind."

They had walked the length of the holding basin and reached the gangplank to the first of the two derelict boats.

Emily stopped and eyed the worn planks. "I'm not sure which boat." She turned from one boat to the other. "All I know is that Kathleen said by the old boats."

As Fletcher began to cross the plank, he suddenly stopped and cocked his head to one side. A muffled noise, strangled, almost muted, reached his ears.

"Did you hear something?" His aunt tilted her head as if to hear better.

"I think so, although I'm not quite sure." He looked across the holding basin and back to the boat. He saw nothing except a coil of frayed rope and the door of the cabin standing ajar. Without hesitation, he started toward the door.

The noise came again. Only this time a thump and then a splash followed the muffled sound. He turned full circle. Emily hurried across the plank and leaned over the far side of the boat.

"Fletcher, hurry! There's something—someone in the water."

Again, the muffled thump and splashing.

"No, no! Fletcher, it's Penny. Come quick. Down there in the water. She must be freezing."

Fletcher rushed to his aunt's side at the gunwale. He leaned far over and saw the top of a wet, bedraggled head. Penny, with her arms behind her back, leaned into the boat.

"Penny!" he shouted as he stared down into the muddy water.

She struggled to lift her head. In spite of the gag half hiding her mouth, she smiled a feeble half smile. Her face looked pale, and her blue lips appeared swollen.

Leaning over the edge of the boat, he stretched out both arms and reached for her. Penny's body, weighted by sodden clothes and mud, resisted his efforts to lift her.

"Aunt Emily, hold my legs. I have to pull her up." Fletcher hitched higher on the edge of the boat, trying to reach Penny without overbalancing. He still could not lift her without falling in himself. He pulled back. Penny's half-smile faded.

"I'll come in and get you. I'll be right there." He stripped off his overcoat and jacket as he ran across the plank. Jerking off his boots, he then slid into the icy water. He winced as the chill seeped through his garments. How long had Penny suffered in this frigid water?

Soft mud squished between his toes as he pushed along the side of the hull to reach her on the other side. Above him, Aunt Emily leaned over the gunwale, monitoring his progress and keeping watch on Penny.

"Oh, child, are you all right?"

Penny nodded, her reply muffled by her gag and her tremors. "I'm-m-m fin-ne. Ju-just so co-cold."

"We'll get you out; never fear. We have been so worried about you."

Fletcher lunged for Penny and pulled her toward him. At first, the water and mud resisted his efforts. Bracing himself, he yanked on her with all his strength. Slowly, she began to move toward him. He pulled harder.

At last, resistance overcome, he scooped her up in his arms and clasped her cold body to his chest. He hoped some of his warmth would ease her chill. "Thank God, you're safe now."

He hugged her tight as he struggled back to the bank. The mud clung to his feet and Penny's added weight slowed their progress. Once he stumbled, and they both fell face forward into the water.

Waves of tremors shook Penny's frame. Fletcher feared the cold might do what her captor had not. "We must get you warm and dry."

He dropped a kiss on the top of her wet head as he lifted her up onto the muddy bank of the basin. Depositing Penny on the grass, he then scrambled up beside her.

Emily hurried up to him holding out his overcoat and frock coat. Fletcher grabbed the heavy overcoat and wrapped it around Penny. Done, he slipped his arms into his frock coat, glad for its protection.

Like a nervous hen, Emily pulled the garment close around Penny and hugged her. She brushed the wet hair from Penny's face and fastened her own bonnet on Penny's wet head.

Fletcher fished into his pocket for a knife and hacked away at the ropes on her ankles and then her wrists. The wet rope, tough yet soft, took several minutes to cut. At last the remaining remnant fell away.

Emily chafed Penny's wrists while Fletcher rubbed her ankles. Feeling her ice-cold, blue-tinged skin he looked at his aunt.

"We must get her somewhere warm. And quickly."

Penny sighed. "Ahh, th-that fe-feels so much better already."

Emily nodded, her face reflecting his own worry. "Yes. Perhaps the O'Briens. They're close by."

Fletcher frowned as he considered the O'Brien's two-room cabin and eight children. "Um, Kitty's is closer still and probably less crowded. We can go to the back door and avoid the common room."

He looked up at Penny. "Can you stand?"

"I think so."

He took one arm and Emily the other as they helped her to her feet. As he looked down on her, his heart turned over. She looked so pitiful—worse than the litter of kittens Jamie Mathews had once rescued. Another boy, Andrew Watkins, he thought, had tried to drown them in the well bucket. Not sure how much stamina Penny had or how long she had been in the water, he wanted to hold her close and share his own warmth with her.

"Never mind, I shall carry you." When Penny shook her head, disappointment knifed through him.

"No, I can walk. I need the exercise. It'll warm me up." She pulled his coat about her. "But you're wet, too. And I've got your coat."

Fletcher smiled down at her, happy she could spare any thought for his welfare. "At this moment, you need it more than I. I have not been in the water as long as you. And if you insist on walking, I suggest we do so. The sooner we get you to a warm fire, the better."

"Here, Fletcher," Emily said and handed his boots to him. He pulled them on and took Penny's arm.

They set off at a brisk pace and soon reached Kitty's back door. Fletcher rapped several times in loud succession and then opened the door. He ushered Penny into a kitchen smelling of Irish stew and hot coffee.

"Mrs. Gottlieb," Fletcher called, "I apologize for imposing on you like this, but our houseguest fell into the holding basin. I fear she will take a chill. Could we dry out here?"

Kitty stared at the three of them for only a moment, then dropped her spoon and bustled over. "You poor, wee thing. Here, sit by the fire." She pulled over a stool and pushed Penny down on it. "A hot cup of coffee with a little whiskey will soon set you right."

She filled three mugs from the granite coffeepot and added a generous slug of whiskey to each. After a second look at Penny's wan face, she added another to one cup and handed it to her.

Penny took the mug and wrapped her hands about it as she sipped the steaming liquid. She sighed.

Fletcher sipped his own mug gratefully. He found it easier to relax as he watched the color begin to return to Penny's face.

"We'd best get her out of them wet things—and you, too. You can go use the first room at the top of the stairs. It'll be unlocked. Miz Dawe and me will take care of the young lady. Now off with you."

Kitty gave Fletcher a push toward the door. After one last look at Penny, he complied. At least he left her safe and in capable hands. Kitty and Aunt Emily would see to her. He sneezed as he closed the door behind him.

CHAPTER 21

The clothing, which Kitty had hung on hooks and across chairs in the warm kitchen, soon dried, although Penny's skirt hung stiff with caked mud and Fletcher's trousers had stains from ankles to knees. Penny watched between bites of the savory Irish stew as Kitty stroked each garment vigorously with a stiff brush. Soon she had them all showing little sign of the abuse they had weathered.

Kitty looked over her shoulder. "How's that stew?" Her voice boomed across the kitchen as she craned her neck to survey Penny's empty bowl. Only moments earlier Kitty had filled it with steaming hot Irish stew.

"Um, good. Thank you, Mrs. Gottlieb." Penny mopped up the last morsels with a crust of bread and pushed the plate away. "Filling and warming. I'm beginning to feel like a person instead of an icicle."

Kitty nodded her head at the pot on the stove. "Nothing like stew for building strength I always told my Heinrich. Would ya like more? Or some coffee to wash it down?"

Penny shook her head as she touched the edge of a napkin to her mouth. "Well, almost as good as new."

When Fletcher entered the kitchen dressed in dry clothes, he drew three pairs of feminine eyes. To Penny, he again looked the prosperous merchant in his frock coat, white shirt, and cravat.

Emily smiled fondly at him. "It's good to see you looking yourself again."

He adjusted a button and flashed a quick smile at Penny. "It's good to feel myself once more. To see a glow back in your cheeks, Miss Barton, pleases me greatly."

"I'm glad, too. For a while there, I wasn't certain I had any chance. When Dan came back—" Penny shuddered and folded her arms across her chest.

"Hudson abducted you, but why?" Fletcher moved to the stove and held his hands near the heat.

"I—" she looked down at her hands and then across the room to where Kitty, out of earshot, busied herself with one of the maids. She turned back to Fletcher. "I tried to warn him to avoid the train, but at the time I was convinced he would die trying to stop a derailment, not plan one. Instead, I heard him plotting with another man to wreck the train." Penny started to rise from her chair. "We've got to stop him. He has a man out prying up track right now."

Fletcher gently pushed her back. "Don't worry about that. I have already sent crews out to check on the tracks. If anything appears amiss, they will be sure to find it. Right now you're more important than the train. Are you sure you feel all right?" His brow showed ragged lines of worry, and his eyes reflected concern.

Penny smiled back, amused he considered her so delicate. "I'm fine, now that I'm warm and dry again. Mrs. Gottlieb's stew is a wonder tonic, good for what ails you." She paused a moment. "Fletcher, after all we've been through, don't you think you could call me Penny?"

He paced the kitchen. "Miss—uh, Penny, why did you go with Hudson?"

Gazing down at her feet, Penny cursed her foolish stupidity. Despite her foreknowledge, Fletcher's suspicions of Dan had proven correct.

"He said he had a package for you at the lockmaster's office.

He asked if I'd take it to you. Then, when we neared the old boat, he grabbed me, and—" Penny licked her lips and looked from Fletcher to Emily. "This sounds ridiculous, but I think he drugged me."

Fletcher and Emily looked at each other with puzzled stares.

"He put a rag, a cold, wet rag, over my nose. It had something on it—something icky sweet. Chloroform, I think. The next thing I remember is waking up inside the boat."

"Chloroform?" Fletcher stared at her, one eyebrow arched. "Chloroform?"

Penny scrambled, trying to remember when chloroform had come into use. Surely by 1854 or '55. "Uh, a recent medical discovery. It makes a person unconscious." She stretched for a better explanation. "Doctors use it for painless surgery."

"Ah, yes." Emily rested her chin on her hand. "I remember reading that the physician attending Queen Victoria used it on her to ease the birth of her last child."

Fletcher frowned, but asked nothing more about the sedative. "However did you get in the water?"

Grimacing, Penny shuddered at the memory of her protracted struggle. "It wasn't easy, but once I got out of the cabin and could see, I wasn't going to stay there and let Dan recapture me or—or kill me. You were right about him, you know. I'm so sorry I didn't see him for the man he really is. Anyway, when I saw him coming back, the water offered the only place to hide. I had no alternative. I thought he might kill me then and there."

"We must have just missed him." Fletcher nodded, his eyes narrow slits.

"Perhaps he heard you coming. He told the other man he didn't want any witnesses to carry tales." Penny looked down. She studied the grain of the worn, wooden table in front of her, still bothered by her misjudgment of Dan.

Moving closer, Fletcher took her hand and helped her out of

the chair. "We must get you home. Then I shall see to Hudson. Can you walk or should I get a wagon?"

Penny shook out her skirts and arched her back to stretch. She rubbed at her stiff, sore wrists where redness from the chafing of the ropes still showed. "I'm fine, really. And the exercise will help get the stiffness out."

Mrs. Gottlieb moved back toward the threesome. "If you're going, then you'll be needin' the likes of this." She tossed Penny a gray woolen shawl, heavy, yet soft and warm.

Rubbing her face against it, Penny wrapped herself in its voluminous folds. "Thank you, Mrs. Gottlieb. I'll return it later."

"Tush, no need to worry. I can send one of me girls by for it tomorrow. Just make sure you don't catch a chill. The weather's none too warm yet, and that north wind'll cut right to the bone. Best take care. You're not really up to roaming about the town." Even though she smiled broadly, Kitty shook her finger at Penny.

Emily took one of Penny's arms and Fletcher the other as they started out slowly for home. As they walked, Penny began to feel more energetic and moved a little faster.

"Don't you think you should take it easier?"

The concern she read in Fletcher's face pleased her, but she hurried anyway. "No. Dan's not going to get away with this. I'm going to stop him."

Fletcher sighed. "Look, Miss . . . Penny, I'll take care of Dan Hudson. Once I see you and Aunt Emily home safe, I'll get John Seton, the sheriff, and we'll settle with Hudson once and for all. I will not risk you again."

"But the train—he told the other man to wreck it. I think he talked with one of the Irish workmen."

Fletcher stopped suddenly and stared at her, his eyes hard points. "An Irishman? One of my crew?"

"I . . . I don't know. I couldn't tell who it was. The man spoke with a bit of a brogue, and said he knew about the track and engines, so I assumed he was one of your workmen."

She stared at Fletcher's ghostlike, pale face. "Which way will the train come?"

"From the east. We had better hurry. Aunt Emily, take Penny home."

Penny jerked her head around and gaped at him, her lips set in that mutinous pout her mother always hated. "No. I'm in this to the finish. I've a score to settle with Dan Hudson."

Fletcher scanned her face as if seeking some way to dissuade her. She glared back, each feature rigid and unyielding. Finally he sighed. "All right, but we'll take a buggy. We can cover more ground that way."

Emily snorted. "Penny and I can meet you at the sheriff's. I'll rig the horse. Now get a move on. We've no time to be dallying. We have lives to save!" Taking Penny's arm, Emily pulled her along. "Come, Penny, I'll need your help with that buggy."

The two women hurried off to the Dawe residence while Fletcher turned toward the sheriff's office.

Twenty minutes later Penny jumped down from the Dawe buggy and left Emily holding the reins. As she entered the frame and brick building that housed the sheriff and the jail, she looked round and smiled. Not much like the tall Columbus City Police Building or the Franklin County Sheriff's Office. Would the local constables even be able to catch a creep like Dan Hudson?

Fletcher stood talking with Sheriff Seton, who looked much the same as he had at the political rally. He chewed on his gingery mustache as he listened to Fletcher. His head turned as she entered.

"We have to hurry," Penny urged. "We don't have much time."

Sheriff Seton nodded. "Mr. Dawe here says Hudson abducted you and held you on the old canal boat."

"Yes." Penny gave him an impatient nod. "But that's not

important now." She tugged at Fletcher's arm. "You can deal with Dan later. Now, we have to stop the train and prevent anyone from derailing it."

Pulled by Penny, Fletcher moved toward the door. "You're right. The train is on its way. We can stop it here at the depot site."

"But, Fletcher," Penny said, dropping his arm, "if the wreck occurs east of town, that'll be too late!"

"Little lady has a point there, Dawe." Seton nodded in her direction.

"I've sent crews northeast and southwest." Fletcher scowled as he ran a hand through his hair.

Penny frowned, her mouth twisted in thought. "But one of your men may be working for Dan. He could easily misdirect the crews."

"Maybe, but not so easily unless he were Carmody or O'Brien."

She pursed her lips, recognizing the truth of his words, but then wondered if the voice she had heard could have belonged to Carmody or O'Brien. She gave herself a shake and straightened her shoulders. "We're wasting time arguing. Let's take the buggy and ride along the track. Someone at the depot site can stop the train there, but I still think they plan to derail it before Coshocton."

Penny lifted her skirts in one hand and sailed out the door, leaving Fletcher to follow or not. Outside, she scooped up her skirts with one hand and hoisted herself into the buggy. Once in, she directed Emily with the other. "Come on, let's get moving."

Emily slapped the reins. The horse, used to more congenial treatment, reared and then galloped off. "Which way?"

"To the depot site and then follow the tracks northeast. I may be wrong, but I think we'll find the problem not too far from town. When I heard the two men talking, Dan said something about causing the derailment as the train entered town. The other man said no, before that. He wanted the train at maximum speed."

Penny glanced back over her shoulder. "Oh, hurry, Emily. Can't this horse go any faster?"

"Not and keep the buggy upright." Emily gritted her teeth and slapped the reins again, her knuckles white. "Don't worry, we'll stop them even if I have to put this contraption on the tracks to do it."

Pedestrians stared as the buggy plunged past, leaving them covered in a thick coating of dust. Penny peered ahead. Despite the racing wheels, the buggy moved too slowly to suit her. When they reached the depot site, Emily pulled on the reins to slow the horse and turned the buggy to follow the broad swath left by work crews constructing the line. Penny saw Jamie Matthews stare openmouthed as they thundered past.

"Stop the train!" she leaned out and yelled to him. "Stop the train!" She pointed to the east, up the tracks.

She couldn't tell if Jamie heard or not. Even if he did, a boy on foot could do little. On they flew, the buggy jolting over ruts and bumps and threatening to throw them out or overturn. Penny bounced in her seat and clutched at the side of the carriage.

The buggy hit an especially deep rut and jolted her upward. She lost her grip and slid across the seat, but managed to reclaim her hold. Emily looked grim and frightened as she jounced in her seat, at times half standing. Penny wondered how she managed to control the horse, which now seemed to be following his own course at a breakneck pace. Her heart thudded in time to the bucking, churning wheels.

Ka-thump, ka-thump.

Would they reach the train in time? The history she knew

said they would, but it also said Dan died trying to stop the train. Penny brushed the back of her hand across her forehead.

Not all the historical details she had read had proven to be true. Now she realized Dan had planned the entire wreck. He had befriended her as part of his scheme. He had tried to use her to gain insight into Fletcher's strategy. She clenched her fists, wishing she clutched Dan's throat and not the buggy side. Somehow, she would even the score with that bastard. But first they had to stop the train. Just hanging on to the buggy took all her strength. They had to stop the train and save its passengers first. If Dan survived, they'd deal with him later.

Emily drove with her mouth compressed into a thin, straight line. Her hands clutched the reins in a death grip. The horse, mane loose in the wind, plunged onward, throwing back a cloud of dust and dried grass.

Tasting loose grit, Penny squinted to keep the flying debris out of her eyes. Ahead she could just make out a knot of men growing larger as the buggy rushed forward to meet them. The workmen, dressed in crude jackets and long coats, stared. Their jaws dropped and their eyes followed the carriage as the two women bolted past. Penny heard the galloping hooves of horses, and two men on horseback dashed ahead. She recognized Fletcher hunched over one horse and Sheriff Seton on the other. She touched Emily on the arm and pointed toward the two men. Emily nodded, saying nothing. Focused only on the horse in front of her, she held the reins taut.

A short distance ahead the two horses reined in and stopped abruptly in a cloud of dust. Emily slowed the horse to a walk and pulled the buggy alongside the two men. Penny could not hear Fletcher's words, but his gestures, as he pointed to the track, made it clear he had found a problem. Emily jerked the buggy to a stop.

The wheels had hardly ceased turning before Penny jumped

down and ran to Fletcher. "What is it?"

"Someone has pulled up a part of the track." He made a sweeping motion with his arm, indicating the faulty track. "If the engine hit this at any speed it would derail the train. I have to fix it before the train gets here."

"Emily and I can ride ahead and signal the driver."

Penny looked to Emily whose hair, blowing about her face in swatches, had come loose from her pins. She nodded and picked up the reins.

Fletcher leaned down to examine the track. "The workmen behind us can mend the track."

Sheriff Seton chewed his mustache, now gray with dust. "I'll ride back and hurry them up." He mounted and rode off as the two women left Fletcher staring at the loosened rails.

Emily shook her head, dislodging even more hair, as she resettled herself in the buggy. "I'm not sure how much longer old Ginger can keep up the pace."

Penny looked at the pitiful beast, sweat breaking through his dust-covered hide. His sides heaved and a thick foam circled his mouth. "You're right. Leave him. I'll take Fletcher's horse."

She jumped out of the buggy and ran to the horse. Grabbing the reins, she hoisted herself up, hitching her skirts to her knees.

"Just where do you think you're going?" Fletcher yelled and grabbed for the reins, but missed.

Penny slapped the horse and urged him forward with her knees. "I'm going to stop that train. You've got to get those rails fixed, and that old buggy horse is almost worn out. I'm not going to do anything foolish."

The roan horse took off. The wind blew her hair back from her face and burned her eyes as she galloped along the track. She squinted and stared ahead for some sign of the locomotive or its smoke.

She had not gone a mile when a horseman galloped toward

her out of a copse of trees near the rail line. He leaned forward on the horse. His dark blue profile made her shudder. The horseman, Dan Hudson, galloped faster and quickly gained on her. She slapped the horse, and he spurted forward. Dan rode the fresher, faster horse and cut her off. Fletcher's horse nimbly darted aside and sped ahead.

Dan shrieked at his horse and lunged toward Penny. He grabbed for her reins and jerked them from her hands. "Well, Miss Barton, so nice to see you again."

CHAPTER 22

Penny glared at Dan, hoping his horse would stumble. "I can't say the same. What do you want?"

He smiled, one eyebrow cocked. "I've arranged transport for us down the river. If we hurry, we can still make the boat."

"Like hell, we will." Penny swung her leg over the pommel and slid toward the ground. She hit hard, and one ankle twisted under her. "Yeow," she groaned as she sprawled in an awkward heap.

"Now, why did you do that?" Dan, still holding the reins of both horses, dismounted.

"I'm not going. You can't derail the train. Fletcher and his crew are fixing the track." Penny tried to stand, but her ankle folded under her.

"That's too bad. But I still have you." He tightened his grip on her arm and dragged her towards him.

"For all the good it will do you. I'm not going with you." Penny pushed him away.

"Ah, but I still have my magic formula." Dan pulled an odorous rag from his pocket.

"Yeah, well, you got me by surprise last time. Not this time."

She pulled her right arm back and let fly a hard punch which landed square on Dan's nose. Surprised, he ducked and loosened his hold. She hoisted her skirts and hobbled toward the trees as fast she could.

"You bitch!" Dan began to mop at his bleeding nose with the

rag and then dropped it as the smell assailed him.

Penny had almost reached the trees when she heard the simultaneous sound of galloping hooves and a whistling train. Dan looked from Penny toward the approaching horseman. She smiled as she recognized Fletcher, coattails flying, racing toward them at a thundering speed. Covered with dust, he bore down on Dan.

Dan grabbed for his horse's mane and scrambled onto its back. Hitting the horse with desperate swats of the reins, he galloped east along the tracks away from Fletcher.

The whistle of the train grew louder, and dark smoke rose above the trees. A rhythmic *shoosh-shoosh* thundered through the air and reverberated in Penny's ears.

Fletcher rushed toward Dan who urged his horse forward, but fixed his gaze on Fletcher. Dan kicked his horse harder to force it to cross the tracks. The animal reared and twisted sideways, throwing clumps of dirt and grass in its wake.

Dan lost his grip on the reins and then slipped in his seat. He slumped to the side of his horse with legs tangled and arms flailing. He fell, head downward. With a thud, his head hit the iron track.

Fletcher reined in his horse and slid off. The train whistle wailed louder. Its ominous warning rent the air. The iron monster thundered down the track. Its bell-shaped stack belched black smoke and live ash, as it roared closer, closer, to the men.

Dan shook his head, dazed. He pushed himself unsteadily to his feet. Fletcher snatched at Dan's jacket and flung him back to the ground.

Penny hobbled forward. "Fletcher!" she screamed, her voice high and thin with fear. "Stop! You'll be killed."

Dan swung at Fletcher and missed. Grabbing Dan by the nape of the neck, Fletcher tried to pull him off the tracks. Dan reared back and shoved him away.

The train, brakes screeching, metal against metal, roared closer. The whistle blew a long warning blast. Fletcher lost his balance, tumbled backward, and sprawled on the track. The engine drove toward the pair.

Penny screamed again.

Time stopped.

Everything moved, but in slow motion. She raised her arm. She stretched it toward Fletcher. Dan ran off. Penny wrestled with an inert Fletcher.

"Oh, God, please help me. Give me the strength I need." She grabbed Fletcher's frock coat and pulled. She pulled harder and saw the fabric strain.

The train whistle screeched.

Penny tugged with all her strength. Desperation fueled her arms. She dragged Fletcher from the tracks and fell with him in a heap to the side of the tracks.

The iron horse thundered past. The wind of its passage ruffled her hair and then a high-pitched scream rent the air. Penny heard a muffled thud followed by the screech of metal as the brakes struggled to stop the mass of the train. She turned her head away.

She had no need to look. Dan had not escaped the murderous weight of the engine. Penny shuddered as she turned back to tend Fletcher. He shook his head as he struggled to sit up.

"Are you all right?"

He rubbed his jaw where Dan had socked him. "I'm fine. Or I will be."

Hot tears rolled down her face and her shoulders shook.

"Are you hurt?" Fletcher stood up and held out his hand.

She swiped the tears away. "No, just my ankle. I twisted it when I fell."

She stared into his brown eyes, thankful that neither of them had fallen beneath the iron wheels. She had never dreamed

Hudson's fate would nearly claim Fletcher, too. The tears flowed unchecked, but whether for their close escape or for Dan Hudson, she neither knew nor cared.

Fletcher pulled her close and stroked her hair. "Hush, it's over. Don't cry. Everything will work out."

"Dan's dead. I know it. I didn't like him, especially after what he did, but no one deserves to die like that." She shuddered again.

The warmth and strength of Fletcher's arms comforted her. She felt the light pressure of a kiss on her head, then Fletcher released her.

"I must see to Dan. You wait here."

In a forlorn daze, Penny watched Fletcher walk toward the stopped engine. The passengers clustered at the windows, trying to see over one another to find the cause of the sudden halt.

A man with a bowler leaned out an open window. "Has something happened?"

Penny straightened her shoulders, glad of a reason to focus on something besides Dan's bloody corpse. "They're just checking the tracks. I think a cow got in the way." She blushed at the lie.

"Drat these farmers. They should keep their livestock fenced in and not let 'em wander. I have an appointment in Newark." The man dragged his watch from his pocket. "I hope this will not delay us long." His face wore a pained frown.

Penny glanced toward Fletcher and a canvas-covered mound next to the tracks. "Just take a seat. The train will continue once the tracks are clear."

Just then the train whistle sounded a long, shrill blast. The man ducked his head back inside. A few minutes later the train jolted forward and rolled toward Coshocton at the rate of a slow walk. The wheels sounded a funeral tattoo.

Chapter 23

From the side porch of the Dawe home overlooking the garden, Penny savored the snowy crab apple blossoms for perhaps the last time. Fletcher stood beside her. Dan Hudson had been buried, and the trains now ran on schedule. The warm weather had coaxed forth flowers from the fruit trees, bushes, and the overflowing gardens. Even the roses had begun to form hard buds. Yet all this beauty and newly awakened life only reminded her of loss and of endings. She had avoided too long the things she must do.

"Now that we have put all the unpleasantness behind us, I hope you will find it in your heart to remain here. I ask from the depth of a sincere admiration and . . . an abiding love."

At Fletcher's words, she pivoted and stared into his eyes. No hard sparks there now. Instead they reminded her of shadowed forest pools drawing her deeper into their luminous depths.

"You must have realized from the first time I met you how attractive I found you." Fletcher licked his lips and gazed down at her, a boyish longing in his eyes. "Our feet lost touch with the earth. You felt it, too."

Determined not to let emotions sway her, Penny crossed her arms over her chest. "Yes, the locomotive as it jerked forward."

Fletcher rubbed the back of his neck and looked toward the sky. "No, a special reaction. A strange, new feeling, not the engine."

He paced to the edge of the porch and back. Late-afternoon

sun glinted off his hair as he fiddled with the shriveled bloom of a tulip.

"After everything we've suffered together, you must believe we're destined for one another."

She sensed how difficult he found his pleading. A proud man, asking did not come easy to him. The softness left his eyes and he turned his broad back to her.

Penny stretched out a hand and then dropped it to her side. "Fletcher, I've never loved anyone so much, ever. But can't you see? It won't work? I'm from a different place, a different time. Somehow I have to go back. I don't belong here. You know that as well as I do. For weeks now I've struggled to do things your way. To say things that wouldn't cause people to question my being here. And until the last few days, I've caused you nothing but trouble." She shook her head and closed her eyes against hot tears.

At her words, Fletcher pivoted to face her, and his gaze softened. "That's over. Things are different now. And it isn't true you caused nothing but trouble. Aunt Emily couldn't do without you now, and—"

Penny stalked to the end of the porch where Fletcher leaned against the post. "Oh!" She clenched her fists. "That's what this is all about, isn't it? Emily asked you to make sure I stayed, didn't she?"

The events of the last week had left her in a muddled emotional state and brought with them the realization any decisions she made now would determine the course of her life. Her judgment of men hadn't improved—first Gerald and then Dan. She tossed her head, trying to shake off her anger and irritation, partly at herself and partly at Fletcher.

"No! No! No! Nothing I say is coming out right. That's not what this is about at all! I've been such a fool, Penny. I couldn't show you or tell you how much you mean to me, because I—"

Penny interrupted him. "Because you're stubborn and unyielding, and you don't know how to treat a real woman!"

His face sobered and then paled. "You're wrong, very wrong." He straightened his shoulders and stared down at her. "I do know how to treat a woman, a lady. Especially one I love."

Fletcher moved toward her, and his strong arm curved around her waist. He pulled her closer until her cheek brushed against the soft fabric of his shirt. Encircled in his arms and unwilling to be released, she leaned into his body, savoring the clean, manly smell of him. Heat radiated through his clothing.

"Fletcher. Before we both regret—"

"Shhh."

He tilted her chin upward and kissed her forehead and then each cheek. Suddenly his mouth covered hers. Instinctively she parted her lips and clung tighter to his powerful chest.

Behind them, out of view on the threshold to the kitchen, Emily hovered, not breathing. This certainly was not the time to ask for Penny's assistance with dinner preparations. Emily stepped back, quietly, on the balls of her feet, as she fixed her eyes on the impassioned couple locked in their tight embrace.

"It's past time, Fletcher," she muttered.

Why hadn't he acted earlier? Emily leaned against the sideboard and stared down at the unpeeled potatoes. His initial interest in Penny and his determination to find her had cooled after his return from Columbus. Instead, he simply said the railroad project and the dry goods store took too much of his time, even when Penny arrived on his doorstep. His anger and distrust had worried Emily until Dan abducted Penny. He had been just a bit too sure of himself about her, determined to believe the worst.

Picking up a potato, Emily vigorously pared away its peel.

She smiled to herself as she strained to hear the conversation from the porch.

A cool evening shower blew a fine mist through the parlor window where Fletcher stood staring out into the orchard at the side of the house. He had neither moved nor said anything for several minutes. Emily watched him, barely able to constrain her curiosity.

"Fletcher, the window. Close it, please." She looked away from her needlepoint and studied the droplets of rain that had formed on the floor near his feet. "Fletcher?" He remained motionless.

"Fletcher?" She spoke louder and leaned forward in her chair. Aggravation colored her tone.

Silhouetted against the bright pane of the window, he finally turned. "Pardon?"

"The rain is coming in the window, Fletcher. Please, close it."

She watched as he mechanically pulled the window shut and drew the curtains tight. He turned and faced her, saying nothing.

"You seem preoccupied this evening." She concentrated on a missed stitch as she went back to correct her error. "I need to speak with you about something. About Penny." She concealed a smile as he jerked to attention.

"Lately, I've given her situation quite a lot of thought, and I'm uncertain she would be happy here." Emily, determined to provoke a reaction from him, tried to look as serious as she could. "We must think of her best interest. Imagine trying to live where you had no friends, no family. You have not treated her well, you know. At times, you've been—well, almost rude." A momentary twinge of guilt made her wince, but she wanted him to react.

"Rude?" He stared at her, shocked and perhaps a bit perplexed. "I have always treated her as a lady. Yes, I distrusted her at first, but it's still difficult for me to believe she's done the impossible. Yet all she predicted about the railroad and Dan Hudson has happened, and she saved us both from certain death." Fletcher shuddered. Perhaps he recalled those terrible moments before Dan's death.

"Penny's best interest? Of course I have thought of her best—" He stopped himself and started over. "I have her best interest in mind. I'm quite able—"

Impatient, Emily stood and paced to the window and back. "The question is her happiness. We must help her find a way to return to her own time. And soon." She turned away from Fletcher, not wanting him to read the expression on her face. "We should plan to speak to her, the two of us together, in the morning."

"Tomorrow I planned to leave early to attend to some business at the store."

"This evening then. Penny has not retired yet, and she should know as soon as possible that she can rely on us. I'll go upstairs and ask her to join us." Emily started toward the stairs.

"Wait!" Fletcher opened and closed his fists.

"Yes?" She smoothed a fold in her dress and tried to look innocent. Now he had to admit he didn't want Penny to leave. He would have to admit he loved her. Taking a deep breath, Emily looked askance at him.

"Not just yet." He held out a hand to restrain her. "Before you ask her to join us, I must tell you something." He motioned for her to sit.

Leaning back in her chair, Emily waited. He looked tired and strained. Deep lines etched his mouth and creased his forehead. Watching him as he struggled to put his thoughts into words made her feel guilty. Maybe she shouldn't have tried to force his hand.

"Yes, go ahead. What is it?" She shifted in her seat and counted the chimes of the clock in the hall. Six, seven, eight.

"I spoke with Miss Barton this evening." Fletcher cleared his throat and jammed his hands into his pockets.

"And?"

Emily could hardly control herself. Penny had been surprisingly quiet at dinner. Had she and Fletcher already discussed her plans to leave? Had his kiss been a final good-bye?

"We shall have to plan on making some arrangements."

"Arrangements?" Emily frowned as she picked at a stray thread on her dress.

"Yes. You see, just this evening I—" He paused. "I asked Miss Barton to marry me. We must make arrangements for a wedding. Something simple. And immediate. We've wasted enough time, Penny and I." Fletcher struggled to continue, but Emily's whoops of delight drowned his last words.

A broad grin crossed her face. She picked up her skirts and flew up the stairs toward Penny's room.

CHAPTER 24

A soft rapping at her bedroom door startled Penny as she gazed out the window. After Fletcher's kiss, she couldn't think clearly and desperately needed to do that. The knocking continued. Unwilling to face anyone just now, she crossed the room with lagging steps. "Yes?" her voice croaked.

"Penny?" Excitement and obvious pleasure sounded in Emily's voice. "Fletcher just told me. I'm so excited. Please open."

Emily's joy only underscored Penny's depression. She opened the door slowly, and Emily burst through into the room. Penny kept her head down, hiding her tears, as Emily pulled her close and hugged her hard.

"Oh, Penny, I cannot tell you how happy I am. When you were missing I thought I would never see you again. But now, I'll never have to worry about that and—" She stopped speaking, and her mouth dropped open.

"Why, you've been crying!" She lifted Penny's chin as she pulled a handkerchief, white and embroidered with tiny purple flowers, from the pocket of her dress.

Staring at Emily, Penny couldn't stem the tears trailing down her cheeks. "Emily, don't you realize I can't marry Fletcher?" Her eyes filled again, and she sank down onto the bed.

"Nonsense. All soon-to-be-married couples go through this. Of course, you can marry Fletcher. There's no problem the two of you cannot solve together." Once again, she stopped abruptly as if the meaning of Penny's words registered. She clasped her hands and stared down at the floor.

"I have to go back, Emily. Somehow. We've never talked about how I came here because I'm not sure myself. For the past weeks, I concentrated on denying the realities of my past life by focusing on April eleventh. But now that's past, and nothing holds me here."

Raking her hands through her hair, she glanced from one object to another. Confusion assailed her, and she dabbed at her tears. Finally, she jumped from the bed and turned her back to Emily. Her shoulders shook as she sobbed.

"We'll work this out." Emily patted Penny's shoulder "You and Fletcher and I. Among the three of us, surely we can make some sense of this situation. Now think. You said you originally met Fletcher on the train. And then?" She tugged at Penny's arm, pulling her toward the bed.

"But it wasn't on a train in this time. Somehow, and, this is the most confusing part, I met Fletcher as he is today, but I met him on the reenactment run, not on an 1855 train. That part you already know. My boss insisted I find Fletcher and . . . I wanted that, too. I asked Ryan O'Connor, and even came to Coshocton—"

At the bewildered look on Emily's face, she tried to explain. "Ryan loves railroads and heads a club of railroad buffs. He told me a lot about Coshocton and the railroad and canals. Everything, except any specifics about Fletcher. The film company wanted him for a commercial. So you see, somehow I had to find him. Besides, I could think only of him from the moment I met him he—he was special. Not just special. No, that's not it."

The more Penny tried to explain, the more confused Emily looked. Penny suddenly realized Emily knew nothing of film companies, commercials, Ryan, or most of what she had just said.

Taking a deep breath, she struggled to find the right words. "I mean Fletcher was someone who could become my special person. Do you know what I mean?" She turned tear-filled eyes toward Emily.

Nodding, Emily relaxed a bit. "Yes, Penny. I do know and remember the feeling well. What you are telling me is that you fell in love with Fletcher in those first moments when you met him."

"Finding him meant more to me than anything else. I never told anyone the real reason I spent so much time learning about the 1850s and Coshocton and the railroads. Through my research I somehow felt closer to him. At the time, I thought he was a practical joker or even a descendent of the original Fletcher Dawe."

Penny twisted her hands together and appealed to Emily with watery eyes. "It's almost as though by wanting him so much and wishing so hard that I could find him, it actually happened. But I don't know how. But if I don't know how I got here, then I can't prevent an unexpected return. I can't expect Fletcher to marry me when I might disappear at any time."

Staring down at the floor, Emily remained silent. Penny, struggling with her own confusion, could understand how much worse all this must seem to Emily.

"I don't know why you opened your heart and home to me the way you did, Emily, except that maybe I reminded you so much of Mary, but haven't you wondered about me? My story about coming here? You accepted it all, even though Fletcher always rejected it."

Emily raised her head and smiled. "Yes, I had some doubts at first, but none of us can know all God's wonders and miracles. I accepted you as a person I liked and came to admire, so I put aside doubts. I expected in time all would be clear. How you came doesn't matter.

"Fletcher loves you and you love him. Maybe you will be whisked away, or whatever you want to call it, by some force neither you nor I understand. But is that any reason to give up the possibility of a lifelong relationship with a man you know you love? What I'm saying, Penny, is take the chance. You must. If you miss this opportunity now, it may never come again." She shook Penny by her shoulders.

"What about Fletcher?" She studied Emily's face, wanting to accept her words, wanting to yield. "This may not be his best opportunity. And if his wife should suddenly disappear, think what that would mean to him. He's a respected member of the community. How could the disappearance of his wife possibly be explained?" Penny's words tumbled one after the other and finally she ended with a long, deep sigh.

Emily shook her head, a grave smile on her face. "Let Fletcher make those decisions for himself, Penny. You cannot decide for him and neither can I, although I would like to ensure he does the right thing. I must tell you I have two very selfish motives for wanting you to stay. You are the daughter I no longer have, but wanted. The daughter Mary, though I loved her, could never hope to be. You offer me the future. To see you and Fletcher wed is my dearest wish. I know he loves you. I have never seen him respond to any woman as he has to you. I want his happiness, but I also want yours."

Emily sighed. "The second reason is perhaps both more and less selfish. I want your help and support in our efforts to free our sisters and improve the lot of women. You come from a time when women have achieved so much more while we still struggle. We have done much in Ohio and have much more to do. Amelia Bloomer, Frances Gage, and Harriet Beecher Stowe have shown us the way. Oberlin educates our new leaders, but so much more remains to be done, and we need all the support and strength we can muster. Please stay and help us."

Unlike Emily, Penny knew just how long and hard the fight would be, but she also knew change would come. Emily was right. These women in the forefront needed all the support other women could give them. Perhaps she had come for a reason, not to change history, but to help it unfold.

She had found the one man she could love and respect. Working with Emily and loving Fletcher gave her life a focus it had not had before. But he deserved to make his decision with the knowledge she might vanish at any time. She owed him the truth.

"You must give him the chance, Penny. Please," Emily said, as if reading her thoughts.

She held Penny with her steadfast gaze for a long moment, then turned and walked to the window. Pushing the curtains aside, she gazed out to the street before dropping the curtain and turning back to Penny.

"Sometimes I just cannot understand that man! Since you came, he has not been himself. And I have known him long enough to know when something is on his mind. What has been on his mind is you. In spite of anything he may have done or said, he loves you dearly. He tried to hide that from me. When we couldn't find you, we feared you were hurt or worse. He was distraught with worry."

Penny shook her head and a lock of hair fell across her face. She brushed it away.

"I know how much he loves me, and there's no doubt about my love for him. I'll speak to him now, though, about my return to my own time. He has to know one day I just may disappear, not because I want to go, but through some force I can't control. After that, I leave the decision to him. There is one other matter, though."

Penny looked down at her clasped hands. "I was married before, but my husband and I found ourselves incompatible and we separated. We got a dissolution."

"A dissolution?" Emily stared at her. "What ever is that?"

"It's a sort of divorce where both parties agree to part. It's like an annulment, but still recognizes that the marriage once existed. Unfortunately, my ex-husband Gerald and I should never have married in the first place. He couldn't accept my career or my interests."

Looking thoughtful, Emily walked the length of the room and back. "Well, this ex—ex-husband of yours is not here, and no one in Coshocton or anywhere else can have heard of him. To us, he doesn't exist. According to you, he will not even be born for more than a hundred years. So it's best to say nothing more about it or him. You may tell Fletcher if you wish, but from a legal standpoint it makes no difference. Besides, Andrew Jackson's wife was a divorced woman. If you and Fletcher love one another, no one else need ever know."

"Oh, Emily, I do want to stay. I want to love Fletcher, and I want to stay with you." Penny closed her eyes and leaned into Emily's comforting embrace.

Penny descended the stairs with dragging feet. She dreaded the coming interview with Fletcher. Reminding him she might disappear at any time would only be fair. Uncertainty would hang over them and risk would color their lives. She didn't want to live like that and couldn't ask it of him. She straightened her shoulders as she entered the parlor.

He looked up and immediately rushed toward her. Taking her hands, he stared down at her. "Sweetling, are you all right? You look so solemn. Has Aunt Emily said aught to worry you?"

"No, no, of course not. It's just—Fletcher, could we sit down, please?"

He frowned, but led the way to the sofa and sat beside her. He kept a firm grip on her hand.

"We need to discuss things. I know you love me, but marrying you—might destroy you."

He stared at her, his eyes filled with hurt. "Destroy me? Don't you love me?"

"Of course, I love you, that's why we shouldn't marry."

"Penny, I don't understand. Surely, if you love me, marriage should follow."

"In ordinary circumstance, yes, but we don't live in ordinary circumstances." She jumped up and walked toward the window. "I don't know how I came here."

"So? You are here, and we love each other. That suffices."

"No, it doesn't. I might disappear at any moment."

"You haven't so far."

"But I might."

"Penny, there are many things we cannot know. I might die. You might die. We have little control over life except to live well and be prudent. I love you, and nothing else matters."

Penny rubbed one hand over the other. She wanted to accept his words, but doubt still held her back. "What if I—disappeared, suddenly snatched back to my own time? What then?"

Fletcher studied her for a moment. "If that should happen, then I would find a way to follow. Penny, my love for you would take me wherever—or whenever—you went. Nothing can separate us, even time."

"I want to believe that, but how?"

"I don't know, but I found you. We met first, you told me, in your time, did we not?"

Penny stared at him as she considered his words. It sounded too good to be true, like a modern romance with a happy ending, not like real life. It stunned her to think Fate meant them to find one another. His reassurances meshed so well with what Emily had said.

Pulling her close, Fletcher held her tightly. She rested her head against his chest. The beat of his heart serenaded and reassured her. The comforting scent of bay rum and herbal soap filled her nostrils.

"Nothing can separate us, Penny, nothing." His arms tightened around her and she melded herself to his body. His strength and warmth gave her hope.

She forced herself back and pulled away. "Are you sure?"

"Yes, I'm sure."

"I want to spend the rest of my life with you, but I don't feel right about accepting your offer of marriage, knowing I might be snatched away at any moment."

"That's a risk I'm willing to accept."

"But what of your friends and—the sheriff?"

"What of them?"

"How would you explain my disappearance?"

"I have no idea. But why should I explain it? Rather, I would follow you."

Searching his face, Penny saw only love. "Oh, Fletcher." She buried her face in his shoulder. "It would be so easy to say yes. But it wouldn't be fair."

"Fair? Is it fair to deny us happiness? Is it fair to run away?"

"No, it isn't, but I can't cause you any more trouble."

"Penny, please, let me decide that. You mean so much to me. I would do anything to keep you."

She searched his face again. "Anything?"

"Name it."

She smiled an impish smile. "Would you let me open a bookstore?"

"But why? As my wife you have no need to work. I can take care of your needs."

"Emotionally, yes. But I need and value my independence."

Fletcher sighed. "You and Aunt Emily." He stared down at her, his eyes probing hers. "All right, if that's what it takes, I'll help you get started."

"And women's suffrage?"

"Anything, Penny, anything."

She laughed. "Too bad, I don't have a long list of demands for you to agree to. Seriously, Fletcher, I have strong beliefs. I've been used to living my life alone and making my own decisions. Things here are different. It will take a lot of adjustment for me. You'll have to be patient."

"I have a great deal of patience, Penny. I'm used to living with an independent female. Aunt Emily has seen to that."

Penny smiled. "Yes, how fortunate for both of us. Fletcher, I'll stay, if after you think over all I've said, you still want me."

"Of—"

Penny placed a finger on his lips. "No, I want you to think about it, alone. I want you consider all the difficulties we may face first. After that, we'll talk again. Tomorrow."

She swept from the room before Fletcher had a chance to say more. How could she ask for anything beyond his love? He had given that.

Gerald had made her cautious. No more impetuous decisions. She wanted Fletcher to fully understand the risks as well as her expectations. She needed something beyond marriage. A bookstore and working with Emily would give her the outlets she needed. If Fletcher could accept that, along with the risk of her sudden disappearance, she would stay.

"My love would take me wherever and whenever you are." Those words had made her heart leap. For Fletcher to love her that much made her pulse race. A man who really cared for her. Guilt at pushing him so hard made her cringe. But she had to be fair to him. No matter what he thought, the problem existed, and they had to face it.

CHAPTER 25

Fletcher smiled as he watched Penny stride across the parlor. Her hips sashayed from side to side, causing the soft folds of her dress to swing gently back and forth. A strong woman, Penny Barton. Stronger than she looked and far more courageous than he expected.

He turned a chair to face the garden beyond the open window. Clasping his hands behind his neck, he leaned back in the chair.

Even as she warned him of the prospect of her unexpected return to her own time, she had looked beautiful. The tears of doubt in her eyes in an odd way had enhanced her beauty and made her even more desirable. Her voice had shaken when she asked how he could ever explain a sudden, unanticipated disappearance of his wife.

Fletcher shifted in his chair. He had told her that what others thought of her disappearance concerned him not at all. If that ever happened, he would find the way to follow her to her own time. Where and whenever she was, he would be, too. They were inextricably linked. Forever.

Another woman in Penny Barton's position would never consider his feelings, if, somehow, she were shifted back to her own time. In all probability, another woman would not give thought to how he might explain the sudden disappearance of his wife. He had underestimated her. He pursed his lips and stared out into the garden, now a lush green with new spring growth.

Leaning forward, he rested his elbows on his knees. Maybe a woman like Aunt Emily would have been as sensitive and realistic, but even his aunt would have acted with more pragmatism. He smiled broadly.

No doubt, Penny would be a challenge for any husband, just like Aunt Emily. But who wanted a docile, dependent wife—like a Sarah Jamison? Fletcher grimaced. Poor Sarah. She would be happy enough, though, and well suited to Clarence Meeks. Why had he not recognized that earlier? Of course, they made the perfect couple.

He leaned back in the chair again. How could he ever have doubted Penny? When she had first come to Coshocton, he had deliberately tried to deny his feelings for her. Fletcher shook his head, wondering at his own actions. He had treated her poorly, at best. Under the circumstances, it amazed him that she had agreed to marry him.

Despite her insistence, he needed no time to consider. Could there really be any doubt? Neither of them could deny the hot desire they felt in each other's presence. At that, a growing ache rose in his groin. Penny, Penny, his copper-haired Penny. Had she really thought he could live without her?

Behind him the door inched open quietly.

"Yes?" Fletcher didn't turn, but tilted his head back to listen.

"Emily's prepared this tea. Apparently she thought we both needed a cup." Penny set the tray on the oval table in front of the sofa.

He shifted in his chair and then stood. "It is not tea I need right now." He crossed the room to her side and grasped her waist with his strong hands. He opened his mouth to speak and then closed it again.

"What? What were you going to say?" Penny's gaze traced the

outline of his face as he watched her study his expression.

He could almost feel a feather-light touch as her sea-deep eyes passed his mouth and lifted toward his eyes. A delicious shiver began in his heart and moved downward.

"You were most gracious to offer me time to reconsider my proposal of marriage. But I had already considered all the problems you raised." He moved closer to her and her hips pressed against his.

"Penny, sweetling, we cannot let this opportunity slip from our grasp. Fate directed you here. Perhaps the real purpose of your coming here was not so much to avert the train derailment, as it was to marry me. Had you considered the train accident served simply as the cause to bring about . . . our marriage?"

He studied her face as he pulled her against him. With his right hand he caressed her back and pressed her hips to his body. He bent closer and nuzzled her neck. Playfully, he licked the shape of her ear and then kissed the swell of her breast just above the outline of her dress. He could feel her respond as she put her arms around his neck. Her hips pushed hard into his body, and she breathed in short, gasping breaths.

Then footsteps sounded in the hall. He released his hand from Penny's waist. The parlor door opened, and Emily, carrying a plate of raisin scones, glided across the room.

"Thought you might want some of these with the tea." She smiled warmly at both of them, but seemed to avert her eyes from either of theirs.

Fletcher, aware of the heat of his face, looked for Penny's reaction. She appeared calm and collected, but a tint of bright fuchsia colored her cheeks. He looked at the scones and back to Penny. The last thing he needed was tea and scones.

"Thank you. They look wonderful, as usual. And you will join us, Aunt Emily?"

He turned to the window as he loosened the cravat at his throat. The sooner they married, the better. He had to make Penny Barton his and fulfill his prophetic dream. He would never be able to get enough of her. Silently, he thanked the miraculous accident that had brought them together.

He watched his aunt pour tea. "Aunt Emily, you are the first to know. Penny has consented to be my bride, and as soon as we can get the license and the preacher, I intend to make her mine."

Emily's eyes shone as she embraced first Penny and then Fletcher. "Nothing could make me happier."

Laughing, Penny hugged them both. "Little did I know when I climbed into that railroad car that it would be my train to yesterday, and even less that it would bring me the love of my life." She smiled up at Fletcher with eyes shining with happiness, ready to meet an uncertain future hand-in-hand with him.

ABOUT THE AUTHOR

A freelance writer and consultant, **Nell DuVall** wrote *Domestic Technology*, a history of household technology. An avid reader, she enjoys reading the classics, romance, speculative fiction, and mysteries. Fascinated by Ohio history, she found a rich lode in the rivalry between the canals and the early railroads. Southern Ohio in the Appalachian foothills provides a bit of paradise for Nell, two cats, five dogs, and Cormac, her pet pig. He has provided material for several children's stories.